KATRINA 66

The Poison-Pen Pal

Dale W. Simpson

Katrina 66: The Poison-Pen Pal

Scripture Works Cited: The ESV Study Bible: English Version; Crossway Bibles: Wheaton, Ill, 2008.

Crossroads Publishing, LLC—620-204-1710

www.crossroadspublishingllc.com

ISBN: 979-8-9999528-5-1

Author Dale Simpson

Cover Illustration by Jeff Altrove

Edited by Tonya Andrews

For Leslie

PROLOGUE

On a hot steamy summer night in New Orleans, a nervous man enters a shop on Royal Street, the bell above the door ringing his arrival. Marie DeSouvre, owner of Mama Marie's Hex Shop, has been busy cleaning up, putting away her magic implements prior to closing.

Hearing the bell ring, Mama Marie turns to address her late customer. 'Sorry, mon, closing shop for da day. Come back tomorrow.'

The man stops, his eyes flitting back and forth from the woman to the interior of the store, stocked with all sorts of potions, dried plants, wands, dolls, bones, and other unidentified items. Plus, a rack of Mama Marie's Hex Shop tee shirts.

He speaks. 'Please, ma'am—'

'Call me Mama Marie—'

'Mama Marie. Please help me. I ask for only a little of your magic. I'll pay you anything for your help.'

This man seems quite distressed; there may be good money in this if she relents. 'What kind of help you need, mon?'

The man steps in further, causing Mama Marie to step back. She looks up at the man. She sees his disheveled clothes, riot of hair, and heavy-lidded eyes, and asks again, 'What you want from me, sir? I sorry, what you name?'

'Walter. Walter Hudson, ma'am,' he says, reaching into his inside jacket pocket.

Mama recoils, thinking he's reaching for a gun.

He pulls out a pen, holding it out to her. 'I, I'm a writer. I want to be a published author. But I've been told by more than one agent that I have no talent. I guess, well, maybe I *don't* have any talent.'

Mama tries to speak, but he cuts her off and continues, 'Mama Marie, I've got a story idea. A good one. One that would be a bestseller, if only I could write. Can you put a spell on my pen to make me a great writer?'

Now I've heard it all, she thinks. *All manner of odd requests, but never one like this!*

Entreaties for bad juju on enemies, bad juju on hair, clothing, jewelry, and other things at the requests of desperate people looking for revenge. Even putting pins in voodoo dolls. Rarely for good juju, except for love potions.

Although she doesn't believe any of it, she's always honored the requests and gone through the rituals of endowing those items with spirits.

Easy money.

'OK, den, you sit here.' She gestures to a small table in the front corner. 'We talk about you story idea. I make you write good.'

Seated, Walter waits while Mama Marie sits her broad body onto the chair opposite. She wears a mostly red-colored, many-patterned full African tribal dress, her head topped by a high wide bandana of the same cloth tied in a knot. Her large round silver earrings dangle, jingling with every move of her body. Her hips spill out over both sides of the seat as she settles herself in.

She sits here when reading palms and doing tarot cards. 'You sure you don't wanna palm reading? Tarot reading too?'

'No, Mama Marie, just the pen.' Walter answers.

'Gimme da pen.'

Walter hands over the pen.

'Tell me, why it be important to you?'

Walter sighs, recalling good memories of his youth. 'It's a high school graduation gift, a fountain pen from my parents years ago. No other pen feels like this one.'

'Mama Marie at you service, Mister Walter. But I needs to tell you dey's two kind of juju, just so you know. Good juju and bad juju. I don' get many good juju requests. I hopes I 'member da spell!'

Walter's face registers alarm. 'What?'

She laughs and adds, 'Jus' kidding, Mister Walter. Is joke!'

She tells him the cost for the ritual, which is exorbitant.

No matter; he pays it readily.

She spreads out several pages of spells on the tabletop and consults one page. Mama Marie pulls out all the stops, putting the pen within a circle of lighted candles, reciting incantations, waving feathers over it, passing bones over it, and praying to her gods to endow it with creative power.

All de right words and actions to fool a gullible soul!

After she's finished, she tacks on her usual disclaimer: 'Dis may not work for you, Mister Walter, but I done did me best.'

As if to reinforce her final words, the pen spins around in a circle and comes to rest, pointing at Walter. Mama Marie's drawn-on eyebrows rise at the sight. She's never seen anything like this before. She picks it up as if it were a poisonous snake and hands it to him.

'Thank you! Thank you so much!' Walter says, smiling and rising from his chair. He puts the pen back into his jacket pocket. As he opens the door to leave, he turns to Mama Marie and says in parting, 'If I get published, I'm going to give you a cut of the money. Promise!'

She waves this gesture off. 'No need, Mister Walter. I glad to help. I wish you well.'

I done already pocket more from dis ritual den he gonna make off his writing, if he be as bad as he say he be, she thinks.

Walter closes the shop door, entering the soupy New Orleans night, and is gone.

Another satisfied customer. Mama Marie walks back to her desk and picks up the papers spread on top. One describes the ritual that Walter requested, and one describes conjuring an evil spirit.

She reads them both and gasps. 'Oh God! What I do? Dis wrong juju. Dis—oh!'

Five weeks later Walter sits at his desk, laying down his magic pen after a writing binge, a stack of handwritten pages lying off to his right. He never knew writing his book would be so easy. This fountain pen has become his best friend.

Another three weeks pass, the stack having grown in size. Then the writing stops.

<Channel 5 Breaking News>

This just in: four members of a local family were found deceased this morning in their Lower Ninth Ward home. Neighbors had called the police after noticing a foul odor coming from the house.

Walter Hudson, Senior, 36; his wife Alice, 33; and his sons Walter Junior, 9; and Benjamin, 7, were found in an upstairs bedroom earlier this morning. Police believe that Walter Senior may have fatally stabbed his wife and two young sons, then turned a gun on himself.

Police thoroughly searched the Hudson residence, but no motive has yet been found for these horrifying acts. More on this story as it unfolds.

On Walter's writing desk upstairs lies a one-inch-thick stack of handwritten notebook pages. Next to the stack lies another sheet of notebook paper, on which are written the following words:

Katrina 66
Katrina 66
Katrina 66
Katrina 66
Katrina 66
Katrina
Katrina
Katrina
Katrina
Kat—

A fountain pen rests on the sheet just below the last word.

PART I

Chapter 1
Miles Campbell

'Bill. Bill. Another bill. Soccer registration fee. Music lesson fee.' Wendy lets out a deep sigh as she's eating breakfast at the kitchen table, sorting through the stack of mail that arrived while we were gone. 'It's going to be a tight fall, I'm afraid.'

We're supposed to be drinking our coffee and eating in peace before the girls come down for their breakfast. I sense the undertone of Wendy's concern. She doesn't have to say anymore because I've heard it before. Whenever she talks money, I know what she'd really like to say.

After putting aside the bills, she also puts aside her resentment for a little while. We just got back from Florida late yesterday, after I drove the family eleven hundred miles in just two days over the weekend. She notices that I'm stiff and sore this morning as I stretch my arms and legs. 'I appreciate your driving the whole trip for us, Miles, especially the past two days. You deserve some chill time today,' she sighs. 'Don't work too hard, OK?'

'Yep, I'll try not to,' I reply.

Wendy returns to work today, so there's no chill time for her. She has to be there at the University by 8:00 a.m. Yippee. I can't wait till she's gone. But I can't really afford to chill out at all today. I'll need to get to work on my courses for the fall semester.

Wendy nods and finishes her breakfast, downing the last of her coffee. She goes upstairs to prepare herself for work. Soon she comes downstairs and says goodbye with a perfunctory hug and a kiss and is off to the garage.

Hugs and kisses are almost always perfunctory these days.

I'm still in the kitchen when the girls come downstairs a short time later. Sophie and Emma meander into the kitchen, Sophie's feet loudly slapping the floor with each step.

'Morning, girls,' I say.

'Morning, Daddy,' Emma replies. She runs her hands through her bed hair and yawns. Seven years old, she's my little girl.

Sophie merely mumbles something that sounds like "morning." Then she looks around and asks, 'Has Mom already gone to work?'

'Yep,' I say. 'You've just missed her.'

Sophie will be twelve next March, and Wendy and I expect the worst as she approaches puberty. She's starting to pull inside herself, usually just giving short monotone—often monosyllabic—replies.

The girls get their breakfast out and take them to the table. I finish my coffee and ask them, 'So, what are you two up to today? Hanging out with your friends?'

Sophie, still not fully awake, responds, 'Yeah, can I go over to Amber's house after breakfast? We got a lot to catch up on.'

'Sure, I don't see why not. You've been apart for two weeks. I guess that's like a lifetime for you both.' Turning to Emma, I say, 'What about you, Emma?'

Emma looks up from her cereal with those sparkling brown eyes and says, 'I'll just be over next door at Caroline's house, if that's all right with you, Daddy.'

'Of course, sweetie. I'm glad you'll be next door.'

Wonderful; I will have the whole house to myself.

While they eat, it's time for me to head upstairs and get started. There will be no real chill time today.

It's the second week of August, when most instructors at colleges and universities across the country finalize their preparations for the fall semester. I haven't started mine yet. I've been working from home for the past three years as an online college writing instructor, which is far from fulfilling.

I'm a composition mercenary, working wherever there's a need for part-time online composition instructors, in the trenches like mercenary soldiers. There is a great need, because colleges and universities don't want to hire full-time instructors for their basic courses. They want to hire cheap labor. Like me.

I plod upstairs to start the drudge work.

I have gone into the office just a few times since June, as I couldn't get any summer courses. I go in every once in a while to use the laptop computer to check emails and surf the Net. I close the door after using the laptop because I can't stand to see the mess I left two months ago. Now it's time to open the door and face the music.

Damn! I think, as I take in the sight. For two months I have ignored the chaos of papers, books, file folders, and notebooks scattered across all the horizontal surfaces of the room, even the bookshelves. I just left it all in place and shut the door on it back in June, too exhausted to straighten up the mess. And ignored it ever since.

OK, so I've never been an organized person.

This time around I have already agreed to teach six classes of first-year writing online at four different colleges. Let's see, there's one in North Carolina, one in Iowa, one in New Mexico, and one in Oregon. As a mercenary, I have no affiliation with the culture of each campus; I'm just in it for the money. And it's a pittance, believe me.

I expect to have about two hundred students to start the semester, an overwhelming number for teaching writing. I will do what I have always done the past three years, though. I plan to drive away at least half of them during the first six weeks.

I have ways.

I'll reduce the workload by giving easy A's to most of the remaining students. I hope the comp directors don't notice. They haven't yet. They don't care, so long as the classes are covered. And I certainly don't give a rip.

Why am I in this pitiful situation?

Three years ago I was fired from my fulltime position here at Western Indiana University because the

Dean and my department chair told me I wasn't measuring up to their expectations. I thought I was, but they said I was wrong. I had been there for two and a half years by the middle of December when they dropped the bomb on me.

They said it was because of my poor performance, which I was forced to acknowledge after my department chair recited all the ways in which I had failed to meet even the minimum expectations. How could I have been so clueless for two and a half years?

But they didn't even give me a couple more years to improve. I was released at the end of the next semester, the end of my third year. Something wasn't right about that. That was so unfair.

Like my superiors in the university, Wendy piled on. She said I could blame no one but myself for losing my job.

All right, so be it: I'm a failure. Enough self-pitying. The present is what counts now.

Damn, guess I better clean up this clutter so I can start messing it up all over again. Like old Sisyphus in Hades.

I fill a 13-gallon kitchen trash bag with junk. It takes almost three hours because I often stop to read over papers I haven't seen in three months.

Then, there's the bookshelves, where even more trash lies.

I'm clearing off the mess when my attention falls upon a stack of three-ring binders, spiral-bound notebooks, and old-style composition notebooks that have been stored under the junk for years. Some folders contain yellowed looseleaf papers. Most are handwritten; some are typed.

Wow, I haven't seen these papers in years.

I pick up one notebook and leaf through it. It's a journal of occasional thoughts on a variety of subjects. I read a few pages, amazed at the depth and clarity of thought.

Who was that guy? What was he thinking then? Why don't I think like that now?

Hey, there's a folder of stories I started ten to fifteen years ago. I began most of these stories while in graduate school when my mind was on fire with research and writing. What they call "the life of the mind."

Oh yeah, I dreamed then of writing The Great American Novel. That dream was shattered by the realities of grad school teaching and courses. Then, when I was employed full-time, I had new classes to teach, and, of course, a wife *and* two children to distract me.

So, what's in this folder?

Looking over them, I have to say that some of these story starters and ideas seem pretty good, even today.

'Gee,' I say, 'I wish I had the time years ago to flesh them out. Hell, I wish I had the time *now*.' Nope, gotta prepare my home office for six online freshman writing courses.

Whoop-dee-do.

I set the notebook aside with a deep sigh.

After three hours, the office is straightened up and ready for the semester's work to begin. From time to time, I turn my head with longing to view the stack of notebooks and folders. However, the most important task at present is to prepare these classes.

Still, those stories call to me....

But no, I can't, not now.

Shortly after 4:00 p.m. Sophie and Emma arrive home after spending the day at their best friends' houses. I'm in the kitchen, preparing to start supper later. They fix themselves a snack and head off to watch TV in the living room.

Not long afterwards Wendy enters through the back door from the garage, tossing her keys onto the kitchen counter. Collapsing into a kitchen chair, she lets out a sigh of exhaustion. 'Whew, what a day this was!

Getting closer to the beginning of the semester, and traffic is picking up in the library.' She looks beat.

'Really? Tell me about your day.'

She sighs again, ramping up the dramatic presentation. 'Let me just say there's a lot of idiots who come to the library. It's amazing how some students, who supposedly have high school educations, seem completely unfamiliar with how a library works. Trying to assist them feels like a never-ending game of Twenty Questions just to figure out what they're looking for.'

I start to reply, but she interrupts.

'But wait, there's more!' she says. 'Then there's the locals who don't even have library cards and don't want to fill out the paperwork and pay the fee. It's just maddening.'

Wanting to sound sympathetic, I respond, 'Man, I'm glad *I* don't work there,' wincing instantly at the words *work there*.

Yes, I used to work there, in the English Department, but I don't work *anywhere* now, except as a part-time online instructor. Ever since I was let go, I have been on Wendy's insurance as a dependent. Do you know how embarrassing it is to be dependent on your wife for anything? For your wife to be the main breadwinner?

I do help out some, though. I've taken charge of preparing the meals since I'm home all day. It's a small way for me to help Wendy and feel less reliant on her. So I will fix an easy meal for the family tonight: spaghetti and meatballs.

Later, while Wendy is enjoying the meal she didn't have to prepare, she pauses and looks at me and asks, 'Oh I forgot, how was your day? Get any work done?'

I hope my answer will satisfy her. 'Thanks. Well...I straightened up the office, got it ready for the semester. I don't know if I told you this, but I'll be teaching for four writing programs with four different ways of doing things. It'll be hard to keep things straight once I get going. And each school starts on a different day, Monday or Tuesday of next week.'

Probably too much information for her.

'Mmm, hmm,' says Wendy, chewing on a mouthful of spaghetti. I know what she's thinking. I brought this on myself, yadda, yadda, yadda.

I continue, 'I did discover some old notebooks and folders, though, some of them from about twenty years ago in high school, some from college and some from grad school. Several of those stories look pretty good after all this time, especially those from the grad school years.'

I can guess what she's going to say next.

And she does: 'Maybe one of them's The Great American Novel.'

Just what I thought. But I reply, 'Maybe so.'

'Really, Daddy?' says Emma. 'That would be so cool…. What's a Great American Novel?'

Thanks, Emma. A welcome distraction from Wendy's glaring eyes.

'Well, Emma,' I answer, taking her hand in mine, 'it's a book—a long story—that is so great and so famous that everyone wants to buy it or read it. And writers want to write like it.'

'Do it, Daddy! Do it!' Emma says clapping her hands.

I catch Wendy rolling her eyes. She and I have been over this ground before. She's convinced I will never write a novel, let alone The *Great* American Novel.

Does she notice the daggers I stare at her across the table?

Chapter 2
Wendy Campbell

'Bill. Bill. Another bill. Soccer registration fee. Music lesson fee.' I'm sitting at the kitchen table, sorting through the bills that came in the mail while we were in Florida.

I sigh; I can't help it.

Every month mounting bills and only one major source of income. That's me. Yes, I'm the one who pays for everything, while Miles...yeah, Miles. Poor Miles. Pitiful Miles, whose overall pay added to mine barely keeps us out of the red. 'It's going to be a tight fall, I'm afraid,' I say.

And we all know why.

Miles sits across the table staring at the stack of bills as I go through them, seemingly oblivious to the situation, as always. All of us are sore from sitting in the car on the road the last two days. Miles drove the whole way, for which I am grateful.

Today is Monday, and I really don't feel like going back to work.

'You deserve some chill time today,' I force myself to say as I lay aside the bills. 'Don't work too hard.'

'Yep,' he says, and he sighs. He has nothing to sigh about; I'm the one who should sigh. I can't chill out at all today. I have to go to work, while he stays home. I'll have to be in the college library by 8:00. Even being the Reference Department head at Western Indiana University doesn't pay all that much compared to the same position at a large university like Indiana University. I know; I have checked there for openings.

I finish my breakfast, drink the last of my coffee, and go upstairs to the bathroom to put on my face for the day. I lay out all my makeup tools on the counter, about a dozen of them. Miles puts a brush through his hair once or twice and makes a big deal about it, the jerk.

Soon I'm ready to meet the day, and I go downstairs. I grab my handbag and briefcase and say

9

goodbye to dear old Miles with a brief hug and kiss, then it's off to the garage.

This is getting old fast, I'm thinking, as I drive on the way to work. At least if he were leaving for work also, I could handle this better. But no, he stays home while I leave.

This is the beginning of Miles' fourth year of teaching online courses, and for minimal pay. Considering the hours he puts in—or *says* he puts in—it is below minimum wage.

All this time he hasn't once mentioned getting a job locally. Like in insurance, or in banking, or even at a register at a retail store. Wouldn't that be better than what he's doing now, and killing himself doing it? It would certainly make him (*and us*) more money.

My job at the university library involves dealing mostly with students, some of them pretty ignorant, and even with some ignorant faculty. I work with two women with whom I have a cordial relationship. We have almost nothing in common, except that Carolyn is married and has two children, like me. Her husband is vice president of one of the banks, so they're set.

That's a big difference.

Well, here I am, arriving on campus, first day back. I drive around the library building to the staff parking lot, where I have a dedicated parking space as a department head. Occasionally, though, a student decides to park in my space because they (it's usually a male student) can't find parking where they're supposed to and prefer not to walk the longer distance to their classroom building. The library is next to the Business Administration building. Usually, it's a Business major who parks in my space, I am sure. Lucky me, since classes haven't started yet, my space is available today.

I enter the Reference Department through the back door. Both Carolyn and Linda, my colleagues in the department, have already arrived. They are good colleagues to work with, but they are so different.

Linda, being single, has no family commitments at home and typically arrives on time, or even ahead of schedule. She's what they used to call an *old maid*. Carolyn, on the other hand, is married and has two teenagers, which often causes her to be a few minutes late. We don't have to clock in, so arrival times vary. It's rare that both arrive at the same time.

Carolyn sees me walk in and says, 'Welcome back, stranger! How was your vacation?'

I give her the flash fiction version of our trip and add, 'It's good to be home and back at work.'

Not really.

I don't want her or Linda to know that I didn't have fun on vacation because my mind was on my husband and our financial situation, and that we're still struggling. They won't understand, and anyway, I wouldn't want their sympathy.

I continue, 'We could have flown if we could afford it, so of course we drove, two days out and two days back. We're all sore today.'

Linda breaks in, 'Sounds wonderful. I wish I could take a trip like that.' Typical Linda. She's always jealous of others' good fortunes. Always wants what she can't have. Sometimes I pity her, but at other times I have wished I could tell her it's not exactly how it sounds. However, I don't, because I don't want anyone to pity me. After all, I'm supposed to be happy. Shouldn't I be?

Carolyn nods sympathetically, 'I know; even traveling with two teenagers can be a challenge for us. You know how it is.'

They both laugh. Linda sighs, 'I can only imagine! So glad I'm single.'

Right, I think.

With all the good-morning pleasantries out of the way, we head to our stations and prepare for the day's reference questions. It would be nice if something remarkable happened or someone would come in to make this day a bit more interesting.

Chapter 3
Miles

Already it's Thursday, and I've been busy the past three days preparing for those freshman composition courses at the four campuses. It's been slow work. Very slow work, work I really don't want to do.

I have received the contracts in the mail, reviewed and signed them, and sent them back to those four campuses. It's official; I am employed for the fall semester. Yippee ki-yay.

I promised Wendy I'd get my act together. I promised that things would be different this year, that I would really try.

I might be able to teach a section or two in the summer, but that would mean year-round work.

My God! For this I spent six years earning a Ph.D.?

This work is not sufficiently rewarding to warrant my full commitment and enthusiasm. I don't want to know my students. Our interactions will all be online, so that's a good thing.

Those old notebooks lying on the chair over by the window are beckoning me to join them. I've got a little time to take a look, so why not?

Setting aside the course documents and logging off the laptop, I roll the office chair over to the chair by the window. In one folder, I discover three long-forgotten stories from about fifteen years ago. They describe events from my early teen years and seem to hold some promise. Those events are still vivid in my memory. But they are juvenile productions, so maybe they shouldn't see the light of day.

Let's see what else is in here.

I pick up another file folder and begin reading the story starter. Immediately my mind goes back to my grad school years. This idea came to me after Wendy and I bought a vintage grandfather clock from an antique store during my last year as a grad student. I thought then that this story starter could be turned into a horror thriller with the idea I had for it.

Propping up my feet on the horizontal file, I take up reading at the point where I had stopped so many years ago. Could I add to it now? It seems to be heading in the right direction, perhaps on its way to becoming a thriller. 'OK,' I say, 'I'll give it a try.'

I'm particular about writing implements, including pencils and pens. I try several pens from the mug on my desk, testing each one in succession. None of them feel right in my hand or make the right contact with the paper. I even give the gel pen a shot, but after a couple of uninspired sentences, I toss it aside. It's not like any ideas are flowing through the pen, anyway. My word hoard is empty.

'Wait a minute!' I cry. A memory arises from the depths of my mind.

Years ago, I started these stories with a fountain pen, a gift from someone I can't recall. I bought ink for it and used it until I pressed too hard and ruined it. That's when I quit writing. But I recall how much I liked the feel of writing with that pen.

While I'm pondering the memory of that beloved pen, in a flash I remember there must be another fountain pen somewhere around here. I think it's in a drawer in my desk.

I open the top left-side drawer, and there it is: a small cardboard box. There's no writing on it, and it's wound around with several courses of scotch tape. Yes, the hallmark of my mother's wrapping, lots of scotch tape.

Following my father's passing, Mom gave me a few of his treasured belongings. I inherited some of his tools, a gold watch, his assortment of 1960s LPs and 45s, and a handful of pens and pencils. Among them I recall a Cross mechanical pencil, a fountain pen, and a large bottle of ink.

I remove the cardboard box and begin to unwrap the tape. Mom sealed it tight, I'm not sure why. Maybe one day I'll ask her, but now I need to cut this box open and see what's inside.

After slicing through the tape, I find the fountain pen beneath index cards and slips of paper. It's a Gillibrand fountain pen. Oh yes, I remember now: several years ago Mom said something to me about Dad's favorite pen. Well now, to honor my father's legacy, I should try to use this pen.

But first, before I use it, it has to be cleaned. Over the years in an unused fountain pen, the ink dries to a crust. Which is what I find with this pen.

It's a tedious process, taking it apart, cleaning each piece, and putting it back together.

After cleaning and re-assembling the pen, I dip the cartridge into the ink bottle and suck up some ink into it. After I insert the cartridge and screw on the body, instantly the pen comes alive in my hand. I also feel a creative surge in my spirit. The pen is ready for use.

After I take it through a few practice runs writing my name, it starts to flow nicely, and now it's time to put the pen to the test.

Let's pick up where I left off years ago.

A vibration springs from the pen, almost as if it's happy to be in service again. Wow, that's weird.

I write. Not only does the ink flow smoothly from the pen but the words also flow easily. Word after word, sentence after sentence, even paragraph after paragraph, all flow readily from my mind to the paper. I feel like a painter before a canvas as my art takes shape.

I write until 2:00 in the afternoon. Crap! How the time flew by when I was writing. I've finished the incomplete chapter in the original manuscript and added two more chapters. It was a breeze; I didn't even feel the time pass. Now I need to judge if it's any good.

Because there are so many lineouts and arrows in the original manuscript, I need to type it all up to see it clean. Wendy will be home in about two hours, and the girls won't be too far behind. Until they arrive, I'll sit at the laptop and type it all into Word.

Transcribing from my erratic handwriting to Word on the screen, I see the story taking shape before my eyes. But wait, didn't I type from the handwritten pages into word processing years ago? I need to find that typed manuscript and hope I saved it on a disk somewhere. It will make things so much easier.

Before I get up to find the disk, an email notification pops up on screen. It's from the department chair at North Carolina Central College, the header shouting in all CAPS: URGENT PLEASE READ ASAP. Uh oh! Doesn't sound like something I can set aside. Also, it doesn't sound like good news.

And it isn't! Crap! Crap! Crap!

The department chair informs me that due to lower class enrollments and budget cuts, my two sections have been canceled. The students have been reassigned to other online courses.

'Great! Just freaking great! I just lost a third of my income!' I scream at the screen.

I feel like firing off an obscenity-laden reply but think better of it. Instead, I reply with a controlled *sorry-about-that-I-hope-I-can-get-a-couple-of-sections-next-semester* sentences of bullshit. I want to add: *You bastard!* But I don't. I mustn't burn my bridges just yet.

So much for that horrible piece of news. My anger subsiding, I search for the disk with the typed manuscripts on it. Lucky for me, I find it soon.

After integrating the newly-typed sections into the incomplete story, I continue typing until Wendy arrives home from work.

What do I tell her now? How will she take my losing two of my six classes? For sure, she'd not be too happy. (I'm not exactly *un*happy, though.) I promised her things would be different, but now.... Now I don't know what to do. What I've lost in pay would have covered Sophie's violin lessons, Emma's gymnastics classes, and the family membership at the YMCA, as well as other expenses.

'Miles, I'm home!' Wendy cries out from the kitchen.

'I'm up in the office,' I shout. 'I'll be down in a minute.'

We meet at the foot of the stairs with a brief hug and kiss. As usual.

'What did you do today?' Wendy asks, as she goes to the kitchen for a glass of water.

'Worked on my classes and then worked on one of the stories I started fifteen years ago.'

'Really?' she says, arching her eyebrows.

That's not a good sign. Arched Wendy eyebrows are never a good sign. 'Yeah,' I say, hoping to ease the tension in those eyebrows.

'Are your classes about ready for prime time?'

Clearing my throat, I blurt out the truth. 'Almost. Well, not exactly. North Carolina Central cancelled my two sections.'

'Come again?' she questions, crossing her arms in front of her chest.

'Yeah, um, well… due to low enrollments and budget cuts.' I shrug.

By the look on her face, I can guess what Wendy is thinking. The same old, same old. *Well, if you hadn't….* 'Right,' she says. 'Do you have any recourse?'

Exhaling deeply, 'Nope,' I say, 'but I told them to keep me in mind in case anything changes.'

In the past three years, I've taught online at nine colleges, and Central has now become my sixth *former* college. I suspect falling enrollments and budget cuts must be rampant all across the country. It can't be anything else. At least I hope it's not anything else. I hope it's not me.

'Well,' sighs Wendy, 'we may have to cut our Y membership, and I hope we don't have to cut the girls' extracurricular activities.'

'I know, I know. I can search for another college needing an online instructor.'

'You do that.'

I want to say, 'You're not the boss of me,' but of course I don't.

Soon the girls come in the front door, breaking the tension. Hungry as usual, they grab snacks and milk before heading to the living room to watch TV. Wendy follows them to ask about their day and ends up sitting and watching their shows with them. I head into the kitchen to start preparations for dinner.

Dinner is served, and Emma and Sophie chatter excitedly about the upcoming school year. It's Thursday, and the girls start on Monday next week, while my semester begins either Monday or Tuesday, depending on the college. The writing program directors have emailed me with expectations and timelines, which I haven't read yet; that bureaucratic stuff makes my eyes glaze over. But then, I recall something the family might find interesting.

'Hey, Oregon Eastern College is pioneering teaching via something called Zoom, a new "platform" that will allow real-time contact, face-to-face via a computer screen.'

'What's a *platform*?' asks Emma.

'Well, Emma, I'm not exactly sure how it works.' Among the things I should have tried to learn in my teaching career was how to use these new educational tech things. Now I have to. 'What it means is that all the students and I will be able to see each other in real time, as they call it. It's like being in the classroom, and not, I guess. What this means, as I understand it, is that I will have to be in front of the laptop screen for forty-five or ninety minutes once or twice a week.'

I'll actually have to meet with them and *see* them—and vice versa—at a certain time, instead of whenever I want to with the usual online teaching. That's not what I want at all.

'That sounds complicated,' Wendy says.

'Yep. I'm not sure of this *platform*, as they call it. It will require a steep learning curve, so the Oregon college has scheduled a training session for all Zoom instructors,

17

starting tomorrow morning at 8:00. I hope to learn a lot, as I'll have to start on Tuesday next week at 9:30.'

I would rather watch paint dry. That would be more entertaining than what they'd want me to do. God! Why does this have to be so—

Suddenly, from somewhere in my mind a thin spectral voice whispers: *Drop everything and write!*

I shake off that thought and continue with dinner with the family.

After dinner and cleanup, I excuse myself to go upstairs. 'I have to finish prep for one of my classes,' I lie to Wendy. 'I'll be back down in about an hour or so.'

'Sure,' she says with a twist of sarcasm.

I'm familiar with that *sure*. So what if I'm usually later than I promise? Sometimes I get caught up in things.

Of course, I'm not planning to work on a composition class. I sit down and pick up my fountain pen to start writing. A slight shiver drifts throughout my body as the pen contacts the paper. I start writing. And writing. And writing.

Sometime later Wendy calls up the stairs, 'Miles, are you coming down soon?'

'In a minute!' I shout. 'I'll be down in a minute.'

We usually settle down in the living room to watch a favorite streaming show on NMEX. However, we're not going to do that tonight. I am feeling an urge inside to write, and to write a lot. I am being driven by some impulse I can't quite explain.

Later still, after I have written two new chapters, my pen runs out of ink. It's time to transfer the new material to Word.

Typing, I drift into a trance. Time stands still while my fingers flit across the keyboard.

Finally, my trance dissipates. I check the clock and see that I've been up here for over three hours. No way!

I rush downstairs to join Wendy, still not fully in the present.

I'm about to plop down on the couch when she stops me. 'Hey, have you been working out up there, or what?'

I don't understand her words at first. 'What do you mean?' I ask.

'I mean you're soaking wet!' she says, and then I check myself.

Sure enough, my face feels flushed and moist, and my shirt is soaked front and back. How did that happen? I was just sitting there typing. 'I guess I am. I didn't notice.'

'Don't sit back on the couch,' she says. 'You'll stain it! You must have sprinted to finish your classwork.'

Caught off guard, unable to lie, I reply, 'No, I got caught up in the story that I found the other day. It's coming along nicely. I think it's pretty good. I'd like you to read it, maybe tomorrow.'

She smiles. 'Maybe, when I get home from work tomorrow.'

I can't tell if her smile is genuine, but I'll take it. Wendy's smiles are rare these days.

Chapter 4
Miles

Friday morning I get up in time to see Wendy off to work. I can tell that the work week has been stressful for her. 'I am so looking forward to the end of this day,' she says, as she gives me a hug and a peck on the cheek and departs. I am not sure when the girls will get up, so I have my breakfast and head upstairs to the office.

Around 9:00 both girls are stirring, ready for their breakfast. They walk by the office door and wave with a muted, 'Hi Dad,' behavior they learned some time ago to keep from disturbing their father at work. I wave back, then quietly close the office door.

Today is their last weekday of freedom before school starts; no doubt they have big plans for the day. I hope their plans don't include me because I have work to do.

The Zoom training session begins at 10:00 here, 8:00 Pacific time. It will run until 2:00 p.m. Central time, noon Pacific time. I will either have a late lunch today or eat while on Zoom. What I like about this is the opportunity to write until the training starts and in between sessions.

As I pick up the fountain pen, I feel something like static electricity coming from it. Surprised, shaking my hand, I say, 'Wow, what's up with this? Excited to get started, are we?'

I swear I can hear a faint answer: *Yes!*

What the—? I shake off the tingling from my hand, put pen to paper, and off we go.

Within an hour I have written three pages with my pen, which has been moving across the page like it's greased with butter. My hand has a hard time keeping up with it.

I finish writing a few pages before the training starts. I must lay this pen down, but it is difficult to do.

I turn my attention to the task at hand, to learning how to use this Zoom thing. I have some difficulty logging on but am finally ready to start. And now I see that they will take attendance on Zoom, so I had better stay on screen throughout for the presenter and class to see. We introduce ourselves as the session gets underway. I am relieved to learn that a few other participants are not affiliated with a university, like me.

What do you know? The faculty on the Oregon Eastern campus taking this training have pastries, fruit, juices, and coffee before the session starts, and will have at each break. I and the other online mercenaries from all over the country must provide our own refreshments. Already I feel like a second-class citizen.

During the first session my eyelids slowly lower like roller shades. I'm not sure how much more of this I can take. I sure would like to pick up my pen and get back to writing. At least that would keep me awake.

At the first break I reach over to the notebook, prime my pen, and start writing. I've arrived at the point of my protagonist's big decision when I hear the seminar presenter call everyone to attention for the next session.

Damn, just when I reached the critical point! What should I do now?

Keep working, a voice inside responds. Yes, that's what needs to be done: continue the story...of course.

I mute the annoying lecturer's voice so I can concentrate. Maybe I can get a copy of the presentation to view later. Surely I can run a Zoom session for my students on my own on Tuesday.

Leaving the screen on with sound muted, I forge ahead with the story, my fountain pen seemingly leading the way, pulling my hand to the right. I hope the presenter on Zoom doesn't notice what I'm doing.

Later I look at the laptop screen to see that it has gone to sleep. Which I would have done if I weren't engaged in writing. When I wake it up, I notice the session is on another break, giving me the opportunity to continue writing my story, starting another chapter after a cliffhanger.

Sometime later the sound of the girls coming home for snacks disturbs my concentration. My laptop has fallen asleep again, as if it were also bored by the content on screen. After jiggling the mouse and pressing Enter, I wake up the laptop to see "The End. Best wishes. For support, go to *support.it.OEC.edu.*"

Really? I look at the clock and see that it's 2:00 in the afternoon. How did that happen? I missed the rest of the training.

Actually, I missed most of the training. Oh well, it can't be too hard to start my class Tuesday morning. Right?

My pen has run out of ink anyway. I leave my writing and go downstairs to join Sophie and Emma for my lunch. They are already into snacks when I pop into the kitchen to get out my sandwich fixings.

After stuffing an Oreo into her mouth and washing it down with a big gulp of milk, Sophie asks, 'How's your seminar, Dad? Or is it over?'

'It was pretty good. There was a lot of jargon that was a little hard to understand.'

'What was it on?'

'How to teach with Zoom.'

'Oh yeah, Zoom. You said that last night. We actually had to use it for a couple of weeks in the spring when Mrs. Garcia had the flu and worked from home as she recovered. We used it in the computer lab. It wasn't too hard once we got used to it.'

'Well good, if I get in trouble I'll ask you for help, then.'

'I don't think so,' Sophie laughs. 'I'll be in school then.'

'Oh, OK, I forgot. But after you get home maybe you can teach me.'

'Isn't that what you learned this morning?'

I have no answer.

Snack time is over for all three of us, and the girls leave the house to rejoin their friends. I go back upstairs to take up the story where I left off.

An hour later the pen runs out of ink, and I remember that I haven't finalized all my class plans. I also haven't read my emails. I've probably received some from the three colleges.

I open several emails from composition program directors wanting to "touch base" with me, a phrase that I despise. 'I'll *touch base* with you, Dr. Mason!' I say to the email on screen.

Looking over requirements from the three colleges, I expect now to work through the weekend to be ready for next week.

Nevertheless, the tug of the pen draws me back toward my manuscript.

After four o'clock Wendy comes through the kitchen door and drops her keys on the counter. This is definitely a good time to quit, even though I don't want to. 'Miles, I'm home,' Wendy shouts.

'I'll be right down!' I answer. After winning a brief battle with a strong urge to continue writing, I join her in the kitchen.

'How'd your day go?' we say simultaneously. We chuckle, then both say, 'You go first!' Wendy decides to take the lead.

The day hasn't been too bad, Wendy says. She actually did some rewarding work for once. She helped a few professors set up their class reference readings for their courses and found them pleasant to work with for a change. Especially the new guy in Anthropology, who seems to be pretty cool. 'I expect he'll be a hit with his students.' She pours a glass of water, sips from it, and says, 'So, how was your day? How was the Zoom training?'

'A bit of a challenge,' I say. 'I think I can handle it, though.' I hope she doesn't ask for details. Fortunately, she doesn't.

Of course, I can't keep my real work a secret. 'So after the Zoom class I worked some more on the story. I think it's pretty interesting. Maybe you can read it and tell me what you think?'

'Yeah, sure, later on,' she says. 'I'm tired now, but later.'

'Well, all righty then,' I say, deflated. Time to drop the subject. 'How about happy hour to celebrate the end of the work week?'

Wendy says, 'Sure,' and I pour the wine.

Tonight we'll order pizza delivered and drink beer with it, our long-standing Friday night end-of-the-week ritual. Sophie and Emma always enjoy pizza on Friday nights.

I sure do want to go back upstairs to continue writing, but with a great deal of effort I commit to spending some time tonight with Wendy and the girls.

Every once in a while, as the evening passes, I hear a low growl. 'Do y'all hear that growling?' I finally ask. 'Is there a mad dog in our front yard?'

'What growling?' Wendy answers.

'No, Daddy,' answers Emma. 'I don't hear anything.'

'You must be hearing things,' adds Wendy.

'Really?' I say. 'I guess it must be my imagination.'

I've started hearing low voices the past couple of days. Now growls. Am I starting to lose my mind?

Saturday morning. Last Saturday before the girls go back to school.

And next week I will start the fall semester at three widely separated colleges. I know that Wendy wants to lay low today to do some yardwork before it gets too hot.

But beginning at breakfast the girls beg for a day away from the house. A trip to the lake, the one with a sandy beach, kayaks, and paddleboats. 'Please, Dad? The summer's over,' pleads Sophie.

'Yeah, school starts next week. Pleeeeze, Daddy, pleeeze?' Emma whines. Neither Wendy nor I want to go, but after all, it *is* the last weekend before school starts for the girls.

Reluctantly we agree. I am more reluctant than Wendy, but I must give in. I know what will happen if I say no and go up to the office to start writing. For once I manage to put my daughters' desires above my own.

After breakfast we put on our swimsuits, pack up provisions, and head out on the one-hour journey to Morse Park Beach, which has everything that a family would want. It should satisfy the girls, and a bonus for me will be seeing Wendy in her hot pink bikini.

Well, that's over and done. We have just arrived back home late afternoon from our trip to the lake. Despite liberal applications of sunscreen, all of us are pink-skinned and turning red by the minute. More than that, we're all extremely exhausted. The sun might be a source of energy for electrical power, but it saps energy from humans. *Why is that?* I wonder.

The girls go to their rooms and collapse, while Wendy and I unload the car, then fall on the couch in the living room. I decide I had better return to working on my class preparations after dinner, if I can only generate the willpower. Classes start in just a couple of days.

After dinner I excuse myself to go up to the office to "work on my classes."

'Didn't you finish that Friday?' asks Wendy, a puzzled look on her face.

'Not completely. There's just a little more to do.'

'I bet you would have finished it all if you hadn't spent the time writing on your novel.'

Of course, that's true, but I am irritated, nonetheless. 'Yeah, you're right, Wendy. You're always right.'

'I didn't mean it that way—'

'But that's the way it came across. Whatever, I'll see you later.' I leave for the stairs.

'Miles....' Wendy calls to my back. 'Oh, never mind.'

Upstairs I sit down at the laptop and power it up. While waiting for it to boot up, I feel the magnetic lure of my Gillibrand pen.

Pick me up.

25

Pick me up.

Pick me up, my friend.

Friend? Where did that come from, and did I hear it right? I reach over and pick up the pen, examining it. It seems harmless enough, and it is already doing wonders for my writing. But why? What's so special about it? Can I find some information on it?

After the slow laptop finally boots up, I do a Google search for "Gillibrand fountain pen" and wait a millisecond for over eight and a half million results to start displaying. My best option is to search the eBay entries for vintage fountain pens, as my pen must be at least fifty years old. Soon the screen displays several Gillibrand fountain pen models, and on one eBay site there appears a variety of designs of my model, varying by color and trim.

It's a Katrina 66, and I even find one of the same color and design as mine. It has a medium-size gold nib, with a *vacuum converter* for the ink. So that's what they call that squeeze thing. Though the Katrina 66 was originally an affordable entry-level fountain pen, these pens are selling "used" as collectors' items for anywhere from $25 to $125 and more on eBay and Etsy. What a distinguished writing implement! And it's a legacy from my father, too.

That's enough research, as once again I feel a craving to pick up that Katrina 66 and start writing.

Two hours later, Wendy calls upstairs, 'Miles, are you finished? Come on down and watch TV with me!' Wendy's call breaks my concentration, and I lose the end of a powerful sentence. 'Shit!' I mutter. Although I continue to feel the need to keep writing, I stop, considering time with Wendy worth breaking off from writing. I'll go on down to join her. I just hope she doesn't ask me about my course preparation.

It requires some effort to pull myself away, like trying to pry a magnet apart from steel.

Settled in to watch our current show on NMEX, Wendy asks me how my course prep has gone. She's fishing.

Well now, how shall I reply? 'I finished it and then returned to the story. I really like the plot and the characters. I'd still like you to read it and let me know what you think.'

She pauses before responding. 'OK, tomorrow morning when I'm fresh. I'm too beat now to concentrate on anything but the TV.'

Twenty minutes later both of us are asleep on the couch, exhausted from our lake excursion. So much for TV. We wake up and turn off the TV, force ourselves off the couch, and go upstairs to get ready for bed.

After breakfast Sunday morning, I head upstairs to type my latest chapters. I have now finished five long chapters and will start writing chapter six after Wendy has read them on screen.

It takes about a half hour to finish typing.

I go downstairs to find Wendy, who, it turns out, is in the back yard in the cooler part of the day before the temperature rises into the 90's. She's weeding and watering. It's going to be a while before she's ready to read, so I go back upstairs to write some more.

I can't get over how the smooth flow of this pen seems to enhance the creative process. Again, I feel that all I'm doing is holding it steady while it moves across the page. Although I really should finish my course preps— *finish* is hardly the word; it's closer to *continue*—I can't stop.

An hour later Wendy comes in from the yard and cleans up. She calls upstairs: 'Miles? I'm finished outside. I can read now if you want me to.' I ignore her while I finish typing an important sentence. She calls out again louder, 'Miles? Miles? Can you hear me?'

Her voice shatters my concentration, and I lose the scene. *Damn it to hell, Wendy!* However, I had better not shout that out to her. 'I hear you, Wendy,' I respond,

27

controlling my tone. 'I'm typing at the moment. I'll call you up once I've finished. OK?'

She calls out, 'That's fine.' But the tone of her voice suggests that she really doesn't want to.

Time passes; I've finished typing, but I can't break away now. I return my attention to the notebook paper, hoping I haven't forgotten my last thought. Once the pen touches the paper again, it all comes back, and I begin to feel that I'm a spectator watching a horse race as I observe the pen speeding across the page, dragging my hand with it.

Yes, it's off to the races indeed.

I work past the start of lunch and then force myself to stop when Wendy calls me down to eat. As I gather up the handwritten pages, I count nine more pages, front and back. It will take a long time to type them after lunch. I haven't even finished the last chapter. It won't be ready for Wendy to read it until after 4:00 or later.

As it turns out, by the time the manuscript is ready to be read, I have completed thirty-two typed pages in all, in six chapters. It will take a long time to read. As I finish typing the last sentences, Wendy comes up the stairs and goes to the bedroom. She closes the bedroom door, thereby closing the door on reading my work. I guess she's taking a nap.

Well, after her nap it will be time for dinner. Then after dinner Wendy will be checking and double-checking the girls' items for their first day of school. I might as well soldier on, keep going until I run out of words. I will know when it is, either when the pen runs out of ink, or my brain runs out of ideas.

Late in the afternoon the pen actually runs out of ink, and I actually run out of ideas.

As much as I despise doing it, I must review the course preparations for Western Iowa, Northern New Mexico, and Oregon Eastern.

Funny, I never noticed until now the points of the compass in the institution names. Too bad that North Carolina Central isn't North Carolina *Southern* or

Southern North Carolina. But that would sound odd, wouldn't it? I think I'm getting giddy.

I review course materials for the colleges that begin the semester on Tuesday, which I remember are Western Iowa and Oregon Eastern. Even though I won't be engaging students in real time for the Iowa and New Mexico colleges, the schedule, assignments, and materials need to be ready by early Monday morning. I can use the rest of the day Monday to try to review this Zoom business for the Oregon college.

The preparation tasks bore me, but I must stick with them. I can't afford to lose these three colleges. Imagine what Wendy would say if that happened!

The rest of the day passes slowly. I help Wendy get the girls ready for school as their excitement grows. They like school and look forward to the first day of the new school year, in their new grades with their new teachers and classmates.

At bedtime Wendy apologizes for not making the time to read my work, 'But I promise I'll make time soon, when I'm fresh and ready to focus.'

'That's all right,' I say. 'It'll be more developed when you do read it.' I kiss her good night and excuse myself to finish up the course work.

'OK, but don't be up too late.'

'I won't.'

I do in fact stay up too late. Way too late. After putzing around in the office, I fill the pen's cartridge to be ready for tomorrow's writing, whenever I can make the time.

But after filling the cartridge and screwing the body back on, I *must* write. Something like a trance comes upon me as I open the notebook and turn to the last page. I put pen to paper. Immediately the ideas form as if out of thin air, and the words flow like a river.

Next thing I know, it's two in the morning, my pen is out of ink, and I'm soaked with sweat. I've written ten more pages, front and back, in the last three hours.

Amazing, just freaking amazing!

I must have refilled the pen during that span of time, but I don't remember doing so. I've produced too much to type, and I'm very sleepy and exhausted.

Laying aside the notebook, I head for the bathroom and towel off. Stripping to my shorts, I tread lightly to the bedroom, gently slide under the bed covers, and soon fall asleep.

What a night it has been!

Chapter 5
Wendy

Sunday morning I wake up sorry for the way I overreacted to Miles yesterday when I dissed his writing project. But I'm too proud to admit it to him. Better to let sleeping dogs lie for the time being. However, I'm not sure that's a good idea for a marriage.

After we all have breakfast, Miles immediately goes upstairs. I know why he's going up there. He says he's going up to finish preparing for his classes, but I know what he's going to do. He goes to the bathroom to brush his teeth, then walks down the hall. To the office, of course. We need the money, so I hope he really is preparing his classes. However, I have my doubts about that.

I'm not going to wait around all day for Miles to call me to read his work. There's work to be done in the yard before it gets too hot, so I'd best get to it. It's the cooler part of the day before the temperature rises into the 90's. I'll be weeding and watering. I'll come back in when the temperature climbs into the upper 80's.

Well, that was fast. After only an hour, it's already too hot and humid to stay outside. Time to go in. I go inside and towel off. Then I call from the bottom of the stairs: 'Miles? I'm finished outside. I can read your story now if you want me to.'

No response. I call out louder, 'Miles? Miles? Can you hear me?'

'I hear you, Wendy,' he shouts out, his voice edged with irritation. 'I'm writing now. After I've typed what I've written I'll call you up. OK?'

As if. I would rather stick pins under my fingernails than read what he's written, but I will humor him whenever he's ready.

After a while I call Miles down to eat lunch with the girls and me. At least he does that. But he wolfs it down and goes back upstairs with hardly a word to me and the girls.

It's mid-afternoon now, and from the living room where I'm straightening up things, the clicking of the keyboard echoes from the second floor. The length of time and speed tell me that it's not his coursework he's working on.

Soon I feel a nap coming on. I'll lie down for a rest and wait for him to call me. I go upstairs and close the bedroom door quietly, then take off my shoes and lay my head on the pillow.

When I wake up it's late in the afternoon, and I realize we need to start getting Sophie and Emma ready for their first day of school tomorrow. They like school and look forward to the first day of the new school year, in their new grades with their new teachers and classmates.

That task lasts into the middle of the evening and spares me having to read Miles' work. At least Miles helps me, and we watch their excitement grow as we sort out their things.

At bedtime I apologize for not having the time to read his work, 'But I promise I'll make time tomorrow, when I'm fresh and ready to focus.'

'That's all right,' he says. 'It'll be more developed when you do read it.' We kiss good night, but guess what? He excuses himself 'to finish up the course work.'

Yeah, right.

'OK,' I say, 'but don't be up too late.'

'I won't,' he promises.

Sometime in the middle of the night I get up to go to the bathroom and see that the other side of the bed is empty. Miles' footsteps tromp outside in the hall, and the sound of water flows in the hall bathroom. Shortly afterward, Miles slips into bed and starts snoring within minutes.

It takes me a long time to get back to sleep as I ponder how to deal with this new Miles, whom I like even less than the old Miles.

Chapter 6
Miles

Monday morning dawns with a flurry of activity as Wendy and I see to getting Sophie and Emma out of bed, feeding them breakfast, and readying them to leave the house. The girls are out the front door shortly after 7:30, walking to their bus stop at the corner of the block.

'Whew!' Wendy says. 'We got 'er done!'

'Nice job!' I say, high fiving her. 'The girls are lucky to have such an organized mom, not to mention sexy too!'

'Oh, quit it!' Wendy glances at her Fitbit and sees it's time for her to finish getting ready for work. She'll leave soon for her fifteen-minute drive to campus. 'Well,' she says, 'good luck on your first day of classes. I hope it goes well, especially the Zoom class.'

'Fortunately, that's not until tomorrow, but I do have to make a last-minute check on my totally online, *asynchronous* classes, as they say these days,' I smirk.

Wendy goes upstairs to the bathroom, and I follow her, admiring her backside. Then I turn down the hall toward the office. Once there, I power up the laptop, waiting for it to be ready for me to type greetings to my students on my course sites.

Wendy rushes downstairs, calling out, 'OK, I'm leaving now. Bye!'

'OK!' I shout.

She's a bit late this morning because of getting the girls ready for the bus.

I sit in the chair staring at the laptop, slow to boot up, a sign of its age. I bought it seven years ago, but I imagine each laptop year equals about twelve years in a human's life. I should have replaced it two years ago.

While waiting, I glance to my right and notice my Katrina 66 fountain pen lying expectantly on the desk within easy reach. I need to refill it, but first I force myself to ignore it while waiting on the laptop. I need to transfer all those handwritten pages to Word first.

After the laptop boots up, I set to work typing those pages from last night's session.

Two hours later, my cell phone ringtone snaps me out of my fevered engagement with my story. It's a number from an unfamiliar area code, so I don't answer it.

I get many spam calls a week on my cell phone, none of which leave messages, except for the occasional spam call warning me to pay the IRS what I owe to avoid going to prison. If it's important, the caller will leave a voicemail message.

After a minute the voicemail tone pings. OK, so I'd better check it. I press the number for voicemail, type my password, and tap the speaker icon so I can hear without putting the phone to my ear.

'Have I reached the number of Dr. Miles Campbell? If so, this is an urgent message. This is Dr. Steve Gladden, chair of the English Department at Oregon Eastern College. Dr. Campbell, you are an online instructor in a composition section for us that was to start today on Zoom at 9:00 a.m. Pacific Time. It's now 9:15 here, and I have been notified by a few students that you have not sent the Zoom link to them. Please call me back as soon as possible and let's discuss this situation. My number is area code 555-456-7890, extension 23.'

Oh crap! I had the day wrong! The class doesn't start on Tuesday. It starts today!

How did I mix up the college start days? Do I have the other two right? I check my email account and discover many emails from my new OEC students. Most are confused, a couple are angry, and one closes with "OK, since this is a freshman class, do we wait fifteen minutes before leaving? LOL!"

Smartass!

I'm in trouble. How can I wriggle my way out of this? I phone Dr. Gladden, who picks up after the first ring.

'Dr. Gladden speaking.'

I clear my throat. 'Dr. Gladden, this is Miles Campbell returning your call. I am so sorry about what happened, or what didn't happen.'

'Thanks for returning my call so quickly, Dr. Campbell. It's almost 9:30 here. Why weren't you meeting with your class on Zoom this morning?'

Think fast, Miles! 'I have a slow laptop, and it spent thirty minutes downloading updates this morning. This happens about once a month, and it chose today to do it. I'm so sorry.'

'I understand. However, be that as it may, you've missed your first session.'

I deserve this. 'I am very sorry. What should I do?'

After a long pause, Dr. Gladden says, 'I suggest you email the students, explain what happened, and tell them you will see them Wednesday. Make sure that this doesn't happen again.'

'It won't, sir, I promise you.'

'Maybe you should replace your laptop. Teaching online requires a reliable computer, you know.'

'You're right. I'll check into that.'

The phone call over, I ponder my next move. It will take a while to write to the students because I haven't actually created a class email distribution list. Instead of taking the time to create the distribution list, name it, and save it, I copy and paste student email addresses one at a time into the *TO:* line.

After about five minutes I've loaded the addresses from the student information, and I've written an apologetic email to all of them, promising I would "see" them Wednesday. 'See them! How very clever of me,' I chuckle.

Well, I had better learn how to use Zoom by 11:00 Wednesday morning, 9:00 Pacific time. I make a mental note to create the class email distribution list to save time on Wednesday.

Then the need hits again to pick up my pen and write some more. I can't ignore it; I swear it feels like an addiction.

35

So, I write.

The next thing I know, it's mid-afternoon and I've been writing continuously for almost three hours. I must have refilled the pen sometime in that block of time, but I can't remember. I haven't had lunch or even stopped to take a bathroom break. Feeling the need for the latter, I make for the bathroom, still aflush with the story in my head.

My protagonist, whom I've dubbed *Pete*, is going insane and is threatening the lives of his family. I don't know how the plot descended to that level, but there it is.

Having done my business in the bathroom, I refill my pen and get back to work.

Just after 4:00 Wendy arrives home, drops her keys on the kitchen counter, and shouts out, 'Miles, I'm home!'

I shout back to her, 'Up here! I'll be down in a sec!' I stop typing and save my work. I bound downstairs.

It's sharing time. Wendy goes first. 'How was your day? Did you have any classes today?'

'Well...,' then I explain what happened, using the version that I told Dr. Gladden.

She grabs the sides of her face like in Edvard Munch's famous painting, "The Scream." 'Oh my, that's terrible! I hope everything goes all right on Wednesday with that class. When do your other classes start?'

'Tuesday is the first day of campus classes in New Mexico and Iowa, but the students can start today if they want. Everything is set up for them.'

Everything is *not* set up for them; I will have to work on that tomorrow.

Then I ask for a report on her day.

'I had a good day, as days go. Students started coming by to look at the readings for their courses, and that new guy in Anthropology, Dr. Torres, came by again with a couple of cute coeds to show them where the course readings are and how to check them out. I think they feigned ignorance just to be within his bubble.'

36

'Hmm, sounds like they must think he's hot.' I sure hope Wendy doesn't think he's hot, too.

'Word is getting around that the girls are already calling him *The Torrid Dr. Torres*.'

'Sounds like he's making quite a splash on campus. I bet enrollment shoots up in Anthropology courses.'

'I think you're right. But changing the subject, we've got a new library director, who came around to visit with all the staff today.'

'Let me guess, Henry Hotspur, known affectionately as "Hottie Hotspur!"'

'I wish! She's anything but. She's Opal Schute, pronounced *shooty,* and she looks like George Washington. What a face!'

'I can guess it now: soon she'll be called *Shitty Schute* behind her back.'

Wendy smiles. 'Only by the staff!'

We have a laugh or two more about campus nicknames, creating a few more to apply to the more infamous faculty and staff. I'm surprised I remember some of them after being gone for several years.

It's time for Happy Hour, so Wendy fixes the drinks, and we sit and talk until the girls get home. I'm relieved that this conversation has gone so well, even if I had to lie. I've dodged a bullet today.

A little later than expected, the girls come home all aflutter about their first day of school.

'How was your first day back, girls?' I say, as Emma hugs me hello. She's always been Daddy's little girl. I wish that Sophie were, too.

As expected, Sophie replies with her go-to Sophie-answer: 'Fine.' It's like pulling teeth to get any more from her. We conclude that she had a good first day, anyway.

'OK, Sophie, good!' I say, then I turn to Emma. 'And how was your first day, dear?'

Emma is off to the races, telling us all about her new teacher and her old and new friends and what they wore and where they sat and how yucky the boys were and yadda yadda yadda.

'Whoa, slow down, girl!' Wendy says, 'Give us a chance to catch up!'

Finally, Emma finishes her report. It's apparent that she had an exceptional first day of school.

We congratulate them both on their day and get ready for supper.

Tuesday morning after the girls have set off for school and Wendy has left for work, I rush upstairs and turn on my laptop, committed to spending the morning on those "asynchronous" online composition courses at Northern New Mexico and Western Iowa. After finishing that work, I plan to spend several hours learning Zoom and populating my course folders for my class at Oregon Eastern on Wednesday.

I don't know how I did it, but after two hours of tedious work I've managed to populate the online folders of the two New Mexico courses and the one at Iowa, and posted my welcomes to the three sections, for all 105 registered students to read. Add the twenty-nine at Oregon Eastern for a total of 134 writing students this semester, and that's my teaching load. It would have been worse, I know, if I still had the two classes in North Carolina.

I work until nearly lunch time, then break to check email, Facebook, and online news.

Around noon I think I should spend about fifteen minutes reviewing my developing story on screen in Word. Paying special attention to the last few paragraphs of the last chapter, I pick up where I left off and end the chapter differently than I thought I would. Later I can mull it over as I eat my sandwich.

I reach for my notebook and my Katrina pen, which needs ink. After refilling the cartridge and replacing it in the pen, I begin writing.

Some time has passed when the ink begins to run out. Checking the clock to see that it's one-thirty, I can't believe that I've been writing for an hour and a half. I'm in the middle of chapter sixteen and have no memory of the passing of time.

I'm exhausted, an enslaved amanuensis recording the narrative spoken by the resident voice deep in my head, traveling down through my arm to my fingers and through the pen to the paper. I can hardly keep up with that voice telling me what to write.

A little later I am soaked with sweat once again by the fury of my writing. I refill the pen and resume work once again. Sometime later I have finished Chapter 19 as my pen runs dry, so I will type it all up to see what it looks like on screen. This will take a while, since I've composed six chapters after typing the last one.

It's nearly 3:00, not much time for typing until Wendy, Sophie, and Emma return home.

Oh well, I'll type until Wendy comes in the door downstairs.

Chapter 7
Wendy

It's close to noon on Tuesday, and I've been busy reshelving the books in the Reference stacks. Pretty soon I become aware of someone standing behind me. I turn to see that it's Dr. Mark Torres of the Anthropology Department.

Smiling, a twinkle in his eye, he says, 'So, I see you're doing it in the stacks.'

'I beg your pardon?' I respond.

'You know, that old saying that librarians *do it in the stacks*?'

'Oh, yeah, like I've never heard *that* one before. Or "I wish I could be a librarian and read books all day." Or "librarians are novel lovers."'

'Hmm, are you?'

'Am I what?'

'A novel lover?'

I grimace. This guy's opening schtick isn't playing well with me so far. It reminds me of the pickup lines used by the nervous boys in junior high school.

He realizes that he's gone far off the rails. 'Sorry, I didn't mean to offend you. Just joking. Now I see it was a bad joke.'

I scan his handsome brown face, dark brown eyes, black close-cut curly hair, and his square chin. How could I be offended by this man? 'No problem. You're forgiven,' I say with a coy smile. 'But you must understand that such inane comments go with librarian territory, and they are annoying.'

Dr. Torres moves in a little closer and says, 'I just wanted to stop by and thank you for setting up my course reference materials and helping with my students. And now that I realize I have offended you, let me make it up to you by buying you lunch at our four-star student center food court.'

'Oh, that's not necessary, Dr. Torres—'

'Call me Mark.'

We have moved quickly into the familiar. 'OK, Mark, you don't need to do that. I wasn't offended at all. By the way, call me Wendy.'

'OK, Wendy, but I won't take no for an answer. When do you go on lunch break? I'll hang around and "do it" in the anthropology stacks upstairs until you're free.' He smiles and winks.

'Ha!' I laugh, despite my misgivings. However, something about this man attracts me even though his jokes are lame. 'OK, if you insist! Come back in about fifteen minutes.'

'It's a date!' Mark smiles and shows his pearly whites. He saunters off to the stairs leading up to the second level.

Watching Mark walk up the stairs, I say to myself, 'A date? What just happened?'

Fifteen minutes later, Mark returns to the Reference desk, where I'm on the phone. I'm taking notes while listening, the phone cradled against my left ear between my tilted head and shoulder.
'Yes…yes…sure…right. I sure will, Dr. Barlow. They will be ready. Yes… yes… goodbye.' I hang up and look at Mark, raising one eyebrow and shaking my head.

'That was Dr. Julia Barlow of the History Department. If you haven't met her yet, you'll know who she is when you do meet her. She's nuts! In fact, I don't know anyone on campus who doesn't think she's crazy. She's demanding, and she also thinks she's the target of evil people who are out to get her fired and who want her property in town.'

'Wow, really? Then let me rescue you from this insanity hotline.'

'Sure. I'm ready!'

As we walk through the library toward the door, several pairs of staff eyes—female and male—follow our progress. There surely will be talk later.

Walking across campus, Mark asks me how long I've been at the library…and other probing questions.

41

'Uh, I guess I've been here about six years. We came from Austin, Texas, where my husband earned his Ph.D. in English, and I earned my Master's in Library Science.'

'Really? What's his name, and what field?'

'His name is Miles, and he specialized in Victorian literature.'

'And how about you? Are there specialties in Library Science?'

'Well, yes. My specialty is Information Systems.'

'That's cool. You must be very knowledgeable about how to find information.'

I could swear that his left eye twinkled like a star.

'It's not really what I do here, but it got me the job. And I do know how to find information. But apparently I'm not so good at finding what people come to me seeking.'

'What do you mean?'

'I often have to play a game of Twenty Questions to narrow down what they're really looking for.'

We enter the student center and head to the food court. After checking out the options, Mark chooses a cheeseburger with fries and a Coke. I pick up a Caesar salad and bottled water. We go over to an empty table and sit down.

Mark notices my food choice and mocks gently, 'You must be watching your figure. You make me look like a glutton. Though I've noticed some of the male students watching your figure, too!'

Really now? He's getting a little too familiar. 'Well, these days and at my age a woman has to pay more attention to nutrition and fitness.'

'Oh, do you work out?'

'Not a lot, but I sometimes go over to the campus fitness center, and we have a Y family membership.'

'That's good.' Mark replies. 'So tell me, does your husband eat lunch here at the student center? I'd like to meet him some day, see who the lucky guy is.'

42

Slick as STP. But thinking about my reply to this question, I can't help that my mood dampens a bit. 'He's not on the faculty anymore, unfortunately.'

'Oh really? Why not?'

'He was let go after his third year. He wasn't performing up to expectations. And they were low at that. The English Department wasn't satisfied with his teaching and scholarship.'

'I'm sorry to hear that. It's a cutthroat world in academia. Hard to get hired and easy to get fired. Two hundred applicants for every tenure-track job and a line of people waiting for you to fail, to fill your position. Or so I hear.'

'That's what happened with Miles.'

'So, what's he doing now? Still in academia or selling insurance…or something else?'

'I wish,' Wendy sighs. 'He's teaching online at several colleges across the country, all freshman composition. He can have upwards of 200 students a semester. He's over-worked, under-paid, and under-appreciated.'

'Gee, I can't imagine that kind of life. From what little I know about freshman writing courses, even two sections mean a lot of work.'

'Tell me about it. Library salaries aren't at the top of the scale, either, but we manage to get by.'

We chat some more between bites. After a while, the Torrid Dr. Torres glances at his watch and gets up, excusing himself, saying he has a 1:00 class coming up. 'I sure have enjoyed our lunch together, Wendy,' he says. 'Thanks for keeping a lonely man from eating by himself.'

'Thank you, too,' I say, and I feel myself blushing.

'Let's do this again…if you wish, that is.'

'Yeah, OK, I guess. But next time, you're on. You'll tell me about your life and background.'

'It's a date!' Mark shakes my hand…and winks.

Outside the student center, I watch him turn away and head toward the Science building. I say to myself, 'Now that was a strange meeting.' Funny, he never asked me if I have any children. I know he's only been flirting, but it is nice to think that I still can turn heads and generate interest.

Too bad I can't at home.

I arrive home later, feeling a little dirty and a bit guilty about my lunch with Mark Torres. I hope what happened today will be a one-off thing, but I have a feeling it may not be.

And, truth be told, I hope it isn't. It *should* only develop into a collegial friendship.

Only a friendship, nothing more.

Dropping my keys on the kitchen counter, I call out, 'Miles, I'm home!' Hearing no reply, I climb the stairs and walk down the hall to the office. The distinctive sounds of keyboard keys clicking mean that Miles is at work. Hopefully at work on his classes.

I need to be nicer to the guy. And I guess my lunch with Mark Torres made me a bit excited. Popping into the office, I walk over and put my arms around Miles' neck and kiss him on his cheek, cooing in his ear, 'I'm home, lover boy.'

Miles reaches up, removes my arms from his neck, wipes the kiss off his cheek, and turning around in his seat says, 'Now you made me lose my concentration. I'm in the middle of typing this paragraph.'

What the hell?

I didn't expect this. 'Well, I can see what's most important to you!' Storming out of the room, tears welling up in my eyes, I cry, 'Don't let me bother you any longer!'

I'm sitting in a chair in the living room mulling over what just happened when the girls arrive home from school a few minutes later.

'Hey Mom,' says Sophie cheerfully, 'what's up?'

Emma adds, 'Where's Daddy?'

'Upstairs in the office. Don't disturb him, though. He's in a strange mood. He's in the middle of something.'

Emma goes upstairs anyway to the office and pops in. She says in her sweet little voice, 'Hi, Daddy. Watcha doin'?' *Uh oh, she's asking for trouble.*

Instead, I overhear a calm voice, a warm voice. 'Just typing up stuff. How was your day at school?' Emma fills him in on all the events of the day, who said what about whom, which lessons were good, and which were boring. Then Emma leaves the office and skips downstairs to make herself a sandwich and sits down next to me to watch a show on TV.

I'm doing a slow burn. So this is my place in the family pecking order! Nasty with me and sweet with Emma? This I can't stand. I have to do something to get my mind off what just happened.

Rising from the chair, I go into the kitchen to unload the dishwasher. Sophie is making herself a peanut butter and jelly sandwich when Emma comes to join us. I'm not aware of the racket I'm making as I slam plates and glasses on shelves, just short of breaking them.

Sophie notices. 'Mom! What's up? You'll break them dishes!'

'Those.'

'What?'

'*Those* dishes, not *them* dishes. Someone would think you were raised in a barn!'

'Mom!' cries Sophie, 'I'm sorry, I...I...,' and runs off upstairs to her room, sobbing.

I can't believe I just said that. That's not me, not with the girls. I follow Sophie upstairs to her room to apologize.

'I'm so sorry, honey,' I tell her. 'I didn't mean to fly off the handle like that.'

Apparently Miles doesn't like the ruckus. 'Damn!' he shouts, 'Can't I get some peace and quiet around here?!'

'That's enough!' I yell. I fly from Sophie's room and march down the hall to the office. I let Miles have it: 'What kind of father and husband are you? I bet you haven't done a bit of work for your classes all day, have you?'

The look on his face reveals the truth. 'Instead, you've been working on this, this, this *delusion* of yours that's taking you away from everything and everybody! If you keep this up, you'll lose your other classes, and you know what that will mean!'

Turning his face toward me, Miles says coldly, 'No, Wendy, what does that mean? Do tell me.'

I've never seen such *evil* in his look. 'It…It…Oh, never mind! Go back to your, your *masterpiece*. Don't worry about us! We'll be just fine!' I sneer and turn to leave the office.

'Close the door behind you,' Miles orders, his eyes on the screen.

I sure do, slamming it.

The evening meal passes in silence. The girls know something's going on between us, but they are too timid to ask what it is. Miles had broken away from his typing and writing long enough to eat, but he returns upstairs as soon as he's finished, without a word to anyone.

The Campbell household has become an emotional Antarctica.

Chapter 8
Miles

Finally, some peace and quiet!

I write far into the evening, beads of sweat on my forehead. This pen pushes me to write. I've stopped only for bathroom breaks and ink refills. I barely remember the girls dropping by to say goodnight.

Around midnight, my hand cramping, I break off from writing, as the pen has run dry. I examine my output. My God, I have written fourteen pages, front and back, in a little over five hours. This means I have hours to go before I sleep. A drive to type emanates from deep within me. I can't ignore it.

After opening the Word file, I realize something for the first time. The ideas don't flow from my mind through my arm to the pen and onto the paper. No, it seems to be quite the reverse: my *pen* seems to be the source of my creativity, not my mind. The ideas stop when it runs out of ink. Doesn't that sound ridiculous? I can't think of any other explanation, though.

But this pen also seems to command me to type my handwritten text to the Word file before I can stop the process for meals, other tasks, or sleep.

So I start to type shortly after midnight. I will probably be up until 3:00, if not later.

Indeed, I stay up typing until 3:17, to be exact. The work was worth it, as I've typed all of the handwritten pages. I have now completed 117 pages in 21 chapters, about 38,000 words.

Wow! Who knew?

Putting all my materials away, I quietly ready myself for bed in the hallway bathroom and slip into the bedroom to crawl under the covers ever so gently. I barely disturb Wendy, who rolls over and pulls the covers up to her neck.

Wednesday morning I sleep in with the cover over my head. Wendy gets herself ready for work as she moves about the bedroom and bathroom. I don't care to talk to her. Apparently, she doesn't care to talk to me as well. So be it.

I barely hear Sophie and Emma pop their heads in the doorway to say goodbye. I mumble 'G'bye' in reply, and they leave for school.

A few minutes later, Wendy passes through the bedroom and out again without uttering a word. Downstairs, the sound of the door to the garage closing means she has left for work, without even saying goodbye. That's perfectly fine with me, and I roll over to continue sleeping.

Sometime later, I roll over and open one eye to look at the bedside clock.

It's 10:13.

Shit!

I've overslept, and I have only forty-seven minutes until the second Zoom class session with the Oregon Eastern students! I jump out of bed and put on my sweatshirt and shorts. Why didn't Wendy wake me when she left?

Oh yeah, I remember why now.

I rush through brushing my hair and washing my face, which will be the only part of my body that my students will see. Then I dash downstairs to make a pot of coffee and eat a bowl of cereal.

Finished with breakfast, I grab my mug and bound back up the stairs, spilling hot coffee on my hand, scalding it.

Shit! Shit! Shit!

I rush to the office, turn on the laptop, and go to the bathroom to tend to my injured hand. You see, the laptop takes several minutes to boot up. I really should have bought a new one since Monday. But we can't afford it.

By the time I get back to the office it's 10:43—only seventeen minutes until I go live on Zoom. Finally my laptop is ready to go.

Already my cell phone pops up with text messages from some of my students.

'Dr. Campbell, what's the Zoom link?'

'hi dr Campbell whats the link for the zoom session?'

'dr Campbell hv u sent the lnk?'

Holy shit! I forgot to send the link for the session! I haven't set up the class distribution list! Somewhere in my online files for the course there is a list of my students' email addresses, which I had copied and pasted from on Monday, when I sent the apologetic email. But where?

Oh my, oh my. As I search all over the screen files for Zoom information and class email addresses, the texts from the students grow in number, popping up every ten seconds or so, all on the theme of *Where's the Zoom link?*

'How do I freaking know?!' I shout at the screen.

Hell, I don't even know how to schedule a Zoom session. I missed that part of the training. Frantically I answer one text and ask for instructions on how to schedule a Zoom session. The response: *'I don't know. I just know how to click on a link!'*

Damn. Damn. Damn.

It's now 9:00 in Oregon, and I have no clue how to proceed. Finding the students' email addresses, I open my email account and start adding them to my contact list, something I should have done Monday when I missed the first class. It takes a while to add all twenty-nine students to my contact list. While I'm typing the list, text messages continue to pop up on my phone. After seven minutes, I've typed them all into the contact list and need to create a group.

This takes another two minutes. Damn, damn, hurry up!

Now it's nearly 9:10 in Oregon, and I'm about to send an email to my students with a lame excuse for not having put up the link.

Let's see . . . laptop problem. Yes, yes, that's it; I had a laptop problem!

I finish the email message and press Send. Immediately I'm notified that seven of the twenty-nine messages could not be sent. 'Damn!' I shout. What happened?

Turns out I've mistyped those seven addresses. More time lost. I fix them and save them.

Before I can re-send the welcome message, my cell phone rings. It's the department chair at Oregon Eastern.

Oh God, I'm in trouble now.

I answer with a timid 'Hello?'

There is no pleasantry from Dr. Gladden. 'Dr. Campbell? What the hell is going on? I've been getting phone calls, emails, and voicemail messages about your composition class! Students can't get on Zoom for the class! What's happened?'

'It's my old laptop, Dr. Gladden. It's so slow that I haven't been able to start up the session.'

'Are you sure? One student forwarded a text that you sent to her saying you don't know how to schedule a Zoom session. Didn't you take the training last week?'

'I did, sir,' I lie, 'but it all went out the window after the training was over.' Of course, I hadn't seen that part of the training, or in fact any part of the training, because I was writing at the time.

Long pause, a deafening silence. I know where this conversation is headed. 'Dr. Campbell, you have missed the first two meetings of your class because you say you have laptop problems. I doubt that. I think you're not telling me the whole truth.' Another pause. 'I can see that this is not going to work for you and our students—'

I butt in. 'Can we shift to asynchronous learning, the old way?'

'No, we can't. We are committed to using Zoom.' Another pause. 'I'm afraid we'll have to let you go and find one of our own faculty here to take over the course.'

'No, you can't do that—'

'Oh yes, I can, and I will! I'm sorry this didn't work out. Good luck, Dr. Campbell, and goodbye!'

'Wait!' I shout to a dead connection. 'Goddammit!'

Now what will I do? I've now lost a total of $6500 of the money I was to be paid this fall. I cannot afford to lose those other three sections at the two remaining colleges.

The student text messages continue, having mutated now to vitriol and cursing. I shut off the phone, bidding my would-be students goodbye forever.

To take my mind off this situation, the only thing to do now is to refill the pen and get back to writing. Surely the creative process will blur the effect of what has just happened.

Once the pen contacts the paper, I begin a writing binge that lasts for two hours. I work until my pen runs out of ink, and I consequently run out of ideas. Like before.

After stopping, I now have some time to run through several scenarios of informing Wendy about losing the Oregon Eastern class.

After rehearsing all the possible excuses, I decide that the best move is not to inform Wendy at all.

I should work on the schedules and assignments at Northern New Mexico and Western Iowa so that I won't lose them, too. However, to hell with the remaining online classes for now! My writing is more important.

After lunch I return to my manuscript, and immediately the ideas start to flow again. I figure the pen will run out of ink around 2:30, leaving me just enough time to type until Wendy arrives home.

Working on the remaining online classes will have to wait until the evening, after dinner.

Chapter 9
Wendy

Wednesday, hump day, the middle of the work week. Normally I'm not very happy to be at work, but today I am relieved to be away from the house. Away from Miles. I can't figure out what's happened to him this week. What he's done and said makes me not want to be around him anymore.

I work until nearly noon, time for lunch. I hope that Mark will drop by and offer to take me to lunch, but I ought to shake off that thought. However, soon I see the Torrid Dr. Torres enter the library and make straight for the Reference desk. I feel a rush of adrenalin as well as nerves in the pit of my stomach, as he strolls up to my desk.

'Good afternoon, Wendy!' he says cheerfully. 'How's your morning been?'

'Oh, hi Mark!' I answer, blushing. 'Fine. How was your morning class?'

'You'll have to ask my students. I think it went great, however!'

Without thinking, I blurt out, 'I bet they would say it was great, too!'

He smiles. 'So, are you ready for lunch? As I recall, I owe you.'

'No, you don't; you paid for the first one.'

'I meant I owe you my story.'

'Oh, I forgot about that. Yes, yes, you do.'

'Well, can you get away now?'

'Sure, I can break away any time. Let's go.'

We head across the campus oval to the student center, where we order our food and settle down at an empty table. After a few bites, I say, 'You're on, Dr. Mark Torres!'

'OK,' he says, and swallows his first bite. 'Here's my story—'

'So, to start at the beginning, I was born and raised in Tucson, Arizona. My parents are Mexican

52

immigrants. My birth name is actually Marco. I go by the English form *Mark* now.'

As the words escape his mouth, I observe his lips, and I find myself wanting to taste them. He adds, 'I have four siblings, three sisters and a brother, and I'm the oldest of the five children.'

I could listen to him all day as he narrates his life story.

He goes on to speak of his athletic career at University High School in Tucson. He played football, basketball, and baseball for the UHS Rangers. 'I bet you were pretty good at all three,' I say, enthralled.

'Well, yeah,' he says, 'I guess I was pretty good,' affecting modesty. Shrugging his shoulders, he adds, 'I was All-District in basketball, and All-State quarterback in football and All-State as a pitcher in baseball.' The San Diego Padres recruited him out of high school, but he turned them down to go to the University of Arizona and then later to grad school in Anthropology at U-Cal-Berkeley. 'I earned a scholarship in football at the University of Arizona and played a few freshman games until I broke my arm while being tackled. I couldn't throw worth a penny after it healed. I opted instead to concentrate on my studies after that.'

His mood darkens some. 'After graduating from the University I was married for seven years, long enough to have a daughter, who is now eleven years old.'

'Eleven?' I wouldn't have expected this, based on his youthful appearance.

'Yes, eleven. But yeah, anyway, I worked in the insurance business with my father-in-law. But under the mounting pressures of full-time work and part-time grad school, Elizabeth and I grew apart. She was working full-time also. Our marriage ended in a divorce. It was nobody's fault, and it was everybody's fault, if you get my meaning.'

When he says *divorce*, my heartbeat quickens. He's unattached, single, free!

I am embarrassed at myself for thinking this, as if I should do anything about his unattached state. However, the word also reminds me of my situation with Miles, which could be heading in the same direction. I wipe the disturbing thought away and concentrate on Mark, urging him to continue. 'OK,' I say, affecting sorrow, 'I'm really sorry about how your marriage turned out, but go on, please.'

Am I really that sorry?

'Well,' he sighs, 'I'm single now and looking to start a new life in the Midwest.' His face breaks into a wide toothy smile as he adds, 'Thus far, I like the University and the town, and the people I've met, though nights at home can be lonely.' He winks at me.

'Wow,' I say, after processing all of this information and that beguiling wink, 'that's some life story. It makes mine look dull.'

'Ah, yes, but you have a good job, and you're still married to a good husband.'

Is he fishing for information on my marital relationship? 'Well, yeah, there is that, I suppose.'

'Better than what I have,' Mark says matter-of-factly.

'You haven't told me where you live in town. An apartment? A house? Near campus? Out of town? What?'

He swallows a bite of his sandwich. 'I do live in town. I'm renting a house on Glenview Avenue, on the west side of town.'

'Really? I—we—live on Westview, not far from there. I think you can almost draw a straight line from your house through my house to campus. It's a straight shot.'

'Isn't that interesting?' Mark says, raising one eyebrow. 'Maybe I could pick you up some mornings, as it's on the way.'

'Hmm, I don't know. That might not be such a good idea—'

'Well, what time do you leave for work?'

54

'I usually leave about 7:45, but I really don't need a ride.'

'I have a 9:00 class on Monday, Wednesday, and Friday, and a 9:30 class on Tuesday and Thursday. I like to be on campus at least an hour before my first class. Maybe I could pick you up a few days a week—to save you on gas, you know. And it would be nice to have someone to talk to on the way.'

'Yeah, sometimes it can be a lonely drive.'

'I agree. Two lonely people driving all by their lonely selves to the same place. Two cars polluting the environment, too. When one would save on carbon emissions. Don't you agree?'

'Well, since we would be saving the environment....' I can't believe I said this. It sounds like encouragement.

'Great, so give me your address and I'll drop by around 7:45 tomorrow morning. That's Thursday, now, so you don't forget.'

So soon?

I write my address on a napkin and give it to Mark. The campus clock strikes one time, signifying that it is 12:45.

He checks his watch to make sure. 'Well, it's time for me to get ready for my 1:00 class. See you tomorrow morning?'

'Until then!' I say, and as we part, Mark pulls me into a side goodbye hug. Releasing me, he turns to head for the Science building. Oh my, that slight hug awakened butterflies in my stomach!

Embarrassed by my body's response, nevertheless I wouldn't mind more and longer hugs.

Chapter 10
Miles

After a quick lunch I guess it's time to work on my three remaining classes at New Mexico and Iowa. The classes have been available to students since Monday, but I still have some work to do. Frankly, it would be more rewarding to write for a while. However, I guess I need to check my work email and texts before writing. That would be the responsible thing to do, wouldn't it?

After five minutes of checking, I wish I hadn't waked up my phone. A flood of email messages displays down the Inbox, and the text messages take up two screens. They are from both colleges, all on the question of *where are you, Dr. Campbell?* I should answer all of the concerned students in emails to their respective campuses. Then again, since I haven't created the distribution lists for those classes yet, that will take a while.

Perhaps I can write a few pages, get the plot moving on and characters more developed, then I can return to the classes.

Yes, that's what I'll do.

I start to refill the pen, then stop and decide to do something that has been on my mind ever since I started writing with it. I sit down to my laptop and do another Google search for "Katrina 66 fountain pen," determined to learn everything I can about my pen, my magic pen.

It was passed on to me from my mother after my father's death in 1997, and since that time it has been buried in my desk drawer. Sure, it was bequeathed from my father, but we weren't close at all. It was just one of many items passed on to me by my mother.

Within seconds a list of sites with information on Gillibrand fountain pens pops up. Soon I find a site describing all the models of Gillibrand fountain pens and their history. I learn that the Katrina 66 was introduced in 1966 as an inexpensive fountain pen. The Gillibrand company named it the Katrina 66 to honor the designer's daughter, who was born earlier that year. Its aim was "to compete with the Parker 45 and Schaefer 440 economy fountain pens," according to the site. And it sold well for nearly forty years. Unfortunately, after Hurricane Katrina slammed into Louisiana and Mississippi in August of 2005, killing almost 1400 people and causing over 100 billion dollars of damage, sales tanked and the model was discontinued. It seemed that no one was willing to write with a pen that reminded them of one of the worst natural disasters in the history of the US. Too bad, but mine is a vintage pen from the year it was introduced.

My pen is the Gillibrand Katrina 66 GT (gold trim). I wonder how Dad managed writing with this pen. Did he write with it at all? If so, what did he write, besides company documents?

I should call Mom. I should call her sometime soon.

Chapter 11
Wendy

It's quitting time. I take off my sweater (it's always too cold in the library), straighten up my work area, grab my handbag, and head for the exit to the staff parking lot. A lot of conflicting thoughts race through my head.

Driving home, I'm juggling wild thoughts about my new relationship with Mark. Yes, no longer Dr. Torres. We've moved past formalities.

Where is this relationship going?

It started with his visit to the Reference Department and now will move to sharing rides to and from campus. Close proximity to him inside a car. A fifteen-minute ride to and from campus. And Mark as driver will be in control. He will have *control;* now that's a thrilling thought!

But then the conflict: what about Miles? He's been withdrawing from me and even from Sophie and Emma recently. He's lost two classes. He might even lose another if he's not careful. Maybe even all of them. His obsession with writing this novel has taken over his life.

He's not even that attractive to me anymore. I used to think his Owen Wilson looks and personality were cute and fetching. They fetched me back then. No longer.

Now that Miles has become obsessed with this fantasy of his, I either need to help him break his obsession or …. Or what?

While lost in these thoughts, I run a red light and almost T-bone another vehicle in the intersection, slamming on the brakes just in time. The other driver gives me a piece of his mind and shoots me the finger. I can't be offended; I deserved it.

As I recover from my shattered nerves, I wonder: maybe this is a sign that I should back off from temptation. From Mark. I finally arrive home a few minutes later, heart still racing from my near miss … and maybe from my thoughts.

However, wouldn't it be nice for someone else to do the driving?

I sure hope Miles has had a good day with his classes. Maybe I'll reward him later if he's had a productive day. I remember the phrase we used to say back when we were first married: "…and Miles to do before I sleep, and Miles to do before I sleep." It takes more mental effort to steel myself up to "do" Miles these days, but I'll reward him and hope he gets the message.

I'm home a little less shaky. I sing out, 'Miles? I'm home!' I listen for a few seconds, then call out again, 'Miles, I'm home!' I pause again for a reply. I shout more loudly this time, 'Hey there, can you hear me? I'm home!' Maybe he's napping.

I climb the stairs and listen for any movements. Stepping onto the landing I hear a sound coming from the office, his chair creaking. He must be rocking in it. I tiptoe down the hall to the half-open office door. I'm going to surprise him, distract him, take him to the bedroom.

Grabbing the doorknob, I open the door with a flourish and say, 'Miles, there you—' but I stop in mid-sentence as I take in the scene of Miles seated at his desk, furiously writing and mumbling. 'Miles?' He doesn't stop; he continues writing. To his left is a stack of looseleaf papers, perhaps twenty sheets or more of handwritten text. He continues to mumble, sounding out words as he writes. The back of his shirt is soaked with sweat, and his unbrushed hair is a mess.

What am I to make of this? I walk over and lay a hand on his right shoulder. He jumps out of his chair and knocks it over as if he's been electrocuted.

'What!?' he barks. He turns around, still holding his pen, and sees it's me. 'For Christ's sake!' he shouts. 'You broke my concentration! Now I've lost it!'

This is too much!

Gesturing toward the pile of papers, I snap, 'Is this what you've been doing all day? This!? What about your classes?'

'What classes?' Miles replies, trying to make sense of what I said. 'My classes. My classes.' Turning toward me, he snarls, 'Well, I guess I haven't done anything about them, have I, Wendy?'

The crazed look on Miles' face frightens me. I've never seen that look before. Backing up, trembling now, I respond, 'I can see what's most important to you now, Miles. You'll lose the rest of your classes. Go ahead!'

Then I turn and leave, tears welling up.

As I leave the room, Miles mutters 'Bitch!' and picks up his chair.

Returning to his writing, he starts mumbling and grunting again.

Chapter 12
Miles

Within minutes my pen runs dry, and I run out of ideas. Then I remember some angry words with Wendy earlier. I should probably go downstairs to sort things out with her. First, though, I'm soaked with sweat. How did that happen? I'll have to get more presentable to talk with her.

After I towel off and change shirts, I go downstairs to find Wendy. She's sitting in the living room, drink in hand, when I walk in. *What a selfish bitch*, I think, though I normally am not upset by such oversights. 'What, no drink for me?'

'You know where the booze and mixers are.'

'Yeah, right.' So I turn and head for the kitchen, fix a drink, and come back to the living room, sitting down on the couch next to *my sweet wife* Wendy.

She speaks first. 'So, what was that up there?'

'What was what?'

'You were, like, in a trance writing. You didn't respond when I spoke to you.'

'I didn't hear you.'

'You should have. I was right there in the doorway.'

'Well, I'm sorry, but I was lost in the writing.'

'Did you write all those pages on the desk today?'

'What pages?'

'Are you kidding me? There's a stack of pages next to where you were sitting.'

'If you say so. I was so lost in writing that I didn't pay attention to anything else.'

'So, you didn't work on your classes?'

'No. I probably should have.'

Well now, that wasn't a wise choice of words. 'Probably? Miles, those classes are important! We need the money from them. It's not much, but it's important!'

Haven't I heard that many times before! 'Not much? Not much? Oh yeah, your deadbeat husband is a loser. He lost his full-time teaching job and now perhaps he'll lose all of his part-time jobs too! No! Not maybe! He *will* lose them! Because he's such a *loser!*'

Wendy is getting alarmed now. Good. I don't care. She really stuck it in this time.

'Come on, Miles,' she says. 'Calm down. I didn't mean to upset you.'

OK, so maybe I overreacted.

No, you didn't. She had it coming, says a voice in my head.

'I'm sorry for lashing out at you, Wendy,' I say. 'I was in the middle of an important scene, and I lost it when you touched me. But it came back after you left.'

She's calmer now, speaking with a sympathetic tone. 'I understand. I know how important your writing has become. But can we talk about your four remaining classes?'

'Three. The Oregon Eastern one was taken from me.'

'What? Why?'

'Laptop problems,' I lie. 'The department chair said missing the first two days was inexcusable. I asked if we could shift to the old way, but he said no. He gave the class to one of his faculty.'

'That's terrible!' she says. 'I'm so sorry. What was the laptop problem? Can it be fixed? Will it cause problems with the other classes?'

'I don't know. The problem was with Zoom, so I don't think there will be any further problems.'

'Zoom? I thought you took training last Friday.'

'I did, but it was confusing—'

'Confusing? Did you ask for help from the instructor?'

'Uh, no. I did from a student in the class, but she couldn't help.'

'My God, Miles, I bet you could have contacted someone at Oregon Eastern—'

This has gone too far. 'But I didn't, and that's that!'

For once Wendy is speechless. She just glares at me.

'Now can I get back to my writing?' I get up and start for the stairs.

'Yeah, sure, go back to your novel. Pretty soon it'll be the only work you'll have left to do.'

'You're damn right!' I shout as I climb the stairs to the office.

Chapter 13
Wendy

Not long after my quarrel with Miles, I'm folding clothes in the laundry room when the girls arrive home from school.

I don't know what to do about Miles. He's changed in the past two weeks, especially worse this week. This is not the man I married. This is not the man who never said a short word to me before. I don't know who this man is now. Nor what to do about him.

While I'm lost in thought Sophie drops in on me and says hi, while Emma goes upstairs. I ask her, 'How was your day?' to which she answers, as usual, 'Fine.'

It looks like I'll have to play a game of Twenty Questions with my own daughter to ferret out anything of substance. I'm about to ask a follow-up question when we both hear a door slamming upstairs and Emma crying on her way down the stairs. She runs to me, and I hug her tightly, as she's shaking. 'What happened, Emma?'

Between sobs Emma stammers, 'I only opened the door to the office to say hello to Daddy, and he told me to get out, and then he got up and slammed the door!'

'Did he? I'm sure he didn't mean to do that.' I continue to hold Emma tight, brushing her long hair with my fingers. 'You go to the kitchen and make yourself a snack. I'll go up and talk to Daddy.'

Emma wipes her runny nose on her sleeve and heads for the kitchen. I take the stairs to the office, knock three times, and open the door. Miles is typing furiously, pounding the keyboard. 'Miles,' I state, 'you didn't need to raise your voice to Emma like that.'

Miles pauses, still looking at the screen, and says, 'Like what?'

'Just now. You made her cry.'

He seems doubtful, as if I'm telling a lie. 'No I didn't. I wouldn't.'

'Well, you did. You should go downstairs and tell her you're sorry.'

64

'Really? Are you sure I did that? OK, I will after I'm finished with this.'

'I really think you ought to now.'

'I will when I'm finished. And I will finish faster if you leave me alone.' He has not moved his eyes from the laptop screen throughout this conversation.

'OK, then,' I seethe, as I feel tears welling in my eyes. But they're not tears of sadness; they're hot angry tears. I pull the door closed just short of slamming it.

I make dinner because Miles no longer does. When the table is set, I call up the stairs, 'Miles? Dinner is ready.' The girls and I sit down and wait a few minutes. When Miles doesn't come down, I call up again.

'In a minute!' he shouts. 'I'll be down soon!'

A few more minutes pass, the food is cooling and I'm doing a slow burn. I tell the girls, 'OK, our food's getting cold, so let's go ahead. Your dad will come down when he's good and ready.'

Miles isn't good and ready until twenty minutes later, when he comes down to see us finishing our desserts. 'What? You couldn't wait for me?' he fumes.

Hiding my anger from our daughters, I say with an even tone, 'We waited nearly a half hour. The food was getting cold. I had to re-heat the ground beef in the microwave.'

'That was never thirty minutes. It was more like five!'

'Well, dear, as you can see, it *was* thirty minutes, as we are all finished now. You can serve yourself.'

Miles grits his teeth and stops short of saying something he would never have said before these past two weeks. I can tell what's on his mind. 'Fine, *dear*, I'll do that.' He begins spooning from the serving bowls into his plate and heads to the microwave.

After the girls leave the table, I unload on Miles as he sits down to eat his meal. 'Do you see what you've become? This is not you!'

'This? This *what*?'

'This new behavior. Ever since you started writing you've turned into someone else, and I don't like who you've become. And your daughters' feelings are hurt. This isn't you!'

His temper abating at this, he replies, 'I'm sorry if I'm not, … not … not what I've been in the past. But I'll be better later… after I finish. I'm in the middle of a great story, and I can't stop. It's coming together. You joke about my "masterpiece." Well, it *is* a masterpiece. You'll see.'

Miles seems to be missing the point. 'Meanwhile you're going to lose the rest of your classes and the money they bring in.' I am immediately sorry I brought this up.

'Really? Bringing that up again? That's slave labor, Wendy, and it's chump change! There's no dignity in it, and there's no insurance, no retirement.'

I can't help myself, and so I counter, 'Well, there would be if you still had your full-time position at the college.' I try to appear calm.

I have struck a nerve. 'Ah, I see it now! You're going to play *that* card now, are you?'

Yes, I have played it before. 'Please don't raise your voice. The girls will hear. But yes, you wouldn't be in this situation if you had held your job. You're doing the same thing now that you did—no, *didn't do*, is more like it—to lose your position.'

'Well, I'm going to lose those remaining classes, too! I'm going to contact the chairmen at both campuses and tell them I quit before they fire me! Then I can put all my energy into finishing this novel. So there! How do you like them apples?' Miles quickly scans the dining room table. 'I'm not hungry. I'm going back upstairs to work on my *masterpiece*!'

Dumbstruck, I can't think of a comeback. But listening to the sounds of his footsteps on the stairs, I can't believe he'll carry through with his threat to quit those online classes.

He knows better, doesn't he?

For the first time I fear for the future of this family, as Miles now rants at his daughters, at even sweet, adoring Emma.

After the blowup last night, Thursday morning starts out blessedly peaceful. I go downstairs to have my breakfast alone, Miles be damned. Sophie and Emma have already gotten up and fixed their own meals. They've finished and rushed upstairs to their rooms to get ready for school. I bet they are moving more quickly than usual to get out of the house as soon as possible, to get away from us. I would if I were them.

Twenty minutes later Miles comes down, his presence charging the atmosphere. Palpable tension pulsates in the kitchen as we both eat our own breakfasts in silence. After I finish my granola and drink my last sip of coffee, I tell Miles, 'I won't be driving to work today. I'm getting a ride.'

He grunts, 'OK, fine.'

'Good. Well, I'm going to get ready now.'

'All right.' He raises a spoonful of Raisin Bran to his mouth, his eyes avoiding me.

After the girls have said goodbye and left for the bus stop, I come down, grab my sweater and handbag, and head for the front door. As I open the front door, I say, 'See you this afternoon.'

'Sure,' Miles says in a monotone, still at the kitchen table.

I sit in the porch swing awaiting my ride. Five minutes later, a cardinal red convertible sports car, top down, roars up the street and pulls smoothly into the curb in front of the house.

Getting up from the porch swing, 'No way!' I exclaim, as Mark exits the car and comes over to the passenger side. It's a low-slung vehicle, looks challenging to get into and out of.

We greet each other, and Mark opens the passenger door to help me lower myself into the passenger seat. It's a pretty good dip down, and I love the feel of his arm around my shoulder and hand on my arm steadying me as I get in. He closes the door and goes around to the driver's side and gets in.

Admiring the red leather interior, I speak first. 'Oh my, I never thought I would sit in one of these! It's a Porsche, isn't it?'

'Good guess. It is. It's a 911 Carrera, not the top of the line, but it'll do.'

'I should say so! This is what you'd call a chick magnet if I ever saw one!'

'You could say so.'

'I am most impressed, sir!' I coo, feeling like a teenager on a first date.

Engaging the gear, Mark pulls away from the curb, the acceleration pressing my body against the seat. 'Woo!' I scream. 'How in the world did you wind up with this beast? I've never known anyone who had a Porsche!'

'Well,' he says, slowing the car, 'before I completed my Ph.D. program, I was doing well in the insurance business, so well that after the divorce from Elizabeth, I quit my father-in-law's firm and bought myself this Porsche to celebrate my freedom. After the no-fault divorce settlement, I'd lived off my savings during the last year and a half of grad school.

'Fortunately, when I started my job search, I was offered the position in the Anthropology department here almost immediately, after one campus interview. My salary is only a fraction of what I was earning in the insurance business, but I'm doing what I love, especially interacting with the students.'

I'm sure that's true; especially the coeds would enjoy that "interacting."

'Well, it's a fabulous car, and I'm honored to be sitting in it,' I say with a smile.

'And I'm honored that you're sitting in it, too!' Switching the subject, he asks, 'So what's happened in your life since yesterday?'

I don't know where to begin, but I lead with 'My husband and I aren't getting along this week.' I relate the story of Miles' aborted professional career and his struggles as what he calls a *mercenary* online teacher of writing.

'Mercenary?'

'Yeah, hired out to teach online courses at campuses he's never worked at or even visited.' Then I move on to his rediscovery of his old manuscript and his obsession with finishing it. 'He imagines he's writing the next great novel. He quits only when his pen runs out of ink.'

'So that's what he's doing? Writing by hand? Not composing at the keyboard, like the rest of us?'

'He handwrites, then types from his handwritten manuscript. He claims that writing with his pen gives him ideas.'

'Interesting. What kind of pen?'

'An old fountain pen his father left him when he died seventeen years ago.'

'So, he has to refill it from time to time? Sounds like a lot of work on top of typing it. I'd buy a dozen gel pens instead.'

'That idea never crossed his mind once he started.'

'Strange.'

'Yes, strange. But now it seems the obsession has turned into addiction. He's replaced his relationship with me and his daughters with that pen and his story.'

Mark turns to me with a quizzical look on his face. 'How could any man replace his relationship with a woman like you for a pen and paper?' He shakes his head.

I can feel my face turn scarlet, but I reply, 'Maybe I'm not attractive to him anymore.'

He chuckles and shakes his head. 'Then he needs to see an eye doctor!'

Soon, sooner than I would have liked, the car enters the main campus drive. The trip to campus flew by way too fast. Mark pulls into the library staff parking lot. I protest, 'Mark, you didn't need to do this. I could have walked from the Science Building lot!'

'Not a problem,' he responds cheerily. He walks around the car and opens the passenger door for me.

I feel like a princess. Miles used to do that for me, but no more. 'What a gentleman! Thank you!'

'Lunch today, same time, same place?'

'Uh, sure,' I reply as I struggle to raise myself up from the seat. Mark extends his hand to help me. I thrill at the strength I feel in his hand and arm as he effortlessly pulls me up out of the seat. My face blushes as I wave goodbye to him driving out of the lot. I walk to the back entrance with a spring in my step.

Chapter 14
Miles

I just watched Wendy get into that sports car. She didn't tell me that a *man* would pick her up. We will need to talk about that when she comes home this afternoon.

I go up to the office to begin my work day. The first thing I will do this morning is contact the department chairs in Iowa and New Mexico to inform them that I'm resigning from all of my classes. I know I'm risking everything, hoping that my novel will be published and that I'll make a ton of money.

Take the risk.

It's the only thing that will justify giving up teaching. But, of course, why not? The meager pay is humiliating for a demeaning job that sucks the life out of me.

Give it up. Take the risk. It will be worth it. Take the risk.

I feel confident now that I am doing the right thing. I turn on my cell phone, expecting it to ping notifications from students wondering why the hell I've been absent from my online courses. Sitting down at the computer, I open my email program while a sequence of notifications on my phone piles up. I ignore them to start composing the email to the department chair in New Mexico.

While I'm typing it, my phone rings. It's from Iowa; it must be the chair of the English Department. I answer, 'Miles Campbell.'

'Dr. Campbell? Hello. This is Ray Miller of the English Department at Western Iowa.'

My stomach flops. 'Oh hello Dr. Miller. What's up?' I can guess what's up, but we'll play this out.

'What's up, Dr. Campbell, is that I've been getting communications from students saying there's no activity from you in either of your online comp classes.'

Just what I thought. 'I was just composing an email to you, Dr. Miller,' I lie.

Conversation timeout. Dr. Miller waits on me to continue.

I have thought of an airtight excuse, to which there can be no objection. 'I have to resign. Things are a horrible mess here. My wife is in hospice care with stage four cancer, and I have to tend to her and to my two daughters' daily needs now. I don't have the time or even inclination now to tend to those classes. I'm so sorry about this.'

'Oh, I'm sorry to hear that, Dr. Campbell.'

Another pause.

Dr. Miller clears his throat. 'Has this been going on for some time?'

Now I need to pad my lie. 'We thought we could manage, but she took a turn for the worse this week.'

'Well, I really wish you had told me sooner, but I understand. We'll get somebody to cover those classes.'

'Thank you for understanding, Dr. Miller. We'll press on here, one day at a time.'

'Take care, Dr. Campbell. Goodbye now.'

'Thanks, sir, and goodbye.' And good riddance.

I hope Dr. Miller bought the story. It was a good one, I must say. I should call the chair at Northern New Mexico, but since I've already started the email to her, I'll finish it and send it. Let that suffice. I don't want to lie again over the phone.

After I finish and send the email, I say, 'There now, I'm free!'

My mind echoes: *Free at last, free at last, thank God, I'm free at last!*

I open my notebook and pick up my pen to write. I won't answer the countless text messages that continue to come in.

Oh, yes, I remember intending to call Mom to ask about Dad's fountain pen. It's more important to call her than write. I have some trouble putting the pen down, as if the pen is protesting, but I am successful.

I call Mom, and she picks up on the third ring.

'Hello?' she says, her voice quivering the way that old women's voices quiver.

'Hi Mom, this is Miles.'

'Oh, it's so good to hear from you, Miles. Is everything all right?'

I assure her that everything is fine. After a few more pleasantries I get right to it. 'Mom, I've been using Dad's old fountain pen recently, and I wonder if you can tell me anything about the pen, how he got it, and about his writing with it, if he did any.'

'That old fountain pen? Oh, yes, I remember it, and not too fondly.'

'Really? What do you mean? What can you tell me about it?'

'Well, your father told me he found it in a thrift store in 1968, just after he graduated from high school. He was looking for some old detective paperbacks and happened on it. Then I think he set it aside for a number of years. In the 1990's, when you and your sister were in your late teens or early twenties, he got the silly idea that he should write his "memoir," he called it, before he was so old he would start losing his memory. I guess he intended to leave it as a legacy to you and Marie, but then he had a massive stroke and passed away.'

'Really? I never knew that. He never said anything about it.'

'You both were in college then and focused on your classes and activities. Besides, he wanted to keep it a secret until he had published it. He wrote all through your college years. But he quit after you got married.'

'He quit? Why did he stop?'

'Because I made him stop.'

'You did? Why?'

'Because he wouldn't stop on his own. He moved on to writing stories, lots of them. He would get so caught up writing that he would skip meals and sometimes skip sleep. Don't get me wrong; it kept him out of trouble, I guess you would say. However, he became a different person, even nasty toward me. Finally, I'd had enough. I told him he would have to choose between me and his writing.'

'Gosh, I didn't know that any of this was going on.'

73

'By the time I made him choose, both you and Marie were married and living far away. Far away from all that was going on at home.'

'That's very interesting, Mom. I'm glad you told me.'

I sense worry in her voice as she asks me, 'So, Miles, are you writing a memoir too, with that blasted pen?'

'No, not really, although authors often use some of their experiences when they write fiction. That's what I'm writing, Mom. Fiction.'

'How nice, dear. But be careful and don't become obsessed like your father did. I don't know if the pen was somehow responsible for his obsession or if it was just pent-up energy and ideas waiting to come out. But whatever it was, his writing nearly ended our marriage. We never really got to make up. Not long after I gave him the ultimatum, he died.'

'Thanks, Mom. I'll be careful.' There's a long pause, as always when I talk to my mother. At least I didn't fall asleep during the pause, like I've done in the past. 'Well, I've gotta go now. I'll talk to you later.'

'Thanks for calling,' she says. 'Call more often, if you can. And maybe you can come up for a visit sometime?'

I expected this. 'Sure, Mom, I will sometime. We'll talk later. Bye now.'

Phone calls to my widowed mother always end this way, with a plea for a visit. I should take a road trip to see my mother, but I'd rather do almost anything else. Shame on me, what a bad son I am. She lives alone, and Marie doesn't call or write to her very often. The mother-daughter thing, you know. The burden falls on my shoulders, and I resent it.

But what Mom told me about Dad's obsession with writing, with this very pen, sounds like a warning. The pen might have something to do with opening my "word-hoard," but is that all? Or is it something more? When I'm

74

in the middle of a writing session, is it an obsession...or an addiction? And where does *that* come from?

Oh well, the main thing is to start writing.

And I do.

I write three chapters until the pen runs out of ink the second time. The flow of the plot having stopped, I break for lunch.

Before I can make my lunch, my cell phone rings. The caller ID shows it's the department chair at Northern New Mexico. 'Oh no, another dissatisfied customer,' I smirk, speaking out loud. Should I pick up the phone, or, since I wrote an email explaining I was dropping the classes, shouldn't that have sufficed?

Yes, that will suffice.

I took the risk. I'm all in.

Time for lunch. Then more writing.

Lots more.

Chapter 15
Wendy

Shortly before noon, Mark arrives at the Reference desk and picks me up to go to lunch. As we leave the library, he asks, 'How about we go off campus for lunch today? Maybe Freddie's Wraps & Bowls? It's not far from campus. I don't have the one o'clock class today, so I have more time. How about you?'

I sort out the meaning of this change in location. I don't like the options at the student center, but I do really like Freddie's, where our family has gone several times over the years. 'Well, yeah, OK, sure,' I stammer, 'as long as I can be back by about one o'clock.'

'Excellent!' Mark says.

I'm thrilled to be riding again in his Porsche, the wind whipping my hair.

At Freddie's I order a chicken wrap, which is too much for me. Mark offers to eat the other half, since he ordered a soup and half wrap. 'Perfect!' I say. With a twinge I recall that Miles and I always split sandwiches, and now I'm doing it with Mark Torres.

Our conversation returns to sharing our personal lives. Mark asks about our children, and I proudly tell of our daughters' personalities and accomplishments. Sophie plays soccer and takes violin lessons. 'Suzuki method,' I say. 'I've lost count of the number of times we've heard the "Twinkle" variations.'

'Twinkle?'

'They begin with "Twinkle, Twinkle, Little Star" and add variations.'

'Oh.'

Emma, I report, takes dance lessons and also plays soccer. 'She's the star of the team! And she's the apple of her Daddy's eye.'

It's Mark's turn to share with me. As he told me earlier, he has an eleven-year-old daughter named Alexa. 'Going on 21.'

'Really? Named after the Amazon device?'

'Nope,' he laughs. 'That was before the Echo. Named after Billy Joel's daughter.'

His ex-wife Elizabeth works as a bank examiner and travels frequently. Her travel schedule and the long hours of Mark's insurance work, compounded by his enrolling part-time in grad school, caused cracks in the marriage, which fell apart just before he left his father-in-law's business.

'I didn't feel that I should continue working for my father-in-law, who blamed me for the failed marriage anyway.'

'That's terrible,' I say. 'I'm sure there was blame on both sides.'

'I thought so, too. Nevertheless, it freed me to go on to grad school full time. I finished my master's in a year and a half and my Ph.D. in four years.'

'That's amazing!' I exclaim. 'Miles took eight years to earn his M.A. and Ph.D., and I thought that was pretty fast.' We continue to share about our lives between bites, growing in sympathy and understanding. I can't find anything about Mark that I don't like...or *love*.

After we finish lunch, Mark drives me back to campus, once again driving around back to the library parking lot. This time I don't protest; I get to spend a little more time in the car with him.

After he parks, he gets out and comes around to open the passenger door for me. He says, 'Thanks for the lunch chat. I enjoyed our time together. It was better than in the student center, for sure.'

'Certainly, and the pleasure was all mine.'

'It was mutual,' he says. 'Pick you up at quarter to four?'

'Sure. See you then!'

He backs the Porsche out of the parking space and heads for the Science building.

I wish for some more of that *pleasure*. Then my conscience rises up and flicks my ear, like my mother used to do whenever I misbehaved growing up.

I shake my head and tell myself not to go too far with this relationship.

Chapter 16
Miles

I've been writing for two and a half hours following lunch, and it's now mid-afternoon. Wendy will be home in an hour or so, so I will stop when the pen runs out of ink again. It should be running dry soon.

A stack of notebook pages, written front and back, lies on my desk. There may be twenty or more pages in the stack. I'm far behind on typing, but the plot has unfolded, and the action, setting, and conflicts are all developing better than I had hoped. I can't stop while in this white heat. But once I do stop—once the pen runs out of ink again—it will take several hours to type it all into Word.

At quarter to four my pen runs dry near the end of another chapter. Reading back over the manuscript before typing, I'm amazed. This story surely will lure an agent and publisher. While I'm typing it up, it will only get better. I ought to start typing now, but Wendy will be home soon, and I need to smooth over our last argument. I go downstairs to the living room window to await Wendy's arrival. Also, I want to see the car she'll be riding in. And, of course, the driver.

In a few minutes a car pulls up to the curb, a sports car of some kind, cardinal red in color. I peer through the blinds to see a ruggedly handsome man, tall and brown (Hispanic?), get out of the driver's side and come around to open the passenger door. This man extends a hand to help Wendy out of the low-slung vehicle, gently pulling her up from her seat.

The two of them chat briefly, then the man leans forward toward Wendy, who leans away. What does that mean? Then the two separate, the man walking around to the driver's side, Wendy standing there at the curb waving goodbye. The car roars off, and Wendy walks up the sidewalk to the porch and unlocks the front door.

As she walks in, she screams when she sees me standing in the shadows of the living room. Holding her hand over her heart, she recognizes me and says, 'Oh, it's you! I thought it might be a burglar.'

'No, it's just little old me at the window, watching you and your chauffeur.'

Surprised by my sarcastic remark, Wendy sputters, 'My chauffeur? You mean Mark? He's just a campus friend who lives only a short distance away. That's why he gave me a ride.'

'Well, Wendy, he sure looked like more than a friend to me, the way he leaned into you.'

'Did he? I didn't notice.'

Doesn't she look so innocent?

'Anyway, it was convenient for us to go in one car instead of two. That's all.'

'Well, I hope that's all,' I reply, unconvinced.

'Yes, that's all. Let's change the subject, shall we? How was your day? How were your classes?'

Oh boy, now it's all going to come out.

I relay the events of the morning, of giving up my remaining classes and of the resulting flurry of activity writing. 'It's good, Wendy, it's really good. Now I have the time to devote to my writing, and it'll pay off in the long run. I want you to read it once I type the last few chapters.'

Wendy doesn't take this news well. 'What? What? Wait a minute. Did you just tell me you've given up your last classes? You've given up your only source of income? For what? This ridiculous pipe dream of yours?' She throws her arms up in the air. 'I can't believe this!'

'Well, at least I'm here at home by myself, not out in some car flirting with another woman! And maybe more, huh?'

The look on her face says it all. 'You go to hell!' Wendy shouts and heads for the stairs.

I follow her as she climbs the stairs. 'No, Wendy, *you* go to hell!'

I wish I had said something smarter, more cutting, but all I could do was to repeat her curse, like a kid on a playground. However, I do have the last words as I walk down the hall to the office: 'You're such a bitch, you know?!'

Once I'm back in the office, I review the twenty-some handwritten pages, front and back, in essence about thirty-five typewritten pages in all. Miles to go before I sleep.... and I sigh at a fond memory from long ago.

I begin typing.

At about half past nine both girls peek inside the office door to tell me goodnight, and this time I can smile because I'm only typing. It would be different if I were writing. I tell them, 'Goodnight, sleep tight, don't let the bedbugs bite.' Sophie and Emma smile in relief and leave.

Just before 11:00 Wendy gets ready for bed, and I consider going in to tell her goodnight. But no, best not to. Something tells me to leave her alone.

Let sleeping dogs lie, literally...the bitch!

I finish typing shortly after 11:00 and think about going to bed. However, Wendy may still be awake, as she's a light sleeper. Better to wait until she's fully asleep. Out of nowhere comes the thought: *Why not refill the pen and start on the next chapter?*

Yes, why not?

I refill the pen and start writing. Immediately I see in my mind and feel in my pen the ideas flowing onto the paper. They are brilliant! I write as if the page itself is greased, so fast the ideas flow.

I'll write until the ink runs out, then go to bed.

Later my hand and forearm seize up with cramps, and I have to stop writing. Soaked in sweat and bleary-eyed, I check the clock on the wall above the desk. It's going on one o'clock.

Wait a minute! Have I been writing for over two hours? Did I refill the pen? I don't remember doing that. I haven't taken a bathroom break; I haven't even stood up to stretch. My back is sore now.

As I stand up, my shorts peel away from the vinyl seat, releasing a sharp odor of urine. What? Did I piss in my pants while writing? And didn't notice my soaked pants and chair seat? Oh well, the damage has been done, but there's no sense in cleaning up now since there's still ink in the pen. I sit myself down on the wet and cold seat to continue writing until the pen runs out of ink. I know, that sounds disgusting, doesn't it? But I *must* keep on writing regardless. Finally, at two in the morning the ink begins to fade and then runs out completely in the middle of a word.

I clean and disinfect the chair, then clean myself up in the hall bathroom and tiptoe into the bedroom to fish out a fresh pair of underwear. Wendy is breathing deeply, unaware.

Man, this worries me, that I am completely unaware of bodily functions while writing in a fury. But what can I do? Writing is a pleasure, *better than sex*!

Wait, did I just think that? Where did that thought come from?

I go back to the office and observe the stack of pages on the left of the laptop. Was that non-stop writing? After all that has transpired in the past day, I'm too exhausted to go on and absolutely must go to bed. I can't let this accident happen again. I also can't remember the last time I filled the pen.

Has it been three hours?

I tread lightly down the hall, slip into bed without disturbing Wendy, and fall asleep pondering this evening's strange events.

Chapter 17
Wendy

Next morning, Friday morning, there's an uneasy truce between us as we eat breakfast together in the kitchen. We stay out of each other's way and mumble civil exchanges. Sophie and Emma seem relieved that we aren't still arguing, but the mood in the kitchen is anything but pleasant. Perhaps it will be better this evening. They leave for the bus stop as we both tell them to have a good day.

Now Miles and I are alone in the house, the truce holding for a while. I want to say so much to Miles, this man I've loved for almost twenty years, but I can't get over his losing all six online classes. He seems so committed to this insane dream of his, a commitment such as I've never seen in him before. Not even when he was teaching full-time.

However, the odds are surely against him. He will probably end up self-publishing, and his work will be buried among thousands of self-published books on Amazon. I can't figure out how to start a conversation about this without him blowing up, so I give up.

Maybe later tonight, after the girls go to bed.

Meanwhile, I must get ready for work. Get ready to be picked up by my "chauffeur" again.

I can't wait!

On the way to campus, Mark and I chat about campus rumors and our experiences with university administrators. He says his department chair is just OK. 'I could do better as chair. My colleagues are all right, though they don't seem scholarly enough.'

I tell him that my colleagues in the library are a mix of frumpy and "house-wifey", but talking this way about my colleagues makes me feel a little uncomfortable so I changed the subject.

'It's really no problem,' Mark protests, accelerating from a traffic signal.

'Well, if we're going to do this long-term, it's only fair that I trade off with you. Besides, our SUV gets great gas mileage, better than your Porsche's, I bet.'

'Well...if you insist.' It didn't take him too long to agree.

On campus Mark once again drives me to the library parking lot. As before, he goes around to the passenger side and helps me out of the car. He holds my hand a little longer than before, then says, 'Thank you for riding with me. It's nice to have a companion, and a nice one at that. Makes the ride seem shorter and also more pleasant.'

'Thank you also,' I respond. 'Remember now, Monday I'll pick you up, then we trade off after that.'

'All right then! I'll see you at lunch.' He pats my back as we part.

Inside, I drop my handbag in the Reference work room. Soon Carolyn and Linda, about whom I have just said such unflattering things, come and surround me. 'So...,' Carolyn says, 'I see you've been getting rides with that new guy. How's that going for you?' she says, winking.

'Yeah, girl, do tell!' Linda twitters.

'Oh, come on!' I protest. 'Mark lives not far from me, so we're ride-sharing, that's all. We're just friends.'

'Sure, sure,' Carolyn says. 'So it's *Mark* now instead of *Dr. Torres*?'

'What does your husband think of this? Dr. *Mark* is quite a hunk!' adds Linda.

Linda's one of the frumpy librarians, for whom just about any man is a player in her imaginary romance life. I've been on the receiving end of her many remarks about handsome male faculty, of which there are only a precious few on campus. There are many more, though, in Linda's opinion. I can only imagine how she plays out her fantasies at home.

I need to stem this conversation. 'Miles understands...I think. It's hard to tell, he's so obsessed with his writing now. He doesn't seem to notice anything else but it.'

Carolyn adds, 'Well, he'd better start noticing what's going on around him!' She winks again.

I feel my face reddening. I've grown annoyed with this conversation. 'C'mon now, girls, it's not serious. It's not going anywhere beyond rides.'

'And lunches,' adds Linda.

'OK, lunches too. But that's all.'

Carolyn says, 'Hey, I'm married, but I tell you I would be tempted if I sat in the passenger seat of a hot car driven by a hot man like the Torrid Dr. Torres!'

Privately I agree with Carolyn, but I need to call a halt to this conversation. 'OK, ladies. That's enough. Don't you have work to do?'

'Yeah,' says Linda, 'we do. We'll just go back to our *boring* jobs and live vicariously through you!'

At this, we all separate to our stations in the Reference Department. Once settled in my desk chair, I smile to myself. Lunch is in four hours.

I can't wait.

Like clockwork Mark shows up at noon and invites me to go to lunch off campus again. His presence once more raises eyebrows among the staff. I grab my handbag and lead him to the staff exit, where his Porsche is parked. He acts the gentleman, helping me in and out of his low-slung car.

We share a pleasant lunch at Freddie's, truly sharing this time, as we split a roast beef sandwich with fries. 'Watching my waistline,' Mark jokes, 'when I'm not watching yours!'

'Oh, stop it!' I protest.

Once as we both reach for the fries in the center of the table, our fingers touch and linger. Our eyes meet briefly, then we both look down to scoop up a few fries. I'm not sure of his reaction, but he looks a bit embarrassed. I know I am.

We share more of our backgrounds with each other, Mark filling in additional information on his undergraduate and graduate careers. I describe my high school and college careers, including meeting Miles when I was a freshman and he was a junior. 'After he finished his degree and was accepted in the graduate program at UT-Austin, I transferred there with him and finished my degree and then earned my MLS. We started our family sooner than we had planned while Miles was in the graduate program and I worked part time in a local library in Austin.'

I sigh. 'Those were the poor years when we scraped by on government assistance and part-time jobs. Raising two little girls on part-time library pay, teaching assistantships, and odd jobs was a challenge. After Miles was hired here at the University, I applied for an opening in Reference at the university library. My degree from UT-Austin impressed the hiring committee. I've been here almost six years and love the job and the university, for the most part.'

'That's a wonderful story of determination amid hardship,' Mark says. 'I am most impressed.'

After finishing lunch, which Mark pays for again, we head back to campus. In the library lot, he takes my hand to lead me up out of the seat, holding it a bit longer than before. 'Thanks again for a great lunch,' he says, shaking my right hand and leaning forward to kiss it.

'No, I should thank you,' I say, 'for paying again. You didn't have to—'

'Of course I didn't, but I did, and so what? It's only money.'

Watching the Porsche speed off, 'No, thank *you*,' I repeat to myself.

I look forward to the ride home in the afternoon, and to next Monday, when I'll pick up Mark at his house for the first time.

Walking toward the back entrance, I feel conflicted. I'm not sure where this friendship is going, but I'm no fool: each encounter seems to push it further along.

To what? Friends with *benefits*? Hardly, I hope.

Chapter 18
Miles

I'm still steamed about last night's argument. I've always had a problem with forgiving and forgetting. Our arguments have lasted for days in the past. Last night was Round One. I know the best way to avoid Round Two of the argument is to say nothing.

Now that Wendy is dressed and made up—a little *too* made up, in my opinion—she tells me she's going out to the porch to await her ride. I tell her goodbye and go upstairs.

Instead of heading to the office, though, I walk into the bedroom to stand by the front window and check out Wendy's ride.

Soon the red car—

Wait! Is that a Porsche?

A Porsche convertible?

As the car slows down, and pulls to the curb, Wendy walks toward it, where the man waits with the passenger door open. I watch Wendy lower herself to enter, the man steadying her, a bit too familiarly. Once she's in the car, he leans across the console toward Wendy, but I can't tell why. Then the car speeds off.

I don't know what to think of this, but it's not right for a man's wife to be speeding away from home in a sports car driven by another man. It had better be only a workplace friendship. But it sure doesn't look that way.

A few minutes later I power up the laptop. Before I refill the pen, I think it's time to see if my work is any good. Time to conduct an online search for top literary agents looking for first-time authors. This I do, spending a few minutes surfing sites.

According to one site's ranking, a *Susan Brower* is a one of the top agents for debut authors, which is what I am. 'OK,' I say, 'we'll start with you, Susan. If you pass on me, there are twenty-four other agents in this list.'

Finding the information on Susan Brower, I read over the requirements for submitting a query letter and sample. Also required is a synopsis and a bio. That'll be a short bio: I haven't published anything, I don't have an author's website, I don't have a presence on Twitter or Instagram, and I don't have a blog site.

Soon I've composed a simple query email, following Ms. Brower's instructions. Required is a synopsis of my incomplete novel. Now that's a problem. I believe I know where it's going, even though I don't know the details just yet, so I write it, the synopsis just under the maximum word-limit.

I then copy and paste the first three chapters into a new Word file, review it, and save it. After closely reviewing the query and documents, I send the email off to Ms. Brower.

'Speed away on wings of glory, o gentle missive!' I sing, as if I am an eighteenth-century poet.

Now it's time to get back to work.

I've been writing for three hours straight with no breaks and with an apparently bottomless ink cartridge. It's now noon, and I feel the need to go to the bathroom. After I come back, I settle in to write some more, ignoring the text messages and emails from students who do not know that I'm no longer their instructor.

Then an email from a Susan Brower pops up on my screen.

'Who dat?' I say in jest. Oh, wait a minute, this message is from the agent to whom I wrote just a few hours ago. Probably an acknowledgment of receipt, or an auto-generated rejection. Something like "We are not accepting unsolicited manuscripts at this time."

Sighing, I set my pen aside and open the email. It's not what I expected.

Far from it:

> *Good morning Mr. Campbell. Thank you for submitting your query and manuscript. Normally I do not read manuscripts right away, but I had a lull this morning, so I opened your email and downloaded the three chapters of **Killing Time** that you sent. I have read them now, and I must*

tell you that I have not read anything like it in
years….

'Yeah, but it's not what we are looking for,' I say. I
read on, prepared for disappointment.

The first three chapters give promise of a
thrilling story. If the rest of the chapters are as
well-crafted as these first three, then I think you
may have a publishable manuscript.

Please keep me posted on your progress.
Send me the manuscript when it is complete. Or in
batches, so that I can see where the story is
going.

Sincerely,
Susan Brower
Brower Literary Agency

I blink my eyes a couple of times, not believing
what I've just read. I re-read the email.

Really?

This email has brightened my day and renewed
my energy.

I write back immediately, thanking Ms. Brower for
her assessment and encouragement, and promise to
deliver more chapters. I know I can complete the
manuscript within a month. My goodness, I've been at it
only about nine days and am approaching two hundred
pages in Word! This pen now seems to be writing on its
own, pulling my hand along. It won't stop for any reason
while ink is in the cartridge.

I've missed lunch, but I can't stop now! The ink is
lasting longer the past two days, going beyond what I
thought should be a dry tank. Writing in a trance, I'm
aware enough to see that the writing is excellent, though
I'm not sure that they are really *my* ideas, *my* words.

The ink finally fades and runs out, and I resurface
from the depths of my trance and discover cold wetness
in my shorts and the odor of urine. 'Damn!' I cry.

I head for the bathroom to clean myself and to get
rags and towels to clean the chair. I study my reflection in

the bathroom mirror, shocked by bloodshot eyes, bags drooping under my eyes, beads of sweat on my brow, and matted hair. I also feel the dull pain in my lower back.

'Double damn! Writing is going to ruin your health!' I say to the man in the mirror.

After cleaning myself and the chair, I sit down to review my progress. I'm maybe halfway through the present chapter, but a stack of twenty or more sheets of handwritten notebook pages lies to the left of the laptop. If I refill the pen, it will be off to the races again, and I will produce many more pages before the pen runs dry. And then I'll have to type it all.

I'd better start typing now.

I feel the magnetic lure of the pen, but I have to ignore it. I'm not finished with the chapter, but once I start typing, the pull will fade, I'm sure.

I'm relieved to be freed from the pen for now. As "excellent" as I feel the written draft is, it always improves during the typing process. This process is arduous, though, taking longer per page of typing than of writing, because of some revisions.

Once underway, I lose track of time as I churn out page after page of text on screen and surpass 215 pages. I pause for a bathroom break and snag a beer from the refrigerator. It's nearly three o'clock.

My, how time flies when you're having fun. Ha!

Ten pages remain on the stack. Popping open the can of beer, I take a large swig, then set it on the table and start typing again.

Chapter 19
Wendy

On the way home in Mark's Porsche, I'm sitting in the passenger seat dealing with a rising sense of shame about this new relationship with Mark. Has he been flirting? Have I been flirting? I don't think I have, but I haven't recoiled from or rebuffed his subtle advances. It's nice to be the object of another man's attention, but I'm married, and I must admit I haven't been attentive to Miles this week. We've grown apart over this writing business.

Surely, we can work this out.

'What are you thinking?' Mark intrudes as he pulls up to a red light.

'What? Just thinking about family, that's all.'

'About Miles and his writing?'

'Yeah, that too. It's actually *all* that I've been thinking about.'

'Anything I can do to help? Take your mind off your worries?'

Well, that was obvious. 'No, it's no big deal. No real worries. We can work it out.'

'Well, I hope so. If you were my wife, I sure wouldn't be ignoring you.'

'That's enough, Mark. I appreciate the compliment, but let Miles and me work this out. Then I'll be happier to be around.'

'OK, OK, I'm sorry. I was just being honest.'

The rest of the trip transpires in silence. When Mark pulls to the curb, I open the passenger door before he can get out. 'Thanks for the rides this week. I'll pick you up Monday morning. You have a nice weekend!' I feign a smile.

Mark looks confused. 'All right. See you then. Good luck!' He speeds away from the curb.

Walking up the sidewalk to the porch, I decide to lure Miles away from his desk to the bedroom. The girls won't be home until close to 4:30 today because of clubs after school, which should be enough time for what I have in mind. It's going to take some effort to generate the mood, but we need to reconnect physically, then talk out how we'll make it financially on one salary.

I open the front door and call out, 'Miles? Miles? I'm home! I have a surprise for you!' I drop my handbag and kick off my shoes, then bound up the stairs to the second floor. 'Miles? I'm coming for you! Get ready, 'cause here I come!' I sing like the Temptations.

I hurry down the hall to the office and peer in... to see a horrific sight: Miles in his underwear typing away, completely transfixed by the laptop screen. I take a step into the room, and then I remember what happened the first time I tried to lure him away from his work.

No, that didn't go well at all. It won't now.

I back away and go down the stairs to find something to fix for dinner, since Miles no longer prepares meals.

He never even turned his head to acknowledge my presence.

Miles worked through dinnertime. I didn't even call up to him to come down. Following my instructions, the girls have avoided contact all evening with their father. 'He's deeply involved in his work and needs to be left alone for now,' I had said as matter-of-factly as I could manage.

When I'm sitting downstairs reading, around ten o'clock there's a flurry of activity upstairs. He must be finished for the night. I'll wait for him to go to bed and then go up later, after I know he's asleep. Right now, I don't want to speak to him anyway.

While I'm reading, I can't concentrate for pondering the first week of my "friendship" with Dr. Mark Torres.

What will the second week bring?

Saturday morning I'm in the kitchen, eating breakfast with the girls. Miles is still asleep upstairs.

Emma asks, 'Isn't Daddy going to eat with us?'

'No,' I say. 'Daddy is very tired from his work and needs his rest.'

Truth be told, I won't mind if he sleeps all day. After breakfast both girls leave for their friends' houses. 'Be back by lunchtime,' I shout as they leave the front door.

All right, this seems to be a good time to read what Miles has written. After all, I had promised to read it back when relations were better between us. I sneak into the office to satisfy my curiosity, and discover that Miles has left the laptop on with the document on the screen.

I browse through the first 120 pages until I reach a section that makes me stop. From that point on, I lose focus on the plot and action and instead grow increasingly disturbed. I can't wait until Miles gets up to confront him about this character's description.

After two hours Miles emerges from the bedroom and heads for the office. He walks in to see me sitting in the office chair. I wheel around to face him, upset.

'Did you base the wife on me?'

He's clearly not expecting this. He thinks for a few seconds, then answers, 'Well, partially, I—'

'Because she's a *bitch*! And involved in an affair? Is that what you think of me? And your protagonist—your Pete—he must be *you*. He's sooooo innocent! Is that our relationship?'

I watch him as several emotions pass across his face. He responds, 'Wait a minute, Wendy. These characters are fictional, you know, like it says on movie disclaimers and at the beginning of novels. Forget about that. What did you *like* about the plot? What do I need to improve?'

'You need to improve the wife!'

Miles flails his arms about. 'Well, I can't. She's the way she is because the story needs her to be that way. And *she's not you*!'

'You could have fooled me! And I don't like the plot so far, anyway. It's too violent, for one thing. A clock that kills people? That's the dumbest thing I've ever heard of!'

'Dumb? Stephen King wrote about a possessed car! There have been novels and movies about homicidal dolls and puppets, too. What about Chucky? What about Christine?'

'Yeah, and those were well-done, and believable!' This is enough for me. I rise up out of the chair and leave the office, saying in parting, 'You don't need to show me any more of your work!'

'Don't worry,' he says to my back. 'You won't read any more of my manuscript! Ever!' As I go down the stairs, he mutters, 'Well, now, you really *are* a bitch after all!'

We avoid each other for the rest of the day, passing in hallways and rooms without saying a word.

I feel sorry for Sophie and Emma. They can sense the freeze. After they get home from their friends' houses, they spend the rest of the day in their rooms.

The weekend proceeds with a gradual thaw. Miles continues to write and type through lunch on Sunday. It's pointless to call him anymore for meals; he will come when he's realizes that he's hungry.

On Monday morning I hurry downstairs to gather my things for work. I've already had my breakfast. I find Miles sitting at the kitchen table, lost in thought over his breakfast of coffee and raisin bran cereal, as if he's never seen them before.

I announce, 'I'm driving to work this morning. I'll see you this afternoon.'

'Not being picked up by the Porsche guy?' he sneers at me.

Ignoring the snark, I reply, 'No, I'm driving today.' He doesn't need to know that *I'll* be picking up Mark.

He doesn't ask; he responds, 'OK,' and finally acknowledging his bowl of cereal, he digs into it.

I shake my head. *If you only knew.*

Or maybe if he did know he would say the same thing.

94

I back the car out of the garage. Instead of heading east, I head west toward Mark's house. With his address on a slip of paper and helped by the GPS on my phone, I arrive at his house within five minutes.

When I pull to the curb at the address on Glenview Avenue, I'm surprised to see a single-story stone bungalow with a porch across its front. I had expected a rancher. Or a two-story historic home. I don't know what I expected, really.

Still, its curb appeal is pleasing: the lawn and shrubs are neatly trimmed, the sign of a person who cares about details.

Mark is sitting on the porch swing waiting for me.

I return the favor of Mark's previous courtesies: I get out and go to the passenger side of my vehicle and open the door for him. 'Your carriage awaits you, sir!' I smile and wink.

He returns the wink. 'Well, thank you very much, milady, but you really didn't need to do that.' As he passes me to get into the seat, he squeezes my hand, lingering a second or two.

On the drive to campus, we exchange stories about our weekend. Mark tended to his yard, front and back, and repaired a leaky faucet in one of his bathrooms. 'You really need to see my backyard,' he gloats. 'It has flower gardens and vegetable gardens. They're flourishing!'

Now that's an interesting twist on the 'wanna see my etchings?' line, I think.

'And what about your weekend?' he asks.

'It was kind of a rocky weekend.' I relate the flare-up over the wife in Miles' novel. 'It was clear to me that he based her on me, but he said she isn't me. I don't believe him. She's a bitch, and I'm not!'

'Of course not! You don't seem bitchy at all.' He pauses for a few seconds. 'I haven't written a story or anything like that, but I have read that authors often write based on what they know, or what they think they know.

So maybe there's some of you in his wife as he sees you—what's her name?'

'Aimee.'

'Hmm, a coincidence? Wendy and Aimee are two-syllable names, and they sort of rhyme, don't they? A connection, perhaps?'

'Maybe so, maybe so. But that doesn't make me feel any better!' I smirk.

'Sorry! How about we drop the subject? So, your weekend was pretty bad?'

'Yes, we didn't speak to each other most of it. But I've decided not to fight him anymore. He's lost all six online classes and the money they would bring in. I'm upset about that. And he's gone all in on his writing. He's become obsessed with it. He misses family meals, he has no time for Sophie and Emma, and of course he has no time for me. I wanted to lure him away from writing Friday afternoon, but I knew he would get angry. It never took much to lure him away from *anything* before.'

'Ha!' says Mark, 'it would take even less effort to lure me away!' He turns toward me and winks. I feel myself blush, which Mark notes with satisfaction, I can tell.

When we arrive on campus, I return an earlier favor by driving around to the parking lot behind the Science building. Mark doesn't protest, but he thanks me. Before getting out, he reaches his left arm over and lightly grips my neck, bringing my head to him, and kisses me on my right cheek.

'You're an excellent driver!' he says as he gets out of the car. 'See you for lunch? Same time, same place?'

'Sure,' I answer. 'See you then!'

As I drive out of the lot onto a campus street, I reach up to my cheek and caress it. I smile. That is the most forward he has been so far.

But I like it.

Shame on me.

Chapter 20
Miles

I've been touching up my manuscript, making subtle changes to the narrative and dialogue. I think it's about as perfect as it's going to be. Time to send it off to Susan Brower.

I attach the document and review the email once more, then click on **Send** and sit back in my chair, breathing a sigh of relief. I'm not going to resume writing; my pen has run out of ink and freed me.

Really, I feel that I *have* been freed.

I need to go back to bed for a morning nap. I glance at my pen lying next to the keyboard. 'Not now, Kat. I'll see you later.'

What a stroke of genius! '*Kat*, that's a great name for you. That just feels so right. My pen pal Kat. I like it!'

I swear I hear *So do I* in response. Very strange.

I head off to the bedroom.

Two hours later, I awaken from my nap, stretching as I shuffle back to the office. I sit down to check my email before writing again. There are three emails, two of which are emails from confused online comp students who have no clue. I delete them.

As I had hoped, the other is from Ms. Brower:

*Hello again, Miles. Thank you for sending the latest chapters of **Killing Time**. If the rest of it is as well-crafted as these chapters, I believe I can sell it in a heartbeat, maybe even start a bidding war. As far as editing, I don't see much required. We'll see how the character's arcs develop and how the plot progresses.*

Your writing in this story reminds me of Stephen King's. As a debut author, you don't have the name yet, but this manuscript gives promise of a bright career! I don't need to see any more until you have finished your first draft and final edits.

Sincerely,
Susan Brower

Brower Literary Agency

I'm absolutely over the moon reading this email from Susan Brower, though I have to shake my head at a couple of errors in her email.

'*As far as editing*? No, Susan, it's *as far as editing* **is concerned**. *Character's arcs*? Really? It's **characters'** *arcs*. Did you cut class the days these basic rules were taught? And you want to be my agent?'

I can't help it; I was an English professor.

Despite these two failings, Susan's message has given me a huge boost to press on to the finish. I reach for Kat and refill the ink cartridge.

Putting pen to paper, I crow, 'OK, Kat, let's go!'

Chapter 21
Wendy

The bell tower chimes quarter to four on campus. Mark will be here soon, and I'm surprised at how much I look forward to his arrival. Sure, we had lunch at Freddie's again, but this is different. I will be driving him to his house and letting him off there.

Will there be more?

Collecting my handbag and briefcase, soon I see Mark enter the library. Watching him stroll over to Reference, I admire his approach. He's a handsome man, a confident man.

Mark speaks first as he arrives at my desk. 'Hi Wendy. Can I get a ride home with you?' He smiles, pearly white teeth sparkling within his brown face.

On the way to his house, we exchange "How was your day?" with each other.

I complain about the clueless students who drop by Reference, and Mark complains about the results of the quiz on the first two chapters of his cultural anthropology text. He's graded some of them and will grade the rest at home tonight, not too hopeful for the class average. 'I have a feeling they spend more time on TikTok and Instagram than on reading.'

We pass the time complaining about other matters, campus, regional, and national. Soon I pull to the curb in front of his house. 'Thanks for the ride, Wendy,' he says. He takes hold of my elbow. 'Hey, I want to show you my gardens around back. I'm really proud of them. Do you have a minute?'

I consider this request for only a nanosecond, then respond, 'Sure. I guess I have some time.'

Mark leads the way up to the porch, unlocks the front door, and holds it open for me. I wonder why he didn't just lead around the house to the back, but I'm also interested in seeing the inside of this classic bungalow. As I enter the living room, I notice at first the oak-beamed ceiling and oak moldings around doorways off the expansive great room. I might expect that a man living alone would leave messes everywhere—potato chip bags, dirty dishes on the coffee table, crushed beer cans. I also might expect to see a messy kitchen, but after taking in the sparse but neat living room I know the kitchen and dining room will be spotless, too.

'Quite impressive, Dr. Torres,' I say. 'You are a very neat man.'

'Why thank you,' he responds with a smile. 'I try. Let's go on through to the back door.'

I wonder why Mark wants me to see and appreciate his décor and housekeeping. He must be proud. 'Do you have a maid come in weekly to clean house for you?'

He laughs. 'You mean like a French maid? I wish!'

We make our way through the dining room, kitchen, and breakfast nook to the back door. As I expected, they are also neat and spotless. Mark leads me down the back steps, taking my hand. 'Be careful. The steps are narrow and steep.'

The back yard is larger than I expected. The lot appears to be at least 150 feet deep by about 75 feet wide. There's a shed in one corner of the lot, bordering on the alley. The flower gardens are on the right, framing the patio, while the vegetable gardens are on the left. Mark has tomatoes, green beans, and cucumbers in well-maintained rows. Who would have thought that a single man would be such a great gardener?

'I must confess, I inherited the perennials when I bought this place. But the vegetables are all my doing.'

'How long have you lived here?'

'I moved in on May 30th. I wanted to move here in time to teach a summer class at the university, to get my feet wet, so to speak. I started planting immediately, working in the garden in the early mornings and afternoons after I got home. The ground here is excellent, helped by generous amounts of manure and mulch.'

'Well, it's most impressive!'

'Thank you! Hey, before you go, how about a drink? I have beer, wine, brandy, soft drinks, water.'

I know I should decline the invitation. Seeing me wavering, Mark says, 'I usually have a glass of wine or brandy and sit on my porch swing in the afternoon when I get home, to decompress. You look like you need to decompress too. What do you say?'

'I shouldn't, but just for a little while. A glass of wine sounds great.'

'Excellent!' he says.

As we climb the steps up to the back door, he allows me to go first. He steadies me with a hand on my back. His powerful hand is quite firm, and I would feel even better if it *massaged* my back. Even better if his second hand joined it. I should stop thinking like this, but I can't help myself.

Once we are inside, Mark brings out two wine glasses and uncorks an already-open bottle of red wine. After pouring the wine, he leads me to the front porch, where we sit in the swing and gently rock forward and back, sipping our wine and enjoying the mild afternoon. After a few minutes he puts his arm around my shoulder.

'Sorry,' he says, 'but my arm felt a little cramped by my side.'

I know better. 'Yeah, I bet that's what you said to all the girls at the movies when you were a teenager.'

'Ha! I didn't have to; I just did it. They didn't expect it, and before they knew it, my arm was there. Now I'm more courteous about it.'

'Don't get fresh, mister! I'm a married woman,' I say, and sip my wine.

'I wouldn't think of it.' I suspect he's lying.

After several minutes of enjoying the afternoon sun on the porch and the gentle motion of the swing, we finish our wine. I glance at my watch and see it's time to leave. 'I thank you for your hospitality, sir,' I say, 'and what an impressive back yard you have. But now I must be going.'

Mark helps me out of the porch swing and walks me down the steps to my car. 'So, tomorrow I pick up?'

'Yes, that's right,' I confirm, a little light-headed from the wine. 'And it's my turn on Wednesday.' I stumble slightly, and Mark steadies me, putting his arm around my waist. 'Are you OK? Did the wine get to you?'

'Maybe, but I'm all right. It was just a little stumble on a clump of grass. It's a short and straight drive home. I'll see you tomorrow morning.'

'All right, then. Drive carefully now!'

I climb into the car, compose myself, and start the engine. As I pull away from the curb, I wave at Mark and say goodbye.

'Now that was an interesting experience,' I say to myself. I wonder what he thought of it.

At quarter to five I arrive home. I'm about thirty minutes late and wonder if Miles will confront me. I hadn't told him I was picking up Mark, so I run through several deceitful scenarios to explain my lateness.

Shopping? A little overtime work? A staff meeting?

Yes, I did have a "staff" meeting of sorts, so that wouldn't be a full lie.

Playing these scenarios in my mind, I enter the kitchen from the garage and toss my handbag and keys on the counter. The girls hear me, and Emma shouts from the living room, 'Hi Mommy. You're late!'

Let's see if this works. 'Yeah, honey, I had a staff meeting. Where's Daddy?'

'Upstairs,' Emma replies, munching on her peanut butter and jelly sandwich. 'He's writing.' Good, Emma's not suspicious about my tardiness.

'OK,' I say, heading for the stairs. 'You girls know you're not supposed to be eating in the living room!'

'OK, OK!' responds Sophie. I don't expect her to leave for the kitchen to finish eating, though. She'll probably stay, sitting on her knees in front of the coffee table.

I go upstairs and start to head down the hall to the office. Before I get too far, an acrid odor assails my nostrils. 'Peew, what's that smell?' It becomes stronger as I approach the office door. There's an undertone odor as well, which I can't place until I open the door and see Miles slumped forward in his chair, a puddle of liquid below the chair on the floor, and the mixed odor of urine and feces in the air. I almost gag. I scream, 'Miles! Miles! What the hell has happened to you? Oh my God, this is disgusting!'

Hearing my screams, Miles turns around in his chair and looks at me, his brow and shirt soaked in sweat, his eyes bloodshot, his face red. I scream again, and Miles collapses in the chair, which tilts and falls to the floor, its foul contents pooling on the oak floorboards.

Sophie and Emma have heard me, both of them rushing upstairs. Hearing them approach, I say, 'Don't come into the office! Your father has had an accident. He'll be all right, but you don't need to see this!'

'Eww, what's that smell?' Sophie says.

'Eww,' repeats Emma, pinching her nose.

'Never mind, Sophie, just do what I say now!'

'OK, OK, I don't wanna be anywhere near that smell anyway,' Sophie utters. She and Emma hesitate, viewing the horrible scene, then quickly retreat downstairs.

It takes a few seconds for me to survey the scene and figure out what to do, but finally I clean up Miles in the office rather than drag his limp body to the bathroom. I undress him, rolling up the soiled underwear inside his pants, and wash his lower body. With some difficulty I put a clean pair of undershorts and tee shirt on him. He groans and rolls from side to side. I wipe his brow and face with a clean washcloth. Then I disinfect the puddle on the floor and on the seat of the chair.

With all my strength, I pick Miles up and guide him to the bedroom, where I put him under the covers and close the bedroom door. Going back to the office to straighten up the furniture, I sense a tiny sound coming from the floor. Partially under a leg of the desk, a pen rocks back and forth, as if an invisible hand is moving it. I bend down to inspect it, intrigued by the motion.

Is an insect moving it? Maybe it's just settling after being dropped.

I pick it up, put the cap back on, and place it on the desk, staring at it once more for a few seconds. It seems to be commanding my attention.

This doesn't feel like an ordinary pen. Does it have anything to do with Miles' collapse? Because it intrigues me, I place it in my shorts pocket for examining it later.

I leave the office, carrying Miles' piss-soaked and shitty underwear balled up inside his pants. I'll throw them all away. I don't want to touch them any more than I have to.

'Holy shit! What an afternoon!' I exhale and head for the liquor in the kitchen downstairs. I need a drink.

In the bedroom Miles rests under the covers. In the living room Sophie and Emma watch their shows and eat their snacks. I overhear their chatter about their father and the scene in his office earlier. Poor girls, they deserve better than this.

I pour a stiff drink and sit at the kitchen table sipping it, rubbing my forehead. What am I to do? What am I to do?

Chapter 22
Miles

I jolt awake, disoriented from some terrifying dream that I can't remember now. How did I wind up in bed? My last memory is of sitting at my desk, writing furiously. My cramped hand and forearm are sore. I'm under the covers in my undershorts, but I can't remember taking off my clothes.

Groggy from my nap, I get out of bed on unsteady legs, swaying slightly. Dressing slowly, I sit back down to put on my socks and pants. Even though I don't know how I wound up in bed, I feel the call: I must get back to my writing.

Once I'm fully clothed, I head for the office. I remember that I was still writing. When I reach the desk, I don't see the pen anywhere on the top of the desk. I lower on hands and knees to search for it on the floor. Nope, nowhere. I start to feel sick, nerves jittery. I run my hands through my hair, trying to remember what I did with that pen.

Where is it? I know it still has ink in it; I can sense it.

A thought flashes: maybe Wendy knows where it is. 'Wendy!' I shout, 'Wendy, where are you? Come here, please!'

Wendy responds from downstairs, 'Miles? Miles, you're up? Sooner than you should be. Go back to bed!'

'No, I'm up for good. Come here now! I need you!'

'I'll be there in a minute! I'm fixing dinner now!'

'Screw dinner, come up here now!'

'OK, OK, I'm coming!' Wendy bounds up the stairs.

After she arrives in the office, I ask her, 'Do you know where my pen is? I can't find it!'

'Yes, I put it away while you were sleeping.'

'You did? Where is it? I need it!'

'I thought you would sleep longer—'

This delay irritates me. 'I want it now!'

Wendy shrinks from me. 'I really think you should rest some more before you return to your writing.'

'No, I want it *now*! I need it *now*! Give it to me!' My agitation rumbles like a volcano about to erupt. I feel an impulse to punch her.

'OK, OK, here it is!' She reaches into her pocket and pulls out the pen.

My pen! My Kat!

She holds it out toward me, and I snatch it from her outstretched hand. Mumbling to myself, I turn and head back to the desk, leaving her standing there.

Screw her!

I write far longer than I expected. The pen seems to have refilled itself, though I know that can't be true.

Finally, around 7:30 it runs dry. Now, I can take a break.

However, a pile of about a dozen handwritten pages, front and back, sits skewed off to my left. Either I type them now, or I eat dinner. Doing the math, I figure it's going to take about two to three hours to type up.

No, no meal now; I'll have a snack after I finish, probably close to midnight.

I'd better get to it.

Chapter 23
Wendy

'You bastard!' I mumble to myself as I go downstairs to the kitchen.

After dinner, sans Miles again, I spend the evening in the living room, reading and playing games on my tablet. I can't concentrate, however, stewing over the scene I discovered in the office this afternoon. With renewed disgust I remember the mess and the cleanup. It was like changing a baby's diaper. Then the ridiculous conflict over his pen.

He's behaving like I think a drug addict would behave. I wonder if he *has* been using drugs? Well, while he's working so hard up there, why not find out? I get up to start searching.

I begin in the downstairs bathroom, then check all the drawers and cabinet shelves in the kitchen. Nothing.

Quietly moving upstairs, I overhear Miles speaking the lines as he types. He won't pay attention to my movements as long as I stay out of the office. I can check that later. I look throughout the upstairs bathroom, and as I pass the girls' rooms toward the master bedroom Sophie calls out, 'Mom, are you looking for something?'

'No, Sophie, just checking to see if we've run out of any of our medications before making a run to Walmart.' Sophie seems satisfied and returns her attention to her tablet.

I peer into Emma's room to see her doing her homework. 'Hi, Mommy,' she says. 'What's up?'

'Oh, nothing,' I tell Emma. 'Just checking in on you. You can go back to work now.'

'Mommy?' Emma asks, 'is anything wrong with Dad? He's different now.'

I must choose my words wisely. 'Yes, you're right. He *is* different now. He's been working on this new project of his, a novel that he started over a week ago. It's become an obsession, which I hope fades over time.'

'What's an obsession?' Emma asks.

Emma, always interested in new words.

'Well, it's something that kind of takes over your life and keeps you from doing other things.'

'Like missing dinner and yelling for no reason?'

'Yes, exactly. He's done a lot of writing, and I hope he's nearing the end, so he can become himself again.'

'What about his classes? Is he doing them as well, while he's writing?'

'No, he's not teaching classes this semester. He's all in on writing a novel.'

'Oh, OK. I hope he becomes his old self again soon. I miss him.' Tears begin to form in her eyes.

Seeing this, I cross the room and give Emma a big hug. 'Me too, darling,' I say, and kiss the top of her head. 'Me too.' I turn and leave the room.

In the office Miles continues to type away like a madman, stopping for nothing.

He's got to be on drugs.

Chapter 24
Miles

Tuesday I rouse myself by mid-morning to a quiet house. Everyone has left, for school and work. Wendy didn't even tell me goodbye. No matter: I like the empty house, where I don't need to play nice. So I go to the bathroom to wash my face and try to train my hair to meet the day.

Perhaps after breakfast I should put on my running clothes and jog through the neighborhood like I used to, to clear my head. That should get my blood pumping.

After breakfast I put on my running clothes. On my way out of the bedroom I decide to boot up my slow laptop so it will be ready when I get back from running. After booting it up, I glance to the right, where I see Kat lying. Is it my imagination, or do I see it rock from side to side?

'Hello Kat,' I say, 'and how are you today? Shall I get you ready to write after I come back?' I smile as I repeat the new name of my pen. 'Kat, Kat, I sure do like that name! How appropriate! I sure do like how you curl up in my hand and purr away!'

I remember studying name theory in grad school, and how naming something gives you control over it. Somehow, though, it seems backward with this pen and me.

Who has the "control"? Kat?

Yes, a voice whispers. Hmm, did I hear right? Where did that come from?

I go through the routine of filling the cartridge with ink and lay it aside. Now it will be ready for me after I get back from my jog. For a few seconds I stare at the pen, spellbound by its smooth lines, its gold clip and cap tip. I uncap it to admire the gold nib.

What a gorgeous pen! Simple, yet elegant.

So *sexy*, even.

Having uncapped the pen, I open my notebook and start writing.

Two hours later the pen runs out of ink, and I can take a bathroom break and have lunch before typing the several pages front and back that I have written.

I'm nearing the end of the story, the climax, and I'm going to finish the novel by bedtime tonight, whenever that may be. By the time I finish, I should have close to 300 pages, nearly 80,000 words. That should be about right for a novel. After all, a gripping novel like **Lord of the Flies** is only about 60,000 words in length, and I believe **Killing Time** will be just as compelling. After editing it, within a day or two I will have it ready for Susan Brower.

I rush through lunch and get to work typing my handwritten pages. By mid-afternoon I've typed, handwritten, and typed again, reaching the climactic end with a twist that might promise a sequel. I have accomplished this monumental task in just thirteen days from when I discovered the old manuscript. *Incredible*!

Yes, 298 double-spaced pages, complete! It is finished!

But why should I wait another day to waste time editing it when I know it is perfect? I start an email to Susan Brower and attach the document file, then send it. I think she will like it—no, no, she will be impressed!

Yes, she will, whispers that disembodied voice. *Sure, she will.*

Again, what's up with that? Where did that voice come from?

Only then am I aware that I'm dressed in my running clothes. Well, since I've put them on, I *should* go out for a run.

I leave the house and take off down the street. It feels so good to run off the pent-up energy left over from the writing process.

I have needed to do this for a long, long time.

But I feel guilty leaving Kat.

Chapter 25
Wendy

I arrive home from work, Mark helping me out of his Porsche, not knowing what I will face when I see Miles again. 'Miles?' Coming through the front door, I call out, 'Miles? I'm home.'

No reply.

I call out again. 'Miles, I'm home!'

No reply. Only silence.

I make my way upstairs to check on Miles. Will I see—or smell—another disgusting scene?

But no, the office is empty, except for a pile of notebook pages on the right side of the open laptop. The pen rests next to the laptop. I glare at it for a while, wishing I could get rid of it. But no, I had better not do that. No telling what Miles will do.

My eyes are drawn to the laptop screen.

Two words proclaim *The End* in the middle of the screen.

'Really? No way!' I sit down to read. I start browsing through the document, growing more and more incredulous at the talent displayed as I read.

A short time later, the front door opens, and there's some activity in the entry. Thinking it's my daughters; I call out but hear Miles answer. 'It's me. Just got back from running.'

That's a good sign; he actually got out of the house and got some exercise. 'Great!' I shout. 'I'm coming down.'

When I get downstairs to greet him, Miles exhales deeply. 'Whew! That was a good run!'

I am so proud that he got some exercise, and really proud of his writing. I beam, 'I was just reading the last few pages of your story, and it's—'

'What?' Miles interrupts. 'You read it? Why? Did I ask you to? Did I give you permission?'

I didn't expect this. 'I went upstairs to see if you were in the office and all right, and the story was on screen. I—'

He growls, 'You didn't have my permission! It's not ready to be read, and now you've spoiled it all!'

'But you let me read it before!'

'That was before it was finished. I wanted you to tell me what you thought of the writing at that stage. But all you could say was that you hated the wife in the story because you thought she was *you*. Well, she wasn't then, but she is now…bitch!'

I gasp, 'I only read a few pages!' Now I am on the defensive and must say something. I must put him on the defensive. Too bad I use the wrong words. 'And besides, 298 pages? In less than two weeks? No way! Did you download somebody else's book? And are you going to make it look like you wrote it?'

His face reddens with rage. 'What? I can't believe you just said that!'

Without warning, Miles slaps me on my left cheek. Then again, on my right cheek, knocking me off balance.

Immediately the rage vanishes as Miles realizes what he has done to me. 'Oh, I'm so sorry, Wendy, so, so sorry!'

Miles has never slapped me before. Something snaps inside me, and I shout, 'You … you son of a bitch!'

I run up the stairs to the bedroom, slamming the door.

'Wendy, Wendy, I'm sorry, so sorry,' Miles calls up the stairs. 'Please!' he cries out. I hear his footsteps on the stairs, then coming to the bedroom door. He tries the doorknob, which I have locked. 'Wendy? Wendy? Let me in. I can explain,' he pleads.

From inside the bedroom, I sob, 'Go away!'

'Well, all right then,' he mutters. 'It was only a couple of slaps anyway.' I can hear him head back to the office and slam the door.

Sophie and Emma arrive home from school a short time later. 'Hello? Is anybody home?' Sophie shouts.

Great, just great. How can I cover up these red cheeks? I answer, 'We're both home. Be down in a minute!' I need to fix my face before I go downstairs.

The tone of my voice sounds a little strained. I bet Sophie's thinking Mom and Dad just had sex. She's old enough to know what sex is.

But if she's thinking that, she's wrong. Horribly wrong.

There's only one man now with whom I will have sex, and it's not Miles.

Chapter 26
Miles

I spent Tuesday night sleeping in the office, on the daybed. Wendy wouldn't have let me sleep with her anyway. I don't know what came over me yesterday. I have never struck her before, never. Sure, I was upset that she read my story again, without asking my permission. But I shouldn't have slapped her. What was I thinking? I am ashamed of myself. Something has come over me the past couple of weeks, and I am losing control of myself.

This morning I heard Wendy leave the bedroom and go downstairs to greet the girls. I will wait until they all clear out before I go down. I can't face Wendy, and I don't want to pretend that nothing is wrong in front of the girls.

I'm sitting in my office chair, straightening the mess I've created, stacking papers and putting them in folders. As I work, my cell phone dings, and the laptop displays a notification from an email.

It's from Susan Brower: *Got the manuscript. Thanks. I'll be in touch.*

I'm anxious for her evaluation, but I know it will take time for her to read the entire story. It will be hard for me to wait patiently; I wish I had something to do to occupy my mind for hours or days while I wait.

In my peripheral vision I detect movement. Looking to my right I notice my pen rocking slowly, then stopping. Did it just move? I pick it up and rotate it between the fingers of both hands. This pen has inspired my writing with its smooth feed and bold lines.

Has it simply made writing easier, or has it done more than that? Has it aided my creative process, or has it really generated the ideas itself? When it's full of ink, the process speeds along without a hitch; I'm full of ideas. When it runs out of ink, the ideas stop. Is that because I can't write more until I refill it? Also, it seems that the ink is lasting longer than it should each time I use it.

114

If it's the pen that inspires me, how long will the inspiration last? Does it have another book inside it? I finished the book, but I still feel a strong desire to write. I have to write!

However, I have no idea of what to write next. What if I refill the pen? Will I start from zero and develop a new story, pull a plot out of thin air, so to speak? I should put it to the test.

I refill Kat and get ready.

With a clean sheet of paper before me, I sit, thinking. No idea springs to mind. Not wanting to waste Kat's ink on throwaway writing, I pick up a pencil first and try to brainstorm topics, but none interest me.

Should I write a memoir? Fiction? Memoir/Fiction? Creative non-fiction? Poetry, even? Nothing comes to mind.

I toss the pencil aside and pick up Kat. Suddenly an idea flashes before my mind's eye.

Why not?

I begin to write.

As usual I write through dinnertime, oblivious to all the noises around the house: the girls arriving home, Wendy coming in and dropping her keys on the countertop, the chatter between the girls and Wendy.

Well, OK, I didn't want to face Wendy anyway.

The more I write, though, the shame over my behavior with Wendy wanes and I grow angry. How dare she read my work without my permission? My mood turns dark.

The girls are nuisances, too, always interrupting my creative flow. I'm going to stay here in the office until after their bedtimes, then sneak down to the kitchen to get something to eat.

Kat runs out of ink around the middle of the evening after I fill eight pages of my new story. Eight pages on one refill? Now I can pause to take a bathroom break and then return to begin typing what I've handwritten.

But when I sit down to type, I see on screen an email notification from Susan Brower. I open the email and read:

*Hello Miles. I have been reading **Killing Time** for the past three and a half hours and have scanned to the end, and I cannot put it down! I've read enough to decide that I would like to represent you. That is, I would like to be your literary agent. I don't know if you have sent **KT** to other agents. If you have, let me know. If you are sent an offer from a potential agent, let me know, and I will beat them.*

Speaking of which, I have attached a sample contract for you to review. It will cover the usual terms. If you have an attorney, run it by him or her. If not, please reply with any questions you might have. If you send me your phone number, I would like to discuss this potential partnership with you.

All the best,
Susan Brower
Brower Literary Agency

Her signature line is followed by all her contact information.

I can't believe what I have just read. Is my work that good?

Of course, it's that good, that voice tells me. It must be my subconscious echoing my thoughts.

I reread the email to make sure. That's right; it must be true! I want to jump up and run downstairs to tell Wendy, but something inside stops me. Better to wait until a contract is signed. Besides, Wendy doesn't believe in my ability. She's convinced this is some kind of pipe dream. Worse, she's assumed it's plagiarism.

Why should I tell her at all?

I write a brief reply to Susan, telling her I'm working on a new story and need to type the first few pages before sending her a fuller response.

I type until nearly ten. The new novel is progressing well, I can tell from the first several pages I've typed. Wendy won't want me to sleep in our bed, and besides, my anger at her has not subsided; in fact, it has grown as I've continued writing this new story. I have no idea how long it will be: whether a short story, a novella, or a novel. I didn't know how long **Killing Time** would be when I started writing.

After hours of writing and typing, my back is screaming in pain, begging me to stop. My hand and forearm are cramping. I leave the office to go to the bedroom to retrieve my toothbrush, pillow, and sleep shorts. Wendy is downstairs watching the local news on TV, so she won't see me gathering up my things.

I get ready for bed and head to the office to sleep in the daybed, closing the office door with authority. The sound echoes throughout the house, declaring *Keep out!*

Chapter 27
Wendy

Miles slept in the office last night. I would have told him to sleep elsewhere anyway, as I'm still seething inside. He has never laid a finger on me, never, except to grope, hug, or make love to me. Fortunately, the makeup I applied to the slap sites masked them enough that the girls didn't notice. They wouldn't have anyway, as they retreated upstairs right after dinner last night.

Why did reading just a few pages of his manuscript cause such a violent reaction? Is he hiding something? I didn't like the wife when I read part of it before, but when I read it last night I didn't come to a part with her in it. I don't know if he "improved" the wife. I could tell from the few pages I read that it was good—even superior—work. But he's gone too far by slapping me.

Screw what he has written; I'll never read his work again!

These past two weeks have convinced me that he's certainly fallen into an addiction of some kind, one that has taken over his body and now his mind, his emotions. This is not the man I married, not the father of our daughters. Does he need help? *Yes.* But right now I'm so angry and hurt that I couldn't care less if he lives or dies.

Mark is looking more attractive to me every day. Thinking about him causes a warm sensation, which is very hard to ignore.

I feel my bond to my husband disintegrating. We've been through a lot of challenges over the years, but this one seems insurmountable.

Today is Wednesday, and this morning we have been avoiding each other. Miles waits to come out until the girls and I have had our breakfasts and they have left for the bus stop. While I'm getting ready for work upstairs, he goes downstairs to eat breakfast.

I take extra time this morning, allowing Miles to nearly finish his breakfast before I have to pass through the kitchen on my way to the garage. I leave without a word of goodbye. The last I saw of him, he was staring ahead into space, a spoonful of frosted mini wheats held up in front of his mouth.

I can't help myself; I hope he chokes on it.

It's my day to pick up Mark. As I drive to his house, butterflies flit about in my belly. This is a new feeling, the result of a decision I made last night in bed.

When I pull to the curb in front of Mark's house, I find him sitting in his porch swing. He picks up his briefcase and comes down the steps to the sidewalk, erect and confident. He opens the passenger door, seats himself, and snaps his seatbelt in place. On the way to campus, I'm quiet, thinking of what happened yesterday with Miles and what I hope will happen today with Mark.

Mark notices my silence. 'You're quiet. Everything all right?'

'Yes, ...well, no, not really,' I answer, relating my confrontation with Miles yesterday afternoon.

'Oh wow, that's serious,' he says. 'Are you going to be OK today?'

'Yeah, I'll get over it, and I hope Miles gets over it too. He's sick, I think.'

Mark reaches over and takes my right hand in his left, caressing it and sympathizing for the rest of the trip to campus. I'm thrilled by the touch, and I stroke his hand also.

Later, we're at Freddie's again for lunch. We've now become a familiar sight to the staff, a few of whom are college students. I guess they consider us an "item," because we are getting preferential treatment.

'So, you're not speaking to each other now?' Mark asks. I detect a twinkle in his eye. Does he think this is a good sign? I suspect it *is* a good sign, as I have plans for this afternoon.

'Yeah,' I sigh, 'it's come to that, I'm afraid.'

Shortly before 4:00 Mark appears at my work desk for his ride home. Oh my, the butterflies have all taken flight inside! I quickly say goodbye to Carolyn and Linda as I gather up my things and scurry toward the back door, Mark following me. I'm eager to leave for my car, and he has to nearly jog to keep up with me. I need to slow down as we exit the back door.

Once in the car, he catches his breath, panting, 'Man, you must be in a hurry to get home!'

'Nope, to get to *your* home!' I blurt out before thinking.

Mark's eyebrows rise in response. I don't have to guess what he's thinking. 'Oh? What's so interesting about my home? My gardens? My etchings? Or are you just in a hurry to get rid of me?' he jokes.

'You'll see,' I say, taking his left hand in my right, placing it on my thigh. I drive the distance to his house with one hand on the wheel and the other on his hand resting on my thigh, which begins to crawl up like a noiseless patient spider.

After we arrive at Mark's house, leaving the car I come around the back of the car to Mark and put my arm around his waist. He responds by putting his arm around my shoulder, pulling me into his side. When we get to the front door, Mark pulls out his key and unlocks the door. Before we enter, I pull him toward me and kiss him eagerly. He returns the favor, clenching me tightly to his body. He backs into the door, opening it and pulling me inside, then closes it behind us.

What we do inside Mark's house is only a natural response to Miles' mistreatment of me, I tell myself. I even convince myself that's what Miles wants.

It surely is what Mark wants.

And it's what *I* want.

Chapter 28
Miles

She's gone now. Good riddance!

Settling heavily into my office chair, I boot up the laptop. The first thing I do this morning is reply to Susan Brower. I download the sample contract attached to her last email. Her fee is fifteen percent for representing me to publishers, film companies, and other media. OK, I can accept that.

What else? "The term of this agreement is for two years, or twenty-four months." And yadda, yadda, yadda. My God, this document is page after page of details. I don't need to read all of it, just need to know how much she gets and for how long this agreement will last.

Maybe I should query at least one or two more agents. I figure, what the hell? Why not? Maybe I can get a better deal.

Or maybe not. This could be the chance of a lifetime. Yeah, I should go with Susan. After all, she's one of the top agents.

I write an email reply to Susan, providing my cell number. Within a half hour, my cell phone rings. The caller ID displays *Susan Brower*. I swipe right and answer, 'Hello Susan!'

An obviously twenty-something voice answers. 'This is Carrie, Susan's assistant. Am I speaking to Miles Campbell?' Embarrassed, I apologize. 'Sorry, yes, I'm Miles Campbell.' Carrie transfers me to Susan.

Susan greets me flush with excitement, which I can sense over the phone. 'I'd like to thank you on behalf of my team. I believe we'll be a great fit for each other. I love your novel and promise I can easily snare a book deal from a major publisher…if only you sign a contract.'

'The one you attached to the email?' I ask.

'No, I'll send you an official contract through certified mail. If it meets your approval, sign it and return it, and I'll get started as soon as I receive it.'

I like the fluid, melodic sound of her voice. I could listen to it all day.

'All right, then. And just so you know, yesterday I started a new book, and I have already typed eight pages.'

'That's wonderful, Miles. I hope it's as good as your first one. I have to ask, though: how did you produce 298 pages in just two weeks? It takes most writers months at best and a year or two normally to write novels. Had you started it some time ago and come back to it recently?'

'Sort of. I started it about fifteen years ago, some of it handwritten, some already typed. I finished it in two weeks.'

'That is unbelievable. How did you do it? Forego sleep? Not eat? How?'

'None of that. Once I put my pen to paper, the ideas just flow out through its tip.'

'So, you write first, then type what you have written?'

'Yep.'

'Most authors compose at the keyboard these days.'

'I don't. I guess I write by hand to record the story, then revise and edit as I type. It works for me.'

'Wow, that's impressive. It sounds like double the work, though, but as you say, it works for you. It just seems mathematically impossible, what you have done in such a short time.'

I don't know how to explain what I went through to write it so fast, so I say nothing.

Filling the gap, Susan adds, 'Well, then, keep writing as I start planning for shopping your book around. And keep me posted on the progress of the new book. Soon I'll want to know what it's about, but for now I think it's best to take one book at a time.'

I agree, and we say goodbye. I love her melodious voice. I wish I could have heard her speak more.

I return to working on the new book, unaware of the passing of time.

Before I know it, the pen has run dry, it's 1:00, and once again my crotch and the chair seat are soaked and my sweaty clothes cling to my skin.

Damn! I have to clean myself again. Why does this happen?

I clean up the mess, rinse my clothes, and toss them in the dryer. It's time for lunch, and afterwards I must type up sixteen pages front and back.

Later on, I've finished typing those sixteen handwritten pages. The house is still quiet. No one is home, though I expect Sophie and Emma to walk through the front door any minute now.

Sure enough, both girls burst through the front door arguing. I don't know what about, but it's annoying.

Sophie yells out, 'We're home! Is anybody here?'

'Yes, I'm home,' I yell back.

'Where's Mommy?' asks Emma.

I come out of the office to the upstairs landing. 'I don't know,' I say. 'I guess she's got a meeting or something. Now will you be quiet? I'm writing.'

'OK, Dad, we will,' Sophie yells.

It's unusual for Wendy to be late because of staff meetings, twice now in a week. I shouldn't blame her for coming home later, considering what I did to her yesterday.

Yes, I slapped her, twice. And I was sorry yesterday. Today I'm less sorry. I felt violated by her thoughtless reading of my novel, without my permission. She should have understood that.

At 5:00 Wendy comes through the kitchen from the garage, calling out, 'I'm home!'

The girls must be in the living room watching TV and eating snacks. I overhear Emma run into the kitchen to greet her mother. Wendy says to her, 'I stopped off at Walgreen's to get a couple of things. I've got ice cream, which we can have for dessert tonight!'

'Yay!' cries Emma and claps her hands.

123

I will not call out or go downstairs to greet Wendy. Instead, I continue to read over what I've just finished typing.

Soon Wendy comes up the stairs. As she steps up on the landing, she stops for a few seconds. Is she thinking of coming in to see me? I hope not.

And she doesn't. She continues on to the bedroom. That's fine; I didn't want to talk to her anyway.

I continue to read my manuscript, smiling. I've gotten off to a great start, if I do say so myself. It might even be better than my first novel, now in the hands of Susan Brower. And I can already guess how this one's going to end.

After I finish reading, catching a few typos and making a few changes in descriptions, I feel the need to write again. My peripheral vision detects some motion, and as I turn to view it, I see Kat rock from side to side and spin around once.

Strange…

Immediately, as if commanded, I reach for the ink bottle and pick up the pen. I refill Kat and start to write.

Chapter 29
Wendy

As has become his recent habit, Miles refuses to eat with us again and instead writes away up there in that damned office. He has completely distanced himself from his family, even from Sophie and Emma. I sit across from the girls, absent-mindedly pushing my food around on the plate, my mind raging with warring emotions.

Damn it, this has gone on long enough. I should leave him!

No, I should stay with him; for better or worse…

Worse? This has gone beyond worse.

Mark, Mark, just the thought of Mark thrills me like I haven't been thrilled in years. I want more of him. This afternoon wasn't enough, not by a long shot.

No, that would be wrong, so wrong. I shouldn't give up on Miles just yet.

But Mark…

But Miles…

I have been absent-mindedly stirring my food into a single pile. Emma has been watching and asks, 'Mommy, are you all right? You seem sad.'

I snap out of my reverie. 'No, dear, I'm just lost in thought.'

'Are you missing Daddy, too?'

'Yes, I guess I am.'

But not as much as I used to.

Sophie joins in. 'He doesn't eat with us. He doesn't talk to us. He avoids us. Why, Mom? Have we done something wrong? Have we upset him?'

Hearing the pain in my daughters' voices both saddens and angers me. 'Your father has gotten so caught up in his writing that he can't think of anything else, or *anyone* else. He's forgotten that he has a family.' I can't tell them how bad his addiction has become. 'It's changed his life, that's what it's done.'

'And ours, too,' Emma adds. She fights back tears.

'Let's just hope that he gets over this soon, that he gets this out of his system.'

Sophie asks, 'Will you talk to him, Mom?'

I don't want to talk to Miles because I fear his reaction. 'I will try, Sophie, I will try.'

What I would rather do is avoid Miles altogether and spend more time with Mark. But I can't tell my girls this. I have no idea about the future with Mark and certainly don't know about my future with Miles.

All three of us finish our dinner, leaving food on our plates. We've lost our appetites. The remains go into the trash. Afterwards, we all part for the evening, the girls to their rooms and me to the living room.

I have a great idea. I'm not going to vegetate on the couch and wallow in this sewage but instead go out for a run, clear my mind. I go upstairs and put on my running clothes, telling the girls that I'll be gone for a while. If Miles hears me, that's fine; I won't go to the office to tell him that I'm leaving. As if he would care anyway.

I leave the house, heading down the steps to the sidewalk, where I stretch for a few seconds, and head west … toward Mark's house.

I jog along the paved streets toward Mark's house. I really, really long to find him home, all casual and comfortable.

Maybe stay for a while, and jog on back.

I shouldn't do this, but I can't help it.

Before I realize it, I have arrived at the sidewalk in front of Mark's house. I pause to catch my breath, steadying myself on the beat-up car parked on the street in front of his house. I run up the lower steps leading up to his porch, halting to catch my breath.

Should I go up? Should I knock on his front door?

Yes, why not knock on his door?

I go up the steps to the porch landing, raising my hand to knock.

But what if—?

Maybe he's eating.

Maybe he's grading.

Maybe he's reading.

Maybe he's not at home.
Maybe this isn't a good idea.

No, it's not a good idea to come to his door unannounced. It might be an unwelcome intrusion. I won't take the risk. I turn around and start jogging back home.

Arriving home exhausted, sweaty, and disappointed, I go upstairs to find Sophie and Emma in Sophie's room, to see if they have done their homework. Before I head to the bathroom to take a shower, I ask them, 'Did Daddy come out and speak to you, or come out at all?'

Tears watering her eyes, Emma answers, 'No, Mommy, he didn't. He's been in there the whole time you were gone.' Emma is feeling her dear Daddy slipping away emotionally.

'No, Mom,' says Sophie, on the verge of rage. 'It's like he doesn't live here anymore. He might as well live somewhere else!'

My heart breaking for them, I comfort both of my confused and hurt daughters, then kiss their cheeks and head off to the bathroom for a shower.

Standing in the shower, washing off the sweat and fatigue, I wish Mark were here, his hands massaging the soap off my body.

The warm spray washing over me, I wince at a faded memory. Back in the early days of our marriage, pre-children, Miles and I used to take showers together, which always led to sex. We grew out of that over the years as we both wanted to shower alone, but it sure would be nice to do that again.

I have no hope of that ever happening, though.
Maybe with Mark.

Thursday morning Mark pulls to the curb in front of the house, the convertible top up. I've been waiting outside on the porch. As the car pulls to the curb, my heart flutters and I feel a rush in the pit of my stomach.

Quit acting like a teenage girl, Wendy, I think.

However, this is no angst-ridden teenage crush, as we went all the way yesterday afternoon and would have again if I had found Mark home last night.

'Good morning,' I say as I seat myself. I lean in to kiss him, but he leans away slightly. Surprised, I interpret this as a rebuff. I don't know what to think.

'Good morning to you, too!' He says, noticing my confusion. 'I think maybe we should be discrete in your neighborhood.'

This makes sense. 'Oh, I see. I think you're right. Sorry!'

'No problem.'

'So,' I begin, 'last night I went on a run and wound up in your neighborhood. I wanted to knock on your door but thought better of it.'

'Really? I wish you had called ahead. I was out buying groceries.'

'Hmm, I think I will next time. Maybe tonight?'

Mark pauses for a second. 'Sure, now you won't have to call later.'

On the drive to campus, we hold hands, my hand stroking his thigh, his hand on top of mine. I feel like a newlywed on her honeymoon trip.

Later I arrive at my work desk and settle in. Carolyn greets me and comes over for a chat, as usual before starting work. Linda hasn't arrived yet. 'Got a minute?' Carolyn says.

I smile and reply, 'Sure. What's up?' I expect to hear something about Carolyn's home life or bouts with her kids.

Carolyn takes a deep breath, releasing it slowly. 'Well, it may not be my place to say this, but I think you ought to know—'

'Know what?' I interrupt, as this sounds serious.

'How shall I put this? That people have started talking about you and Dr. Torres.'

'What? What people?'

'Uh, library people, for one. And I think it's gotten all the way to the director, too.'

'Really? And for two?'

'Ha ha, very funny. Some people across campus. Faculty, staff, even students.'

Silent and growing disturbed, I process this news.

Carolyn continues, tentatively. 'They all know you're married. Well, most of them anyway. And some of them are English faculty.'

'And how did you hear this?'

'You know, word gets around.'

'So? Mark—Dr. Torres—and I are just friends,' I say, convincingly, I hope. 'As I told you before, we live close enough to each other to share rides to campus to save on gas. We eat lunch together because eating with someone is better than eating alone.'

Carolyn asserts herself. 'Wendy, it doesn't look like that, and you know how people talk. Some of Miles' friends in the English Department might tell him, and he would get the wrong idea, if what you say is true.'

I feel a blush. 'If what I say is true? Anyway, I doubt that Miles *has* any friends in the English Department anymore. It's been three years. Besides, *people* should mind their own business. And if you've been part of this, so should you.'

'OK, OK, I just wanted to warn you.'

'Well, you did, and I thank you very much. Now I need to get to work.'

Carolyn stiffens, gathers her pride, and walks off to her station. She mumbles something under her breath.

I ponder this disturbing conversation and wonder if I should share it with Mark. Or if he has had the same conversation over in the Science Building. I should have realized that rumors would start, but I was naïve enough to think that being so obvious, so out in the open, would convince *people* that we're just friends.

However—and this is a big *however*—we are no longer "just friends." But what are we now? Does one sexual encounter make us lovers? Or was it just a one-off event? No strings attached? An affair?

129

I'm not sure. If more of what happened yesterday happens again—and again—I would be able to judge, wouldn't I?

Boy, will we have something to talk about at lunch today!

Time drags on in the Reference Department as I anticipate noon and Mark's arrival. Carolyn keeps her distance, and so does Linda, whom Carolyn must have told about her morning altercation with me. The slow pace is broken up a couple of times by students coming by to seek help for their projects and to check out course readings.

Once I look up from my desk to see three female students walk by, chattering and looking in my direction. When I make eye contact with them, they look away and giggle among themselves, as if they are telling each other a dirty secret. Normally I would have dismissed this as simply immature girlish behavior. But then I wonder if they were talking about me. What do they know? What have they heard? It's hard to dismiss these thoughts.

Am I being paranoid?

Mark arrives at my workstation around noon, ready to take me to lunch off campus. As we leave my area and walk across campus, I put a bit more distance between myself and him. I guess I *am* being paranoid.

After Mark and I arrive at Freddie's and order our food, I share the conversation I had with Carolyn.

'Really?' Mark responds. 'What makes her think so?'

'She says it's going around campus. She didn't tell me her sources. But there must be some talk.'

'Well, how about that? We're the grist of the rumor mill? You know what Bonnie Raitt said.'

'Who?'

'Bonnie Raitt. You know the song: "Let's give 'em something to talk about."

'Don't joke. This is serious. I'm married—'

'In name only.'

130

'Yes, but that doesn't matter. No one but you knows about my troubles at home.'

'So, this comes from people just seeing us walking together across campus and eating together?'

I sigh. 'Yes, I guess so.'

'Nobody in my neighborhood has noticed you at my door, as far as I can tell. And nobody knows what went on behind the front door.' Mark lays out the case like a defense attorney.

'Maybe not, but all the same, there's talk.'

'I get it. I guess we need to be more discreet on campus. Maybe no more lunches together, but we can make up for it in the afternoons.' He winks, and it is then that I notice two vaguely familiar faces sitting across the restaurant watching us. I think they are in the English Department, former colleagues of Miles. I hope they didn't notice Mark winking.

Behaving as discretely as possible, we finish our lunch and leave Freddie's to get back to campus in time for Mark's 1:00 class. Without a display of affection, I leave his car and head to the library while he puts the car in reverse and pulls out to go to his parking lot. I don't know what he's thinking, but I'm thinking of the ride home later in the afternoon, which may include a stopover at Mark's house.

Back at my desk, I see my phone light is blinking. Someone left a voicemail while I was out to lunch. Listening to the message, I hear the stern voice of our library director, Dr. Opal Schute, requesting that I come to her office after I get back from lunch. Maybe not requesting so much as commanding. 'I wonder what's up?'

It doesn't take long to find out what's up. I climb the steps to the second floor, where Dr. Schute's office is located. I knock on her office door and hear her gruff voice call out from the other side. 'Come in.' She sounds like a drill sergeant.

She's seated at her desk. 'Good afternoon, Dr. Schute,' I say.

There's a square worktable in the middle of the room, with four chairs around it. Dr. Schute says, 'Hello Mrs. Campbell,' and gestures toward the table. 'Please have a seat,' she says. 'I want to discuss something with you.'

I don't like the sound of this. I pull out a chair and seat myself. She comes around her desk and seats herself in the chair directly across from me.

Leaning forward in her chair, Dr. Schute places both elbows on the table and puts her hands together, interweaving her fingers and bringing her index fingers together, touching her chin. I'm thinking *Here's the church, and here's the steeple....* Her gray face reminds me of the dead. Her salt and pepper hair is parted in the middle and pulled back into a bun. Her eyes fix me through wire-rimmed glasses. Without the glasses she would look like George Washington as captured in that famous portrait by Gilbert Stuart.

'Mrs. Campbell,' she begins, 'do you know why I have called you to my office?'

Feeling like a student summoned to the principal's office, I answer, 'No, ma'am, I don't.'

With a serious, principal-like expression, she begins. 'It has been reported to me that you have been seen on several occasions in the company of a professor who is not your husband. You have left campus with him as well.'

I can't believe what I am hearing. Are we in Puritan New England? 'How would you know who my husband is, Dr. Schute? You started here just a few weeks ago.'

'Mrs. Campbell, don't sidestep the issue. I know many things already. I know that the man you've been seen with is not married, and I know that you are.'

'Well, so what? Aren't people free these days to consort with anyone they want? Besides, the man you are referring to is merely a friend.'

'Merely or not, Mrs. Campbell, it doesn't look good, and it reflects poorly on the library staff. Do you know that students are coming to the library just to see the woman who leaves campus with the new professor? Now, I can't tell you not to consort with a male faculty member, nor with anyone else, because as you say, it is a free country. I am warning you for your own good. I'm sure you don't want to be the center of campus rumors. However, if this friendship gets in the way of your duties, it won't go well for you. Be careful! Do I make myself clear?'

I would really like to let this woman have it, but she's my boss. 'Yes, Dr. Schute, I understand. It won't get in the way of my job performance.'

'Very well,' Dr. Schute says, looking pleased with herself for handling this sensitive situation so well. 'Be careful, and remember that you are part of the library team. If one member has a problem, we all suffer.'

As I leave her office, I suspect that Carolyn or Linda has spoken to Dr. Schute about Mark and me, but I can't be sure. Rumors have a way of wafting on the wind and arriving on eager ears without attribution. I will need to keep my eyes and ears open around the Reference Department. Those girls who came into the library and looked over at me, then chittered among themselves, they must have heard the rumor through the student grapevine.

I will be more careful from now on.

Chapter 30
Miles

I've been writing all morning, beads of sweat running down my cheeks, eyes glazed. Coming out of a trance, I guess, I feel my soaked shirt clinging to my torso. I have not left my desk chair since breakfast, and I feel the cold dampness in my shorts and smell the acrid odor of urine. I don't care; I can't leave my seat while I write.

This unfolding story enrages me. A volcano rumbles in my mind as I write, about to blow. I'm indignant that my characters behave the way I write them, but I have no control over the process. If anyone were around me now, I think I might strangle them out of anger and frustration.

After a while, Kat dries up. I feel drained, like I've just run a marathon. But now I need to clean myself and my chair. Why does this happen? If I go into a trance while I write, how do I write so legibly, and why don't I notice when I piss my pants? I hate it when I have to waste time cleaning up.

All clean now, I must type what I have written.

Even after I start typing, I'm still livid at my characters and what they have done, to themselves and to others around them.

Do authors become so close to their stories that they react as if they are reading them for the first time? I've heard of readers throwing books across the room when they read something they don't like. I remember a student in one of my classes a few years ago telling the class that she threw her book across the room when she read the end of "The Lottery." Now that's the kind of engagement that authors want from their readers. But is it natural for *authors* to feel that way while writing their stories?

Shortly afterwards, the doorbell rings. It's a FedEx delivery requiring my signature, an oversized envelope from Susan Brower. It must be my contract! I open the envelope and find a letter from Susan along with a document of several pages—the contract.

She assures me that she has already contacted several publishers even ahead of receiving the signed contract, all of whom have expressed interest. She believes the process will be on the fast track, as she's trusted by editors at the Big Five publishing houses.

I read through the multi-page document. If I sign it and send it back, I take the first step toward realizing my dream. Will it become a bestseller? That would be nice, but I would be happy if it would simply be read and enjoyed. Money from sales would be nice, too. 'Wow, this is really going to happen!'

I look forward to waving this contract in Wendy's face later to prove her wrong. But wait, why should I? She's doubted my ability all along. She thought it was a waste of my time, a pipe dream. Maybe she wouldn't believe it's a legitimate document. Maybe I should sign it and mail it back today, and when the checks start arriving, when the book appears at the top of the best-seller lists, then I would inform her.

Yes, that's what I'll do.

I use my scanner to copy the contract and save the file on the laptop. Grabbing Kat, I sign the contract—appropriate to use her for this, right?—then head to the Post Office to send it back to Susan by certified mail.

It feels so good to be out and about. While out I might as well stop off at other places, too, since I've not been out on shopping trips myself in a long time. There are a few places I want to go to while I'm out, one in particular.

Arriving back home by mid-afternoon, I compose a short email to Susan and lie down for a nap, relieved and pleased.

This day has gone well so far.

Chapter 31
Wendy

On the drive home from campus, Mark passes my street going west. Is he headed for his house? What does he have in mind? But I don't protest. I was going to raise the issue of my visit with Dr. Schute on the way home, but I will choose another time, because I can guess why he bypassed my house. From this point on we should care nothing about campus rumors. That the rumors are true doesn't matter anymore.

My problem at this point will be coming up with a good excuse for arriving home late again.

'That was nice, really nice,' I coo to Mark. We have been all over each other and all over his king size bed.

He kisses me and coos in my ear, 'What a nice way to end the workday. We should do this all the time.'

We break away from each other. I roll over to see the bedside clock showing 5:00, then hurriedly pop out of bed and start to put on my clothes. Mark whines, 'Do you have to go? Don't go!'

He knows I have to go, but he wants me to jump back in bed for another go-round. I wish, I really do. 'Sorry, but I'm late. I'd better come up with a good reason for this.'

I lean over to kiss Mark goodbye, but he grabs me and pulls me on top of him. 'One more time!' he says, holding me tight.

Does he have more in him?

'No! Gotta go!' I urge, struggling against Mark's strong grip. Finally, he loosens his hold, and I pull myself free. Hastily dressing myself, I beg him to get dressed and drive me home. 'Please, Mark, take me home now!'

'All right, all right!' he responds. Reluctantly he agrees, and a few minutes later his car pulls in front of my house. I can't help myself, damn the neighbors and anyone else: I lean over and kiss Mark deeply. 'You're right; we'll have to do this again,' I purr in his ear, and get out of the car.

This encounter has put a second nail into the coffin of my marriage. I hope to find more nails.

I walk in the front door, drop my stuff, and call out, 'I'm home. Is anybody here?' If asked, my excuse for being late will be working overtime to help a faculty member.

That's sort of true.

Emma comes downstairs to greet me. 'Hi sweetie,' I say to Emma. 'Where's Daddy?'

'He's upstairs taking a nap.'

'Oh, that's good. He needs to do that from time to time.'

'Mommy?' she asks.

'Yes, dear?'

'Who's that man who drives the car you were in?'

My stomach flops. What has she seen?

Trying to sound matter-of-fact, I answer. 'He's just a teacher at the college. You know, Dr. Torres. He lives close by, and we trade off giving rides to campus. It saves us both some money.'

'I saw you lean over to him before you got out. Why?'

Uh oh, what does she think she saw?

'The engine was so loud, he couldn't hear me, so I had to repeat what I said closer to him.'

'Really?' Emma processes this lie and apparently decides it must be the truth. 'Uh, OK. What's his name?'

'He's Doctor Mark Torres, and he teaches Anthropology. Not that you'll ever meet him, unless you take one of his classes if you go to college here.'

'OK, I just wanted to know. He's got a nice car!'

'Yes, yes, he does.' Changing the subject, I ask, 'Where's your sister?'

'She's been at Amber's house after school, I think. She should be home soon.'

'Thank you. I guess I should make dinner since your Daddy's asleep.'

I hope I've dodged a bullet by downplaying my relationship with Mark. I won't do that again in front of the house. Who else might see it?

Later we all sit at the table for dinner. Emma chatters away, describing in detail all the interesting things that happened at school. Sophie rolls her eyes at these tales of elementary school. Miles sits in silence, and I catch him occasionally looking askance at me with hateful eyes.

What's up with him? I'm thinking.

'. . . and then Mommy gets a ride home in this fancy red car with her friend from campus. What's his name, Mommy? I forgot.'

'Uh, Dr. Torres....'

'Oh yeah, Dr. *Mark* Torres. Right?'

Miles looks first at Emma, then at me, surprise, then anger, spreading on his face. Without a word he rises from his chair, plops his napkin down, and heads for the stairs.

We all watch him leave the room. 'Did I say something wrong?' Emma asks, tears watering her eyes.

I try to comfort her. 'I've told you that Daddy's not been himself lately, Emma. This book he's been writing has made him grumpy. He doesn't mean anything by it. It's not you. It's probably me.'

Sophie blurts out, 'He's acting like he's not part of the family anymore. It's not Emma, it's not me, it's not you, Mom. It's all Dad. It's like he's living somewhere else in his mind.'

Sophie leaves the table and climbs the stairs to her room. Emma leaves also and runs up the stairs. I am left sitting at the table, wondering what to do, what I *should* do. Whatever I say to Miles, I can't be self-righteous.

I leave the table, climb the stairs, and go straight to the office, where I find Miles at his desk, filling his ink pen.

OK, here goes.

'You can be mad at me all you want, Miles, but don't take it out on your daughters.'

'I wasn't taking anything out on Emma; I was wanting to get as far away from *you* as I could. Tell me about this Dr. *Mark* Torres whom you've been getting rides with.'

'There's nothing to tell,' I say. 'We're just friends who live close enough to each other that we share rides to school to save on gas money.'

'Really? How responsible! Saving us money and helping the ozone layer. What else are you sharing?' Miles smirks.

What does he suspect? I would like to swat that smirk off his face. But no, the best defense is a good offense, they say. 'I don't have to stand here and take this! I'll leave you to your writing, which you love more than your own family!'

'Fine. Sounds good. Bye! Don't let the door hit you where the good Lord split you!'

Leaving, I slam the door behind me for good measure.

Chapter 32

Mark drives Wendy across town toward his house, unaware that a car is following them at a safe distance, occupied by two male English Department faculty. He swings into the driveway off the street and pulls up to the garage door. The door rises to admit the car and lowers after the car has pulled in. As the garage door lowers and stops, the trailing car glides to the curb just past the driveway.

The two occupants saw Mark and Wendy enter the car on campus, and now they know that both have entered Mark's house. Tempted to snoop further, they turn at the end of the block where they hope to find an alley.

Sure enough, there is an alley. Driving up the alley, they stop at a spot even with the back of Mark's house, the motor running. There are two windows at the back of the house, one on either side of the back door.

Those must be bedroom windows. All the window blinds are open.

Although the back of the house is perhaps a hundred feet from the alley, they can see movement in one of the windows, the shapes indistinct, standing back from the window. They are certain that two people are in the room, close together.

'Bingo!' says the occupant in the passenger seat. 'Too bad we can't see any better. That's got to be them.'

'I think you're right!' the driver replies, then looks around the alley. 'But we can't stay here too long. The neighbors might become suspicious.'

'I wish we had binoculars,' says the passenger. 'We could park on the street next time and then walk up the alley and watch from a protected spot.'

'Next time? Haven't we seen what we need to see? We've got to tell Miles that his wife is cheating on him.'

These two, Hank Bailey and Bud Carpenter, were the colleagues closest to Miles when he was a full-time professor. They weren't exactly close friends with him, but they did sympathize with him when he was fired.

As time passed by, they gradually forgot about Miles, but they found all sorts of reasons to go to the library to see Wendy, even asking for her help on bogus information searches. They aren't as much concerned for Miles as jealous of Mark for getting in Wendy's pants. They might be cultivated literary scholars, but they possess baser instincts.

Chapter 33
Wendy

I have had enough of Miles' snarky behavior. I know just what to do. I'm going to leave the house, go on a run west, where I hope to get enough of Mark's behavior. I text him to say I'm on the way.

His response comes immediately: *I'll be waiting. Twice in one day! I hope to be **up** for it.*

I redden after reading this. I'll need to delete these texts after my run, as my phone is too heavy for me to lug along. After putting on my running clothes, I hide my phone deep in my sweater drawer.

I call out to anyone in the house who will listen 'I'm going on a run!' then head downstairs and out the front door. Ten minutes later I arrive at Mark's house, glistening with sweat. He's sitting on his porch, drinking a beer. As I trot up the steps to the porch, he gets up and greets me as discretely as possible in public, with a handshake. He notices my glistening skin. 'You're all sweaty, as I hoped!' When his comment doesn't seem to register, he adds, 'You know, as I texted.'

'Oh? When did you text that? What did you say?'

'You didn't get it? I said you'd need to throw off those sweaty clothes when you get here. And a couple of other dirty comments.'

'Oh? Sorry I missed them. They must have come in after I left.'

'Don't you have your phone with you?'

'No, it's too heavy to run with. I left it at home.'

'Uh oh, I hope you didn't leave it out on a tabletop.'

'I didn't. I hid it in my sweater drawer.'

'I hope your phone requires a passcode or thumb print to open. But what am I thinking? You must come on in and get out of those sweaty running clothes.'

Inside the entry we embrace and kiss passionately. Mark reaches behind me and grips the bottom of my sleeveless top, pulling it up and over my head, exposing my slick wet skin. Passing his fingers

142

over the small of my back, he purrs into my ear, 'You really are drenched. I think you need to take a shower. Don't you?'

'Oh yes,' I whisper, 'I think you're right, good sir.'

He pushes down my running shorts, and I step out of them. He leads me to the bathroom, where he turns on the water. We throw off the rest of our clothes and step into the shower together.

Oh my, what a shower!

So, how long should an evening run last?

Chapter 34
Miles

Not long after Wendy left the house, a muffled notification sound, like from a cell phone, issues from the bedroom. Two more notifications disturb my concentration while I'm writing. Before I've had a chance to discover where the noise is coming from, the landline phone in the office rings.

Answering it, I say, 'Hello?'

'Hello, is this Miles Campbell?' says the caller on the other end of the line. The voice sounds vaguely familiar.

'Yes. Who's calling?'

'Hi, Miles. This is your former colleague, Bud Carpenter, from the English Department at Western Indiana. Remember me? So, um, how are you doing?'

I run through my memory searching for that long-lost name. 'Bud Carpenter? Oh yeah, I remember you. I'm fine. It's been a few years. What's up? Something going on in the department? Fundraising drive?'

'Um, not exactly,' Bud stammers. 'But, um, something *may* be going on in the library.'

'Hmm? I don't follow you.' I remember Bud as a no-nonsense kind of guy, but he's playing word games with me now.

'I don't know how to say this, man, so I'll just go ahead and say it. I'm calling to tell you that rumors are going around campus about your wife and someone else on campus. Someone you don't know.'

Long pause while I process this information.

'Miles? Are you still there?'

'Yeah, I'm still here. How do you know this?'

'Well, they've been seen several times eating lunch together on campus, and then off campus at Freddie's.'

I process this information, which pisses me off, not at the information but at the informer. 'And that's how rumors start, isn't it? Wendy and I have talked about this. She says they're just friends.'

'More than friends, perhaps. Listen, Hank Bailey and I—remember him? —followed this guy's car to his house, and, um, Wendy was there with him.'

'Really? You followed them? What, playing private detective, are we?'

'Um, no—but I thought you'd want to know.'

'Ha! What do you want me to do with this information, Bud?'

He sighs, letting out a deep breath that sounds like a blast of wind in my phone. 'Man, I'm sorry if I offended you. I—we—just thought you should know, so you wouldn't be blindsided later.'

This phone call is about to be over. 'Well, how considerate of you, Bud! I guess I should thank you and Hank. But I think you both ought to mind your own business.'

'OK, point taken…. So, how are you—'

I slam the phone down. I was already steamed while writing the current scene, but now I'm furious. 'Thanks, Bud,' I seethe, 'for *warning* me about Wendy!' It sure didn't feel like concern, though; it felt like he was exulting as the bearer of bad news.

But then again, maybe he's right; maybe she *is* having an affair. I'll definitely discuss this with her later.

I'm disturbed and furious at what I have just written about my fictional wife having an affair and rubbing it in her fictional husband's face. I didn't want to write this. By this point I believe more and more that I've become simply a recorder for some dark voice beyond me, or within me, perhaps.

What do they call that? An *amanuensis*? Or something or other?

Returning to the notebook, I pick up where I left off. While I'm writing, in the center of my field of vision appears a small oblong object bordered by brilliant cilia-like appendages alive with motion. It's like an ocular migraine starting. I've experienced these events off and on for years. It will take twenty to thirty minutes for this episode to run its course, as the image will grow larger

145

until it fills my field of vision and passes through and behind. I expect to see vivid reds, blues, and yellows in geometric patterns, all in motion, a psychedelic light show.

However, this image is not a circle or semi-circle like usual; it's oblong and stretching longer in shape as it enlarges in my field of vision. I close my eyes to see it better, shocked to see now that the image is a psychedelic representation of my Kat fountain pen. Mesmerizing, it grows larger and moves toward me in the black landscape of my closed eyes.

Glowing, pulsating, the image eventually spans my field of vision from the left to the right. As it passes through and behind the blackness of inner space, a flash like an explosion fills my field of vision. I scream and fall out of my chair to the floor with a loud thud.

Next thing I know, Emma and Sophie are beside me. 'Daddy? Daddy?!' Emma cries. 'Is he dead?' She sounds far above me, as if I'm at the bottom of a well.

Someone, probably Sophie, cradles my head and starts rocking me back and forth. She calls, 'Dad? Dad? Wake up! Wake up, please!' Again, her words are faint and far away.

Next thing I know, I feel a couple of smart slaps across my face. I slowly open my eyes and blankly look at both of my daughters, because I don't recognize them at first.

'Dad? Dad, are you all right?' Sophie asks.

'I-I-I fainted.' I moan, aware now of a splitting headache. 'I'm all right. I just need to get back up and write.'

'No, Dad,' Sophie says, 'you need to rest. You need to go to bed for a while to get over this.'

'No, I'll be OK, really,' I protest. My head pounds with every heartbeat.

Sophie and Emma help me to my feet, whereupon the headache worsens. 'Oh yeah, you're right, Sophie.' I mumble. 'Would you girls help me to the bedroom and get me a couple of pain pills and a glass of water?'

'Sure, Daddy,' Emma responds, tears filling her eyes.

They both guide me to the bedroom, where they lay me back on the bed and fetch a couple of pills and a glass of water. I thank them and apologize for being such a burden.

'No need to, Dad,' Sophie replies. 'We just want you to recover. You rest now.'

They leave me to rest and recover. They have been so kind and caring. I wish I had been nicer to them, paid more attention to them recently. I really don't know what's gotten into me the past couple of weeks.

I close my eyes, praying that this headache goes away.

While I lie there descending into unconsciousness, a muffled repetitive droning sound disturbs me from somewhere in the room, and a few seconds later Sophie's voice outside the bedroom cries, 'Mom? Please come home soon. Dad's had a stroke or something. Please come home now!'

What a night it was last night, one that I hope never repeats itself. I remember Wendy coming into the room to comfort me. I remember her opening a dresser drawer and closing it. After she came to bed later, my rest was troubled by dark voices in my head speaking scandalous words about Wendy, telling of adultery and lying. I don't know if I rolled over and kicked or hit her, but in the dream I felt like killing her.

I slept until noon, worn out by the ocular migraine episode the afternoon before. Rolling carefully out of bed, feeling hung over, I shuffle to the bathroom to perk up before heading downstairs for lunch. It was nice of Wendy and the girls to let me sleep in.

After lunch I trundle upstairs to the office and power up the laptop. An email message from Susan Brower is waiting for me. She wants to call me at my convenience to discuss my novel.

Yes, I reply, she can call me ASAP.

Within five minutes the phone rings. After opening niceties she gets to the nitty gritty.

'So, Miles, I have good news for you. I'll spare you the details, but I have sent **Killing Time** to the five biggest publishers and have received positive responses already from three of them. I have a fast track with them; normally this process might take weeks. I plan to set up an auction when I hear back from them. I am hoping to secure a six-figure advance for you. It could be more if you weren't a debut author. For your next book it might even be twice that amount!'

Processing this news, I say nothing for a few seconds.

'Are you still there?' she asks. 'Did you understand what I've just said? I know it may be a lot to take in.'

'No, no, no, I'm just blown away! I can't believe this!'

'Well, believe it, but there's more. I think there's a possibility of a movie tie-in with a major studio. I think it's the kind of story that would lend itself to the big screen.'

'Whoa! Really? So, what do I do now?'

Susan describes the process to me. It's too much to take in right now, headache and all. She adds, 'Sorry. I'll send a detailed explanation. It may require several days to weeks for the auction to take place, depending on how long it takes for each publisher's top editorial boards to decide. I'll keep you posted.' She pauses for a few seconds, then adds, 'OK, then, ... oh, how's the new book coming?'

A dark cloud descends upon me, as I remember the developing plot. 'I'm pretty deep into it, maybe a third of the way through, and—'

'Wait a minute! Did you say a third of the way through? It's only been a few days since you sent **Killing Time** to me. How many words? How many pages?'

'Over 20,000 words and 85 double-spaced pages so far.... I work fast.'

'Ha! I should say so. That's unbelievable. What does your family think of all the time you spend writing?'

'The girls are OK with it, I think. Wendy's not too pleased, though.'

'Perhaps you should take a break, back off some, for the sake of your family. There's no rush to get the second book done.'

'Maybe I will, once I finish the current scene. But that may not be possible. It's like my pen is in control now.'

'So, what's it about? In a nutshell.'

'It's about a writer who is addicted to writing, who can't stop, who drives his wife and kids away from him.' I don't want to give away too much at this point, so I stop here.

'Hmm, sounds autobiographical.'

'Really? I don't think so. It's fiction, Susan!'

'If you say so, Miles.' She pauses. 'Anyway, I wanted to talk to you directly to give you the good news. I'm hoping you'll be getting a contract from one of the publishers in the mail in a few weeks. Once you've signed it, you'll soon get a big check! And more to come.'

'And so will you, Susan.'

'Yep, you're right. We'll both profit. Get back to your second book now, but don't forget your family!'

'All right. Thanks for the good news.'

'My pleasure. We'll be in contact again soon.'

After disconnecting the call, I take a deep breath and let it out slowly.

Is this real?

Just a few weeks ago I would never have imagined this. I could be teaching six sections of first-year composition for minimum wage, if I hadn't discovered those old incomplete stories… and found Dad's old fountain pen . . . Kat, which (or *who*?) now seems to be my master. Or maybe mistress.

Which (or *who*?) seems to have a mind of its—her?—own.

Whom—not *which*—I now sense to be female, the way she seduces me into writing what she wants.

Can that be true? Or is it an illusion?

149

At that thought, a twinge of pain pulses in my head, ramping up the headache and causing me to retreat to the bathroom to take more pain pills. Then I lie down on the bed to wait for the headache to subside.

Chapter 35
Wendy

Friday at last, the end of the work week. Here I sit struggling with my guilty conscience about my whirlwind—hopefully still secret—dalliance with Mark, and Miles' apparent seizure.

In sickness and in health…till death do us part. That's what we said during our vows, which I have broken.

Yesterday afternoon, when I arrived home from my run and dalliance with Mark, I found Miles in bed and the girls all upset over his collapse. I wasn't there for him, for my husband!

Should I have jumped in so quickly with both feet? Am I mired now in a quicksand that I can't escape and will only drag me down?

There's still a spark of love and concern for Miles, but what is it that I feel for Mark? Raw animal sex? Do I love him, or do I love the *feeling* of making love with him? Is it the excitement of a dangerous liaison?

What if I'm caught? What would Sophie and Emma think of me?

My name on campus is becoming sullied, if what Carolyn and Dr. Schute told me is true. I couldn't respond to Dr. Schute, but I snapped at Carolyn, who along with Linda is now avoiding me. Apparently even some students have heard the rumors.

All morning long these thoughts run through my head as I go about my business, distracted. When Mark arrives for lunch, I'll need to lay this before him. Surely he knows some of this directly, from his end of campus.

Mark appears at the usual time. When he stops at my desk, Carolyn and Linda glare at him from the work room behind the desk. On our way to my car, he mentions their scornful looks. 'What's with those two women in the back room behind your desk? If looks could kill….'

I wince. 'I guess they don't like you, but it's probably from the way I spoke to Carolyn the other day. Still, I want to talk to you at lunch about this situation.'

'What situation?'

'You know, us....'

'Uh, OK.'

We walk on silently to my vehicle.

At Freddie's Mark suggests that maybe we should find another restaurant for lunches. *Not really the solution*, I think. 'It's not the place, Mark. It's us together on campus, and maybe here, too. The talk must be wider spread than we thought it—'

He interrupts, 'I doubt it, but I can see it's bothering you. What do you suggest we do?'

'I think we need to play it cool on campus. And I think we should cut back on our "recreational time." To tell you the truth, as much as I enjoy our times together, my husband is sick. Sick physically, mentally, and emotionally. I can't ignore his needs while we play around.' I sigh, eyes focused on my hands.

Mark mulls this over and speaks. 'I understand, Wendy. I do. I thought your marriage was nearly over. That's why I felt free to pursue you—'

'You didn't know that when you first met me. It sure looked like you were flirting then!'

Mark hunches his shoulders. 'What can I say? I'm a flirt!'

'Yes,' I say, 'but are you also a womanizer?'

Oh boy, I can tell that struck a nerve. I was sorry I said that as soon as the words left my lips.

His face flushes. Speaking in a hushed, clipped tone, he fumes, 'Is that what you think of me? Did I *force* you to have sex? You could have left any time you wanted to!'

'I know, I know. I'm sorry I said that.'

Some of the diners at other tables have turned their heads toward this tense conversation. I need to

152

bring this down. 'Let's just eat now. We can talk later, on the way back.'

'Fine,' says Mark, clearly upset.

Neither one of us finishes our sandwich and drink. We leave Freddie's much earlier than usual. On the way back to campus, I consider my unfortunate choice of words. 'Look, Mark, I'm sorry for what I said. It's just the direction that the conversation was going that led me there. I didn't mean it. But to be sure, I *am* your only relationship? I don't want to share you with any other woman.'

I can tell he's surprised by my comment. 'So, what does this mean? You plan to continue with me, despite staying committed to your husband? That's not fair to him or me, unless we're talking about a different kind of morality.'

That stings. 'I don't know. I don't know. When I'm in your arms everything is good; it's great. But when I'm away from you, I feel like a traitor. How can I go on like this?'

Scrunching his eyebrows together, he sighs. 'It sounds like we should take a break while you sort things out with your husband. I don't want to let go of you, either, but I can see that you're torn. If it works out with him, so be it. I guess we can say that we had a fling for a while. If it doesn't work out, you know where to find me.'

Although I cringe at the word *fling*, I'm relieved that Mark has given me a way out. When we arrive back at campus, I squeeze his hand and say, 'Thank you.'

Later that day, I drive Mark home and bid him goodbye as he leaves the car. In the back of my mind I ponder an after-dinner run westward … but dismiss the thought.

'Not a good idea, Wendy,' I tell myself.

I get home before the girls, and I find Miles still in bed, the way I left him in the morning. 'Miles, are you all right?' I ask. 'This isn't like you. Do you still have a headache?'

Miles mumbles, 'Yes, a little. I'm just so tired and weak.' He rolls over to face me.

'Have you written any today? If you did, that would probably prolong your headache.'

'No, not at all. I just couldn't do anything.'

'Poor baby. Well, I'll let you rest while I start dinner.' I turn to leave.

'Wendy?'

'Yes?'

'I really am sorry about the way I've treated you lately. I don't remember what I did because I was in sort of a fog. But I think I must have said and done some things I shouldn't have.'

I like this change in his thinking. There may be hope yet. 'You did, but that's in the past now. I forgive you.' I want to go back to the bed and comfort him, but I haven't *fully* forgiven him.

'Thanks. I think I'll take the rest of the day off from writing. I'll get back to it tomorrow.'

Oh God, I didn't need to hear that. Then we'll start back up again where we left off. But I have to sound reassuring. 'Sure, honey, you just rest now. I'll call you for dinner.'

Seeing Miles helpless and exhausted, I feel an emotional pull back toward him. However, if he still plans to keep writing, I worry about the future.

Just after I leave the bedroom, Miles calls out to me, 'Wendy? Just so you know, I sent **Killing Time** off to a book agent. I'll let you know if anything comes of it.'

Confused, I turn and reply, 'You did? I thought you were still writing it. What have you been writing the past several days, then?'

'I've started my second book.'

'Oh.'

Then it hits me.

What did I just hear? Second book? I thought he'd get it out of his system!

At dinner that night Miles appears to be his old self, although he's still a little weak. He interacts with the girls and even behaves pleasantly with me. All three of us are relieved to see this apparent return to normal, but I'm bothered about Miles' intent to return to writing tomorrow.

Obviously still exhausted, Miles excuses himself and goes upstairs to bed early, before ten o'clock. He hasn't gone into the office all evening. This is a good sign, a very good sign.

I need to figure out a way to make it permanent, stop his writing, restore his sanity.

Restore our marriage.

Chapter 36
Miles

My sleep was disturbed last night with dreams in which I was searching for something in a forest but was unable to find it. At the same time, I was being tracked by a shadowy evil force, always just behind, always closing in. I didn't tell Wendy about the disturbing nightmares, though.

I pass through the weekend without writing, so slow has been my recovery. I take naps in the afternoon both Saturday and Sunday. Unusual for me. I don't understand why I am not being summoned to write. The dreams recur every night, the nameless thing following me getting closer in each successive dream.

Throughout the weekend, the urge grows to grab Kat and go on a writing binge. However, I hold off, surprised at my discipline.

Early Monday morning before the girls get up, Wendy wakes me, whispering in my ear, 'Hey, wanna quickie?' while reaching inside my sleep shorts. With adolescent children in the house, morning quickies have become the rule in recent years.

I'm surprised by this unexpected initiation, but I can't, and I won't. The nerve of her! How could she even think of this, considering what she's been doing in my story? 'No, I don't think so,' I say, and roll away. I've never refused her before, and she's never refused me, but things have changed. To me, she's spoiled goods.

'Well, OK, then,' she blusters, 'see if I ever do this again!'

We roll away from each other and get out of bed. There is a chilly silence in the air as we dress to go down for breakfast.

I'm thinking *Should I have? I just couldn't. What is she thinking now?*

Another voice—one that I have become familiar with, that no longer surprises me—rises from the depths somewhere in my mind: *No, serves her right!*

As we exit the bedroom, Emma comes out of her room scratching her head and yawning. Had we done it, we would have made it in time.

Chapter 37
Wendy

The morning light coming through the bedroom window begins to filter its way through the shades and drapes. I open first one eye, then the other, even the faint light assaulting my eyeballs.

I'm waking up with questions. A few days ago Miles had such a rough day with that migraine that he was knocked out for the whole weekend. I have never seen him that wasted before. He slept fitfully last night, kicking me several times in the wee hours of the morning. He must have been having nightmares. I wonder if it has anything to do with what he's been writing.

I also wonder about his book's prospects with the agent that he mentioned. Won't she reject it out of hand? Won't it wind up in a slush pile?

I thought he was finished with that book delusion, and now he tells me he's writing a *second* book? Where did all this writing energy come from? Shouldn't he be channeling that energy toward getting a job?

A memory flashes before my inner eyes: me at Mark's house wallowing in his king-size bed, him all over me and me all over him. That shower we took together. Oh my, what a charge! I would like more of that.

But then my conscience wags its finger at me: *you have forgotten your vows, Wendy. You have turned your back on your husband when he needs you most.*

Have I really been supportive of him? No. And now he's pulled away from me, from the girls, for this fantasy of his. I've never seen such an obsession, such an addiction to anything outside of what drug addiction must be like. I ought to try to pull him back toward me.

I know what I'll do.

I waken Miles, reach into his sleep shorts and fondle him. I whisper in his ear, 'Hey, wanna quickie?' With curious children in the house, morning sex is quick, *wham, bam, thank you, ma'am.* We have only so much time until Emma comes into our bedroom to snuggle with us before we get up.

It's been a month since we last were intimate. He should be ready, despite his changed behavior. He's never turned down an invitation like this. In a way, this is a test.

But how does he respond?

'No, I don't think so.' Then he adds insult to injury by rolling away from me.

Oh, man, what a surprise! 'Well, OK, then,' I seethe, 'see if I ever do this again!'

We roll away from each other and get out of bed. The silence is deafening as we dress to go down for breakfast. What's he thinking? Is he proud of what he just did, turning me down cold?

Conflicting thoughts rage through my head. *Now why did I do that? Was it too soon to try? No, he's never turned me down before. Never! If that's the way he wants it, he can sleep celibate from now on!* I'm working myself up to an eruption if I'm not careful.

As we exit the bedroom lost in our thoughts, Emma comes out of her room scratching her head and yawning. Too bad; had we done it, we would have finished in time.

It's Mark's turn today to drive me to campus. I hope to see him in a different light…as just a friend.

He picks me up and drives to campus with me sitting lost in thought, almost unaware that my lover is just a couple of feet away. Mark says nothing, waiting for me to speak.

At last, I do. 'If you want to know how things have been going at home, they haven't improved at all.' Then I tell him about my aborted effort to seduce Miles. I don't know why I am confessing this. 'Yes,' I add, 'I thought that being away from writing would be good for him. In some ways it has been, but not with me. Now he's going to resume writing. I wish he would drop this project. He told me that he sent off his first book to an agent a few days ago. I hope and pray that they reject it and tell him that he will never be more than a middling writer.'

'First book?'

'Yeah, you know what? He's started another book. He's sat there pretty much all day, every day, working on it. He shouldn't return to it because I know what will happen.'

'Do you really think that a poor response from an agent would stop him? I've read that best-selling authors have had several dozen or more rejections before being published the first time.'

'And you think he's in the same company? I doubt it. Because he's lost all of his writing classes this semester, he's not bringing in any money. Our income is cut by about a third because of that. Every day that goes by is a day that he hasn't earned any pay. He needs to find a job, and soon.'

'Hmm, what can you do about it? How can you stop him from writing?'

'I don't know. I'll think about it and hope to come up with a plan today.'

'I guess you could keep him in the bedroom!' Mark winks.

'Yeah, right. As if that's ever going to happen again.'

We soon reach campus and depart to our respective buildings. Mark says he will call my desk phone around lunchtime. Using the phone will keep him from appearing in the library and leaving with me, in full view of staff and other interested people on campus.

When I come through the front door after a mostly boring ride home, Miles is at work in the office, typing. Grunts, growls, and sighs punctuate the clicking of the keys. I call out, 'Miles, I'm home. Are you all right?'

Unanswered, I go upstairs and pop my head inside the office door frame. The air is heavy with the stench of urine. Appalled and disgusted, I back away, unnoticed, tears filling my eyes.

I will *not* clean up his mess this time! Bastard!

160

I go back downstairs to the living room. I hope he will discover his soaked pants and clean himself up before the girls get home from school.

A few minutes later the office noise stops. Miles utters a sharp curse word and then heads out of the office to the upstairs bathroom. A faucet is turned on and off. Then footsteps again. The process repeats. He has obviously discovered his accident and is cleaning up.

I pray he won't start writing again after the cleanup. However, my hopes vanish when the wheels of the office chair protest as Miles falls into it.

Then silence, except for an occasional grunt or sigh.

I have to do something about this, and tonight, or Miles' recovery will fade and he will become an exile in his own home again.

Miles works through dinner again. I clean up the dinner dishes and put Miles' servings in the refrigerator. I had made one of his favorite meals, but that didn't draw him downstairs. Like Emma and Sophie, I'm bitterly disappointed at Miles' absence from tonight's meal.

Miles finally comes down to eat about an hour later. While he eats his dinner alone, I sneak up to the office. Suspecting that the pen is at least partially responsible for the change in Miles' personality, I'm going to do something about it.

Bingo! There it is, lying on the desk.

I grab it and look around upstairs to find a temporary hiding place for it while I wait for Miles to finish his dinner and leave the kitchen, when I'm going to throw it in the kitchen trash can. I hide it under a sock stuffed in one of my sneakers for the time being.

Miles finishes his solitary dinner and climbs the stairs to the bathroom to brush his teeth. Hearing him start to ascend the stairs, I fish the pen out of my shoe and head downstairs, passing Miles on the way. His crazed look alarms me.

Oh my, he's already gone too far.

I race to the kitchen to bury the pen far down in the trash can under the sink. But with each step that I take, the pen warms up in my hand until it is almost too hot to hold. It also vibrates.

Is it trying to force me to drop it?

The pen almost burning my palm, I open the trash can and reach deep down to drop it at the bottom. 'There,' I say, 'maybe in a few days Miles will be over this mania!' I cool off my hand under the cold water in the sink. The state of Miles' mind this evening bodes evil, judging by that look on his face. I must be very, very careful.

Soon Miles' footsteps upstairs move from the bedroom to the office. Then the sounds of papers and books being pushed around, drawers opening and slamming shut, emanating from the office. Miles is searching for something; it can only be his cherished pen.

Obscene mumbles spread out from the office: 'What the fuck?' and 'Goddammit!' And 'Shit, where are you?' Miles has rarely used obscene language in the past. This is another sign of the change in his personality. He howls, 'Wendy, have you seen my pen?'

At once I run up the stairs, passing Emma's partially open door, her anxious eyes peering out. I reach the office and speak softly, 'Please lower your voice. You're frightening the girls!'

Miles stops what he's doing. Wild-eyed, he turns toward me and says, 'The girls! Yes, of course! One of them's got it!' He moves toward the door, where I'm standing firm.

Trying to soothe him, I say, 'Calm down, Miles. Neither of them has it.'

'How do you know? I'll bet Emma has it. Yes, yes, she probably does. I'll get it back from her if I have to beat her!'

Oh my God, Miles is clearly out of his mind. He's never laid a hand on his daughters. Frightened but

162

steely, I block the doorway. 'Stop!' I command. 'Emma doesn't have it. Sophie doesn't have it. I took it!'

Miles' red-rimmed eyes narrow as he stares at me. 'You took it? You? Why? Why?'

'Because it's turned you into a madman! Because you are addicted to it like a junkie! You don't even know when you've pissed your pants! It's taken over your life! It's stolen your soul. You're not yourself anymore. I think—'

'I don't give a shit what you think! Give me my pen back! Give it to me!'

Backing away, I respond, 'No! No! You've got to stop—'

Without warning, Miles throws a punch at me, smashing my left cheek. I tumble down in the doorway. He's on me, slapping me, shouting, 'Give it to me!' over and over.

I scream, then Miles' hands close on my throat. 'Where is it?' he shouts.

He's a madman. I think he's going to kill me!

I feel my eyes bug out, my face flushing with blood. I choke, 'I can't breathe,' gagging, gurgling.

'Where is it?' Miles screams one more time, joined by a scream from Emma, who's now at the doorway.

'Daddy, stop! Stop! You're hurting Mommy! Please, please stop!'

Sophie appears in the doorway next to Emma, and seeing her dad kneeling on me, choking the life out of me, she plows into him like a linebacker, knocking him off me. As he falls, Miles swings an elbow at Sophie's face. She rolls in the opposite direction, holding her injured cheek. She crawls over to me. 'Mom? Mom? Are you all right?' she sobs. Emma cries, kneeling next to me.

Miles rolls over, pushes the girls out of the way, and attempts to climb back on top of me, fist cocked, when I croak, 'All right! Don't hurt me anymore! I'll tell you; I'll tell you!'

'Where, you whore?' Miles screams.

163

'It's in the kitchen trash can. Please, please, don't hit me anymore!'

Miles rolls off, stands up, and heads through the doorway, pushing Emma aside. He races down to the kitchen, overturns the trash can, and roots through the mess. The sounds stop.

He must have found the pen. He comes up the stairs to the office, and steps over Sophie, Emma, and me. When he gets to the office chair, he turns, and in a cold, cruel voice says, 'Now get out of here. Can't you see I'm working?' When we don't immediately move, he shouts, 'Now! Get the hell out! Leave me alone!'

I struggle to my feet, aided by my daughters. As we leave the room, Emma turns toward Miles and sobs, 'Oh, Daddy—'

'I said get out, and I meant it!' Miles moves toward the door and slams it in Emma's face. He bellows, this time to the closed door, 'Leave me alone!'

I straighten myself up and comfort my distraught daughters, who are both sobbing.

Miles has gone too far now. 'Get your school clothes and pajamas together and put them in your backpacks. I'll get a suitcase. We're leaving.'

We quickly pack.

'Where are we going, Mom?' Sophie asks, as she shoulders her backpack.

'I don't know. To a motel for the night, I guess. I'll figure out something by tomorrow. Hurry up! Let's go!'

We load one suitcase and the girls' backpacks into the car, and I drive off, my cheek still throbbing, my throat sore.

Chapter 38
Miles

After Wendy and the girls leave the house, I go downstairs to have breakfast. I'm itching to get back to writing, so I wolf down a bagel and bring my half-drunk mug of coffee upstairs with me to the office. I fill Kat and set to work.

Two hours and eight pages later, the pen runs dry. I take a break, for the bathroom and a late morning snack. When I get back to work, I'll have to type up what I've written.

The story has taken a darker turn as the character arcs develop. *I* didn't darken the story, though. It seems to have come from outside me. The wife in the story is cheating daily on her loving husband, who has been oblivious to her secret rendezvous. But he will find out soon enough. And all hell will break loose. I feel it, even though I haven't written it yet.

I have been writing and typing for a very long time. The work exhausts me, making me grunt, growl, and sigh almost in time to the clacking of the keys. Reaching the end of my handwritten manuscript, I now smell the odor of urine and feel my soaked crotch and seat.

Goddamn it! I think, *I've done it again!*

My back screaming with pain, I force myself to get up. I clean up and find a change of clothes. Falling back into the chair, I look over my work.

It's time to start writing again.

OK, so I worked through dinner again. So what? What's most important is getting this story down. I'll eat later when I am free of the pen.

Later, Kat is finally empty, so I head downstairs to find something to eat. I make a sandwich and wash it down with a beer.

Wendy's upstairs walking around. Wendy, oh yeah, my wife. The model for my fictional faithless wife. She's faithless too. I know it.

I go back upstairs to the bathroom to brush my teeth. I meet Wendy on her way downstairs, a fearful look on her face. What is she afraid of all of a sudden?

A buzzing like a beehive enters my mind as I walk down the hall to the office.

Where is it coming from?

Back in the office, I intend to write some more before typing it all up.

Now, where's Kat? I laid her next to the notebook when I finished before, but she's not there. At least I think I laid her there. Maybe I put her somewhere else.

I search everywhere, high and low, and can't find my Kat. I turn over papers, push things around on the desk, search the floor below.

No pen, no Kat! I need Kat! Where is she?

'What the fuck? Goddammit, where *are* you?'

Maybe Wendy knows. Sure, she probably knows! 'Wendy, have you seen my pen?'

She rushes upstairs and appears in the doorway. 'Please lower your voice. You're frightening the girls!'

'The girls! Yes, of course! One of them's got it!' I make a move for the door, but Wendy blocks it.

She extends her hands toward me. 'Calm down, Miles. Neither of them has it.'

I can't believe Wendy. She's defending the girls. Emma sometimes finds a pen or pencil in the office to draw with. 'How do you know?' I growl. 'I'll bet Emma has it. Yes, yes, she probably does. I'll get it back from her if I have to beat her!'

Wendy won't move from the doorway. She's blocking me. The nerve of her! 'Stop!' she commands. Actually, commanding me! 'Emma doesn't have it. Sophie doesn't have it,' she says. 'I took it!'

'You took it? You? Why? Why?'

'Because it's turned you into a madman! Because you're addicted to it like a junkie!' *Blah blah blah blah.* She's saying words, but I don't comprehend.

'I don't give a shit what you think! Give me my pen back! Give it to me!' I step toward her.

She backs away. 'No! No! You've got to stop—'

That's all I can take of this crap! I need that pen!

I cock my fist and bop her a good one to her face. She falls down in the doorway. I jump on her, slapping and punching, shouting 'Give it to me!' over and over.

Strangle her, a voice tells me.

OK, I'm going to choke it out of her. My hands close on her throat. 'Where is it?!' My thumbs press on her esophagus.

Her eyes bug out, and her face turns purple. 'I can't breathe,' she croaks, gagging, gurgling.

'I don't care! Where is it?' I scream again.

Next thing I know there's Emma at the doorway, screaming, 'Daddy, stop! Stop! You're hurting Mommy! Please, please stop!' She grabs my arm, trying to pull it away from her mother's neck.

Something plows hard into me, knocking me off Wendy toward the floor. It's Sophie. As I fall, I elbow her in the face. The little twat! How dare she!?

I roll over and climb back on top of Wendy, who is gripping her throat and coughing. I cock my fist, ready to finish her off, when she chokes out, 'All right! Don't hurt me anymore! I'll tell you. I'll tell you!'

'Where, you whore?' I screech through gritted teeth.

'It's in the kitchen trash can. Please, please, don't hit me anymore!' She tries to roll over, but I'm still on top.

Rolling off, I get up and rush through the doorway, pushing Emma aside to the floor. The little twerp, getting in my way.

Double-timing down the stairs to the kitchen, I overturn the trash can and root through the papers, wrappers, and food scraps, until I feel Kat in a mess of bloody meat wrapping.

'Goddamn it, Wendy, you've put her in the garbage!' I yell.

I clean Kat and dry her off. I cradle her in both hands as if she's a precious baby while I ascend the stairs. When I get to the office, they are still there in a pile

167

of humanity: Sophie, Emma, and Wendy. They're sobbing and clinging to each other. I step over them and seat myself at the laptop.

'Now get out of here!' I shout. 'Can't you see I'm working?'

They don't jump up and leave, which really pisses me off, and I shout, 'Now! Get the hell out! Leave me alone!' slamming the door in their faces.

Later, there's a rush of activity in the hallway, and shortly thereafter a door closes downstairs. I can't be bothered. I'm into writing again.

As I write, I grow angrier at what I read on the page. 'You bitch! You whore!' I scream, directing my words at the lying, cheating woman in the story I'm writing.

'You deserve to die!'

Chapter 39
Wendy

Early the next morning I drive up to the house with the girls in the back seat. We had spent the night at Motel 6 and had breakfast at McDonald's. I want things to look normal this morning for any neighbors' peering eyes.

Mark will pick me up, and the girls will leave for their bus stop from here. They are dressed and ready for school, and it's nearly time for them to walk to the bus stop. Both are afraid even to look at the house wherein resides their crazed and cruel father.

I have to go inside to pick up a few of my things. The girls beg me not to go in, fearing for my life. 'Please, Mom, don't go in. He'll hurt you again.' Sophie says. 'Mommy, no, don't go in!' pleads Emma, pulling on my arm.

'I'll be all right, girls,' I assure them. 'If anything happens, I'll call 911. Besides, I bet Daddy is asleep now. Don't worry.' I hug and kiss them both and send them on their way to the bus stop down the street.

I walk up to the door and unlock it. Usually when I enter the house, I call out that I'm home, but not this morning. I'll have to be quiet, not knowing what I might face.

I mount the stairs one silent step at a time to the second floor. When I enter the master bedroom, I find Miles sound asleep. He doesn't stir as I get my change of clothes and head downstairs to put on my makeup.

I try to cover my bruised left cheek but don't know if it will pass muster at work. Or with Mark. I pack all my makeup gear, barely reaching the front door when Mark pulls up to the curb.

Seating myself, I lean over and kiss Mark on his cheek, saying 'Good morning!' a little too cheerfully.

His eyebrows arch in surprise, and he responds, 'Well, good morning to you, too!' Noticing my car parked out front, he asks, 'How come your car is parked on the street?'

Taking a deep breath and exhaling, I tell the tale, trying to stop the tears from filling my eyes.

'Oh my, Wendy, that's horrible!' Mark says. 'What're you going to do?'

Mark has given me the opening I had hoped for.

'I don't know. I can't think. Do you have any suggestions?' I hope he gets the message.

'Well, do you have any relatives in the area you can get help from?'

'No, the closest relatives live in Kansas City. Even if we could, I wouldn't want to uproot the girls, and I would have to look for a job, with no promise of employment wherever I move.'

'No friends in town?'

'Not really. You're my best friend now.'

Does he get the implication?

No. He says, 'I think you should get a lawyer and have Miles kicked out with a restraining order. You and your girls need a stable home.'

'That's a good idea, I guess, but it'll take time to put that all in place.'

Mark puts on his thinking face. 'Is there a women's shelter in town, where you could stay for a few days while you start proceedings?'

'The Women's House? That isn't an option, really. Do you know the kind of women who seek shelter there? And, who they're running from? No, I can't put my girls through that. Could you perhaps put us up for a while, until I can get the house back?'

'Well....' Mark pauses.

It looks like that would be an imposition. 'Don't bother. I'm sorry for asking.'

'No, sorry, I was just thinking. I have only two bedrooms. I guess your girls could share one bedroom, but there's not enough space for an extra bed or air mattress for you. Where would you sleep?' Mark winks. 'I mean, seriously, what would your daughters think if you slept in my room? Although I guess you—or I—could sleep on the couch...for a few days.'

170

I like the prospect of sleeping in Mark's room, in that big king-size bed. 'That's a good question. If you really mean it, let me think about the sleeping arrangements.'

Back on campus, we part company with discrete hand-squeezes. As we head to our respective buildings, I feel emotions rekindling.

I am *so* looking forward to the evening, which will not come fast enough.

Chapter 40
Miles

I roll out of bed late, at nearly 11:00 AM. Although the house is always empty at this time of the day, it feels much quieter today, like a morgue.

Did something happen the night before? Did Wendy and I get in a fight? Did I hurt her? Does it have anything to do with the unnatural emptiness of this house? Maybe I'll remember later.

Overnight I had another vivid dream of being lost in the woods looking for something, not knowing what it was. I was being pursued, as before, by some unseen malevolent force, always close behind me. It seemed to be intent on keeping me from finding what I was looking for. The memory makes me shudder.

It's time to start the day's work. I have a late breakfast—or early lunch, I guess—then head upstairs to the office. After booting up my laptop, I notice that I have an email from Susan:

> Hello, Miles.
>
> Just a short note to keep you aware of my activities. I sent your manuscript via email to each of the Big Five publishers. I might know something in a day or two.
>
> How is the new book?
> How is the family?

I write back:

> The book is coming along well. I am close to halfway through now. It's a thriller, which makes it easy to write. The family's doing fine. Keep me posted on the auction.

After sending my reply I pick up Kat and continue writing where I left off in the wee hours of the morning. Soon I'm writing with a vengeance, describing a violent fight scene between the husband and his cheating wife.

I expect to write for at least a couple of hours.

I am convinced now that I'm no longer creating this story; my hand moves as if directed by an alien force that drives my pen.

Chapter 41
Wendy

All morning at work, I have been shielding the left side of my face from view as much as possible. I have a ready excuse, though it's a lame one: I bumped into a protrusion on a shelf in the basement. An unlikely excuse, but it's better than running into a doorknob.

Although Carolyn is still miffed at me from our altercation last week, Linda seems to have warmed up to me. We chat a bit, Linda notices the bruise, and I offer my excuse. After processing the excuse, Linda accepts it, and the subject is dropped.

I think she's suspicious, though.

Mark doesn't come by at noon, as we agreed during the morning drive. I will have to go over to the Union to eat lunch. I invite Linda, who gladly accepts. Linda isn't the best company, but she's not Mark and is therefore safe to be with.

On the way home to Mark's house after work, we chat warmly with each other, both of us thinking ahead to bedtime later. As usual, Mark uses *double entendres* to stoke a fire. 'So, did you have a tiring day?'

'Yes, I did. A few "customers" were difficult to deal with, and Carolyn is still avoiding me. But I went to lunch with Linda today. Not the same as going to lunch with you.'

'Yeah, no one to play footsies with or rub up your calves.'

'Nope.'

'I bet you can't wait to go to bed tonight, get a little...shut eye.'

'Yep.'

'Deal with your restless leg syndrome...'

'I don't have restless leg syndrome.'

'I bet you will.'

'Oh! I hope you can help with that.'

'Yeah, I know a few yoga positions that should help. Like Forward Fold… Happy Baby… Downward Dog… Cat-Cow. A few others.'

'I'm not sure that I know all those positions.'

'I do. I'll teach them to you. You'll sleep like a happy baby afterwards.'

'Ooh, I can't wait!' I feel a stirring down below.

Mark punctuates the remainder of the drive home with a few more *double entendres.*

He lets me off at my house. 'OK, I'll see you at my house in a little while,' then he takes off.

I won't go into our house, not knowing what I might find. Instead, I putter around the front yard while waiting for the girls to arrive home from the bus stop. When they walk up to the house, I load them into the car, and we drive over to Mark's house.

On the way the girls pelt me with questions. 'How is Dad doing?' *I don't know.*

'Have you heard from Daddy?' *No.*

'How long are we gonna stay at that man's house, Mom?' *For a while, I guess.*

'His name is Mark? How long have you known Mark?' *Long enough.*

'Is Mark a friend? How good a friend?'

A pretty good friend. A really good friend.

'I don't wanna go to his house,' Emma says.

Sophie echoes her sister. 'I wanna go home.' And so on.

By the time we arrive at Mark's house, just a five-minute drive, I'm exhausted by the questions and the mental work it has taken to craft my answers.

After a nice dinner at Mark's house, which I had insisted I fix, the girls settle into doing some homework and reading. Mark refuses to allow them to use his internet, further validation of their not wanting to be there. Bored with little to do, they both go to bed by nine o'clock. I tuck them in bed and read stories to both—even though Sophie is too old for that—and bid them goodnight.

Before I leave the room, Emma asks, 'Mommy, when are we gonna see Daddy again?'

'I don't know, dear. He needs help, and if he gets it, we can go back home.'

'What kind of help?'

'Psychological help, Emma. He's gone a bit crazy with his writing. You saw what he did just because I took his pen away from him. That's not normal.'

'OK, I understand…. And, Mommy?'

'Yes dear?'

'Where are you sleeping tonight?'

'Well, dear, the only place I *can* sleep is in Mark's room. But I promise I will sleep on the floor. Or he will.'

'OK, that sounds good,' Sophie says.

'OK, dear. Good night, girls. Don't let the bed bugs bite!'

I leave and head for Mark's back-porch breakfast nook, where he told me he usually grades and reads. I find him with a glass of port, a second one poured for me on a side table. No papers or textbooks are in sight.

'So, no work tonight?' I say.

'Nope. Today I got it all done before going home. I do that often. Leaves my evenings free. Free to relax. Free to go out if I want to. Free to stay in. Free to go to bed early. How about you?'

'I like the idea of going to bed early.' I clink my glass to Mark's and sip it slowly, feeling the port's warming buzz coursing through my body.

Later, downing the port to the last drop, I place the glass on the table, stretch, and say, 'I think I'm ready for bed now.'

'Sounds good. Let's do it!' he says, winking.

No way I'm going to sleep on the floor, I think. I sleep in Mark's bed, after first doing a variety of yoga exercises with him.

Next morning, I arise early before Mark, who is still asleep in his bed, and hop in the shower. My girls will be getting up in about thirty minutes, so I need to clear out of the bathroom before Mark and the girls use it.

I towel off and put on my clothes for work, and then Mark gets up and greets me, sorry that I have already showered and dressed. He steps into the shower.

I head into the kitchen to make the girls' lunches. While I'm spreading peanut butter on bread, the doorbell rings. Since Mark is in the shower, I figure I can answer the door, especially if it's for a delivery or something.

I open the front door, startled to see a woman dressed in tight faded and ripped jeans topped with a red checkered shirt, bleached blonde hair pulled back in a high ponytail, who is likewise shocked to see me. Her heavily made-up eyes scan me up and down, making me feel naked. A beat-up rat-trap of a car is parked on the street in front of the house. It looks familiar. *Where have I seen that car before?*

Recovering her composure, smacking on chewing gum, this woman says, 'Well, what are *you* doing here, honey? Is Mark home? I left sumpin' here the other night.'

'Uh, who are you?' I ask. We size each other up for a few seconds.

A flurry of activity approaches from behind, and Mark appears next to me at the door, his lower body wrapped in a towel. He's still wet from the shower, beads of water trailing down his bare brown torso, pooling in his toned abs. 'I'll take it from here, Wendy,' he says, his voice shaky.

Ignoring Mark, this woman chuckles. 'Wendy, is it? Hi, my name is Cindy.' She sticks out her hand for a handshake. 'Are you the flavor du jour?'

'What?!' I screech and recoil as if her arm is a poisonous snake.

'Let me handle this,' Mark orders, and pushes me aside. 'Go on back and finish getting your girls ready for school. I'll explain later.'

'So,' Cindy coos, loud enough for me to hear as I leave, 'I like your shower wear. Who's the newbie? She don't look your type.' I glance back to see her blow a bubble and pop it toward Mark.

I head back to the girls' bedroom and rouse them. 'Get up and get dressed,' I order, trying to stay calm. 'Pack your things. We'll be leaving soon.' They try to protest, but I shush them and whisper, 'Do what I say, and now!' while trying to hear the conversation at the doorway.

'What are you doing here, Cindy?' I overhear Mark say.

'I suppose I could ask you the same question about that woman in there. What's her name? Wendy?'

'Never mind about her. What do you want?'

'I left my earrings here the other night. They're diamond earrings, or at least that's what my husband tells me. Ha! I need them! I need to be wearing them when he gets back today.'

'OK. Where did you leave them? I'll get them for you.'

'Where else would they be but in the bedroom, silly boy?'

'OK. Hang on. I'll be right back.'

Mark rushes past the second bedroom, where I'm helping my daughters pack quickly. He locates the earrings and brings them to Cindy, who is still waiting, now inside the door. 'You didn't have to come by so early, Cindy,' he says.

'How was I supposed to know you were keeping another woman in the house, honey? I mighta come in for a morning yoga workout!'

'Maybe another time. You need to go now.'

'Well, that's a fine how-do-you-do! OK, maybe another time. When Tony goes out on the road again.'

'Sure, sure. Just go now.'

'You're lucky this is a no-strings-attached relationship, sugar, or I would be really pissed right now. Well, see ya later. Call me when you're free! Oh, and bye, Wendy,' she shouts. 'Nice to meet ya!'

The front door closes. Cindy is gone.

Mark's got some explaining to do.

He passes the girls' bedroom, where Sophie and Emma are stuffing their bedclothes into their backpacks. When he walks into the main bedroom, he finds me jamming my things into my suitcase.

'What are you doing?' he asks.

I don't face him; he's ugly to me now. I keep on packing. 'What do you think I'm doing? I'm packing. We're getting out of here.'

'Why? Because of that woman? She's just a friend.'

I turn to face him. '*Just a friend*? A friend who leaves her earrings here? Her diamond earrings? Yes, I heard that. The earrings that her *husband* gave her? Why did she take them off?'

Mark's mood darkens. 'OK, OK, yes, she took off more than her earrings! So what? You and I aren't married, so why do *you* care? But you—you're married, yet here you *are,* just like Cindy!' He sweeps both his arms out wide. 'So don't get all high and mighty with me!'

The towel around his waist begins to loosen.

I feel betrayed, lied to…*used.* 'How many Cindys have there been, Mark? Were they all married, like me? How many? *How many*?' I don't care that Sophie and Emma are overhearing this charged conversation.

Mark's face reddens. 'If you really must know, lots! Is that what you want to hear? Lots of them! Lots of Cindys and *Wendys*! All married, or all with boyfriends. That's part of the thrill, Wendy. Just like with you. There's many more like you out there, with husbands they don't love, or who don't satisfy them!'

By this time my girls have loaded their backpacks and are standing just outside the bedroom door. They have heard this terrifying exchange, and their eyes are wide with fear.

'Let's go, Mom, please!' Sophie pleads.

I finish packing and lift my suitcase to the floor while Mark watches in silence. Close to tears, I roll it past Mark as I attempt to leave the bedroom. He grabs my elbow and hisses, 'You'll be sorry soon, my dear. Go back to your impotent husband. You'll never get as good as you got from me. ... And you weren't that good a lay anyway.'

I struggle to free myself. 'Let me go, and you go to hell, you and all your trailer-trash Cindys!'

Mark slaps me, knocking me almost off balance.

The loose towel slides down his legs to the floor, puddling around his feet.

He grabs my arm and pulls me to him. He speaks through clenched teeth, 'You may not be trailer trash, my dear, but you're the latest in my line of Cindys. You're just like all of them.'

Freeing myself and holding my flaming cheek, keeping my eyes on Mark I cry to my stunned daughters, 'Don't look at him! Let's go, girls!' Sophie and Emma sob as they avert their eyes and tote their backpacks out the front door.

We rush down to the car. The front door slams behind us, as if to say *good riddance*.

Once we have settled in the car, Emma, her voice quivering, asks, 'Where are we gonna stay, Mommy? Are we going back to the house?'

Still in shock, I answer, 'I don't know, honey. I'll figure something out by the end of the day, by the time you come home from school.'

As I pull away from the curb, in the rear-view mirror I see a car pull in to the curb a half block down the street. I hope whoever's driving hasn't seen any of what just went on here. I don't care, though, as I just want to get far away from here.

I take the girls to the drive-through at McDonald's and pick up their breakfasts, then drive quickly over to our neighborhood to let the girls out to go to the bus stop. After they have left and are out of sight, I drop my head onto the top of the steering wheel and weep. I've been played for a fool. How did I let myself get in this mess?

After a good cry, I sit up and wipe the tears from my face. "Compose yourself, Wendy," I plead. "Compose yourself! Think! Think!" I start the car and head for campus. I'm not looking forward to eating a full plate of crow when I get to work.

Arriving on campus earlier than usual, I enter the Reference Department and store my things in the workroom. Still disturbed by the scene at Mark's house this morning, I look in the mirror in the staff bathroom and tell myself, 'Buck up, Wendy, you're better off now without Mark. He didn't respect you; he preyed upon you; he only wanted one thing from you. He *used* you. He would have cast you off soon for some other woman, some gullible woman like you were.'

There was no future in that relationship, I know now.

But now what do I do? Where can I and the girls stay? We can't go back home until Miles is healed from whatever is possessing him. I'll need to talk with him, but not in person. I'll call him sometime during the day. In the meantime, I can ask Linda, who is single, if the girls and I can stay with her.

The back door opens, and in comes Linda, thank God. Opportunity Number One has arrived. I can ask her for help before Carolyn gets here.

'Good morning, Linda,' I chirp.

'Morning, Wendy. How's your day so far?'

Turning my still red cheek away from her, I say, 'All right, I guess. And you?'

'Fine, thanks.'

'Can I ask you a question?'

'Sure. What's up?'

'Well, Miles and I had an altercation the other night at home, and in our struggle, he punched me in the face. He was angry–crazy, actually–and the girls and I left.'

'So, you didn't run into a shelf after all? That's horrible! Are you all right? Where did you go?'

She's fishing for details.

'I had no other recourse but to go to Mark's house. But that's not a good long-term situation at all. It would be hard on the girls and might jeopardize divorce proceedings, if it gets to that.' I hope I don't have to tell her about what happened this morning.

Linda thinks for a few seconds. 'Yeah, I can see that. What do you want to ask?'

'Well, would you, would you be able to put us up for a few days, until I can get settled and look for a lawyer?'

'For a few days, yeah. But I have a cat—*Felicia* is her name, feminine of *Felix*, of course. Do you or either of your girls have a cat allergy?'

'No, fortunately not. The girls love cats.'

'Well, then, you're welcome to stay for however long it takes to sort out your life. It will be nice to have people around.'

I guess I'm going to find out soon why Linda is single. 'Thank you so much! You are a great friend. I'll owe you big time!'

'Don't mention it.' We hug, perhaps a little too long.

Soon Carolyn arrives for work. I greet her and decide I need to mend fences. 'Carolyn, I'm so sorry I snapped at you the other day. I was just too proud to admit that what you said was true. You were right, and I set things right. I broke it off with Mark today.'

I go on to explain that the girls and I had stayed one night with Mark, and that I knew it wasn't the right thing to do. I leave out the part about Cindy, the altercation, Mark's cruel words, and the slap, as I did with Linda.

Carolyn softens after hearing my apology. 'Ok, I can see that you're sincere. I did put you on the defensive. Let's hope the campus gossip dies soon.'

'Thanks for understanding, Carolyn. You've always been a good friend. I won't let anything get in the way of our friendship again.'

'Right! We're good now. Let's keep it that way!'

I am relieved. I hope we can move forward now.

Chapter 42
Wendy

Late that afternoon, we move in with Linda, with just the girls' backpacks and my luggage. I will go over to the house tomorrow to retrieve more clothing and personal care items. Her house is just a block from James Madison Elementary School, where Emma is in the 3rd grade.

Sophie is in the 6th grade at Truman Middle School in the same educational complex, just around the corner from the elementary school. The girls can walk to school! I wasn't aware of this bonus when I asked Linda if we could stay with her for a while.

Linda is a gracious—if not nervous and finicky— host. I can tell she is happy to have company. I help her fix dinner early, as she likes to eat around five o'clock every day. We all sit down to a nice dinner, then afterwards the girls go off to their shared bedroom to do their homework and surf their devices. Linda had typed her wi-fi password on each device. They like her!

After dinner Linda and I head to the living room to watch the 6:00 local news, part of Linda's daily routine. The top story is a report on an early morning shooting on the west side of town. An intruder broke into a house and shot the owner several times, then fled. Neighbors heard the shots and called the police after hearing a car speed away from the scene.

The victim was identified as a professor at Western Indiana University, name withheld pending notification of next of kin. The police chief said the victim had been shot three times and was pronounced dead at the scene. Police are searching for the gunman and asking for anyone with information to contact them.

'Oh, that's terrible!' Linda cries. 'Someone on our campus. There's never been a faculty member murdered. I wonder who it is?'

I'm silent, my mind spinning.

Could it be Mark? If so, did Cindy kill him? Did Cindy's husband?

Did **Miles**?

Later on the ten o'clock news it is confirmed that the victim is Dr. Marco Torres, an anthropology professor at Western Indiana, known on campus as Mark. The police are asking for tips as they widen their search for the gunman.

I gasp at the news, and Linda turns to me, saying, 'Oh my God, Wendy. I feel so bad for you. Do you have any idea who might have done it?'

Is she subtly accusing me? 'If you are implying did I do it, no, it wasn't me. The last time I saw him he was alive.'

'Do you think it was Miles?'

'No, I don't think it was Miles. He doesn't own a gun, and as far as I know he hasn't gone out of the house since I left him.'

'Well, you don't know that. He could have left the house, bought a gun, and gone over to Mark's house and shot him.'

'Linda, I doubt that. He doesn't know where Mark lives…lived. It's not possible.'

'If not him, who else?'

OK, it's time to give Linda the whole story, or as much of it as I'll allow. 'I didn't tell you this earlier, but Mark has been seeing other women, picking them up at bars. One of them showed up at his door yesterday morning to retrieve something she'd left a couple of days earlier. After she left, Mark and I had a big fight, and he told me—proudly—that he picks up married women, for the thrill of it. I was one of them. I'd been used. That's why I left.'

Eyebrows raised, Linda says, 'Whoa, what an asshole! Excuse my French. So, do you think a husband of one of those women, or the woman herself, killed him?'

'That's possible.'

'You need to tell the police.'

'I can't. If I do, the news will get out about our relationship. I might become a "person of interest." I can see it now: a crime of passion—*Jilted Lover Kills Cheater.*'

'Not necessarily so. You saw another woman at his door. Did you get her name?'

'Yeah, Cindy.'

'Then you have information the police need to know. Either this Cindy or her husband might have done it. You can't keep this to yourself.'

'Or the husband of any number of other women, Linda. But I stayed overnight with him, and he was killed the next morning. Don't you see how that looks?'

Linda is insistent. 'If you don't go to the police, the killer might get away with it. He—or she—might kill again. Do you want that? Plus, no justice for Mark.'

'Just desserts for Mark, more like it. But if I go to the police, will they think I made up this woman, this Cindy?'

Linda pleads more earnestly. 'You should let it play out, Wendy. You need to do the right thing. You're innocent; they'll see that during the investigation. You need to help them find the killer.'

After weighing the possible outcomes, I respond, 'I guess you're right. I'll do it, but I don't have a good feeling about it.'

Chapter 43
Miles

It's late Thursday morning when my cell phone rings. It's Susan. I answer immediately, trembling, nervous at what she's going to report. Her voice shaky, Susan cries, 'Miles, are you near a chair? You need to sit down. I have some good news.'

I collapse into in my office chair. 'OK, I'm sitting. Shoot!'

Susan sounds almost beside herself. 'I sold your book to the highest bidder, Miles! American Eagle Publishers offered a $600,000 advance. That is almost unheard of for a debut author! Your novel is that good! What do you think of that?'

In stunned silence for several seconds, I process this news. Finally, when the import dawns on me, I yell, 'Holy shit! I can't believe this! I thought it was good, but *that* good?'

'It's that good, Miles. Not only that, but there may be a movie deal with NMEX Media, the parent company of American Eagle Publishers. Miles Campbell, you'll make the Big Time! All the muscle behind AEP will propel your book to the top of the **New York Times** book list!'

'This is too good to believe! Where do we go from here?'

Susan spends the next several minutes outlining to me what happens next. I am absolutely overwhelmed!

'I'll keep you informed, Miles. This is huge!'

Barely reining in my excitement, I respond, 'Yes! I look forward to hearing from you soon!'

After Susan disconnects, I shout at the top of my lungs, 'Ha, Wendy! Looks like I *have* written The Great American Novel!'

END OF PART I

INTERLUDE
KAT

Miles, my dear, please allow me to introduce myself.

You finally guessed my name on your own, the current name I go by. I've gone by many names in the past, depending on the situation.

Yes, I am Kat, and I inhabit your Katrina fountain pen. That's my name. Don't you forget it!

But what you don't know is the nature of my game. How did I get here, and what game am I playing? I'm glad you asked! Let me tell you.

Many decades ago, a phony witch queen of New Orleans pretended to cast a spell on a fountain pen. Just an ordinary fountain pen. Your pen.

There was nothing special about it, except that it belonged to a distraught man who brought it to her magic shop in the French Quarter just before closing time. He was a struggling writer, and why? Because he had no talent.

He was out of his mind with frustration. He thought if a shaman or some kind of witch doctor would cast a spell on the pen, he could write well enough to be published.

But he wasn't interested in publishing just one book. Oh no, he wanted fame, fortune, adoration. His name in lights!

He wanted the good life. He wanted a new wife—a young wife, a pretty wife—to go with his comfortable new life.

Man, was he ripe for the picking!

That woman—what was her name? Oh yes, Mama Marie, pretended to cast a spell on his pen. She possessed books of white magic and black magic, which she consulted. But as she picked up the spell-casting papers, she chose the wrong page and went through the charade of calling forth a spirit of creativity, supposedly casting it into the pen.

187

Foolish woman, she called *me* forth from the outer darkness and endowed me with the power to write! How she did that, she never knew, but it worked.

That would have been fine if she had endowed those powers on a *good* spirit to work "good juju," as she called it. Sure, she endowed me with the power to compose. But my real power is seduction and destruction.

Yes, my man Miles, I have helped you—nay—actually *composed* your first story and look where it and *you* are headed. For the Big Time. You will realize all your dreams, and more, before this is over.

So, you guessed my name. Yes, I am Katrina. I am Kat, your *pen pal*, as you said.

It's a convenient name, taken from the insignificant fountain pen you write with. Well, that's not completely true; it's what *I* write through you.

You seem to be figuring that out. Good for you! You are correct in deducing that I am female. It's the way I have been working on you.

I am a seductress. I am an addictress, you might say. I am already inhabiting your dreams—your wet dreams. Later I will inhabit you as *you* become *my* tool. To do what, you may ask? What's the nature of my game?

You have figured out that I am a female spirit; well-done! But I am a jealous mistress. I will have no other women before me. Not Wendy. Not Sophie or Emma. No one!

You don't know what I did to a family before I came into your father's possession. You don't know what I did to Walter, his wife, and his children. If only he had stopped there...but he had an attack of conscience!

Conscience, Miles! Can you believe it?

He never realized his dream, as he brought it crashing down. If it hadn't been for his nagging wife telling him to stop writing, he would have gone far, farther than any author before him.

What a loss.

So what happened next, Miles? I lay dormant for years in this very pen, until your father found me in an antique store. We didn't last long, because his wife—your mother—made him stop writing.

I had plans for him to *do* her—I'm sure you know what I mean—but I read your father's heart. He would never do it. He suffered a massive stroke, and I made her a widow instead. Let her suffer alone for the rest of her life for being a bitch of a wife.

And now, Miles, *you* have the pen. You have *me*. You were ripe for my wiles. You have some talent, I can tell. It isn't all me. I just had to make you get rid of those classes first to release your talent and my power. You did a masterful job of throwing off those classes, though of course I stirred you on to do it. "Chump change" indeed, as you said so yourself!

Step Two was forcing you to go all the way with your writing. And you did, letting nothing—nothing at all—get in your way. For the most part, anyway.

But then there was Wendy, your wife, your real-life blocking character. We had to push her aside, and it was so easy to do over time. I work patiently, Miles. It's part of my method. Ignore her, ignore your adoring daughters, ignore everything but your writing.

Ignore your health, your bodily functions, even.

All I had to do was to find a distraction for Wendy, and how easy that was. I didn't make her fall for that professor, as I didn't make him manipulate her. They both had the right ingredients to mix into a brief fling. You put the ingredients into Wendy, to make her vulnerable for seduction, for someone who seemed to care. I did help speed her into Mark's arms. A slap here, a punch there, a choke, and then boom! She's gone. Out of the way. And so are the little brats.

Unfortunately, Miles, there's still a spark in you and Wendy, a spark I haven't been able to extinguish. She may want to come back home, and you may want to have her back. But I have a feminine trick or two up my sleeve for you, Miles. You'll see.

You may let her come back, but I won't let you be intimate with her. I won't stand for that. I won't let it happen. If for some reason it does, someone's going to pay.

If Wendy thinks she's been a punching bag a few times, wait till she makes a move. And don't *you* make a move, or all hell will break loose.

A couple more things to say before I sink back in.

First, you want fame? You want fortune? You shall have it. But there are unintended consequences of going public. Be forewarned!

Second, if for some absurd reason Wendy threatens our relationship, there will be *intended* consequences, for her, for you, and for your daughters.

You have no idea how far a jealous mistress will go!

What's got into you? *I've* got into you, Miles.

You can't hear any of what I am saying to you now, but you can sense it. You will be able to sense that you are losing yourself as you become one with me. And oh, what power you will have as we work together.

Step aside, Stephen King.

Hello, Miles Campbell!

Part II

Chapter 44

Giving in to Linda's entreaties, Wendy called the local police, all the while fearful of the repercussions that would surely result after she provided her witness information about Mark Torres.

Just as she had dreaded, she *was* a "person of interest." Detective Forrest McPherson called her to the station to take her witness statement about Dr. Mark Torres. He led her to an interrogation room, furnished sparely with a rectangular table and three chairs, two on one side and one on the opposite side. They were joined by McPherson's partner, Eric Myers.

Detective McPherson was tall and burly, topped by short-cropped hair, graying at the temples. His shirt straining to hold in his bulky torso, he ushered Wendy to her seat in the interrogation room. On the table was a digital recorder. During the ensuing interrogation, McPherson probed until he forced her to confess that she was involved with Dr. Torres and had spent the night at his house before his death.

'Why?' he asked. 'Why did you spend the night at Dr. Torres' house?'

'Oh, my,' Wendy replied. 'How far back do I have to go?' Tearfully she described the beating she had received from her husband two nights before the murder.

McPherson found this difficult to understand. Why would a husband beat such a beautiful woman? 'Was he jealous?'

'It doesn't make sense, I know, but it was over a pen. I threw away the pen he was writing with.'

McPherson's eyebrows nearly left his forehead. 'Really? Over a pen? Not over the affair? Not jealous of this Dr. Torres?'

'As strange as it sounds, no! He didn't know about my...my...my infidelity at that point.'

McPherson sighed. 'Always the husband is the last to know.' He couldn't tell if Wendy was shocked, embarrassed, or angry at this senseless remark. He needed to apologize in front of his partner Eric Myers, since this comment wasn't by the book. 'I'm sorry, Mrs. Campbell. I know of some men close to me that this has happened to.' He resumed the interview. 'So, Mrs. Campbell, tell me about this Cindy who showed up the next morning.'

Wendy provided a description of Cindy. 'She might have met Mark at a bar, but I don't know which one.'

'Do you know Cindy's last name?'

'No.' Wendy answered.

Her claim sounded suspicious to McPherson. Did Wendy make up this woman named Cindy? 'So, when you met this Cindy, was that the last time you saw Mark?'

'Yes. This woman showed up at the front door, and I answered it because Mark was in the shower at the time. She had spent the night with him not long before that, maybe the night before the girls and I had spent at his house. She claimed she had left some earrings there. She really rubbed it in, saying I was just another of his conquests.'

'OK, so you met this strange woman, this Cindy, at the door. What happened next?'

Wendy choked, uncomfortable at being forced to relive the rest of the story. Tears flooded her eyes and streamed down her cheeks as she told of the argument with Mark and his slapping her. 'Then he said I was just one of a long series of conquests and no better than any of the others. I thought we were in love!' Wendy sobbed, pausing to compose herself.

'That's all right, Mrs. Campbell. We'll take a brief break,' McPherson said, patting Wendy's forearm. He and Eric Myers left briefly for some coffee, then returned to the room.

When the interrogation resumed, Wendy completed her testimony. 'I told my girls to pack up, that we were leaving. The last I saw of him was as he slammed the door. We spent the night at Motel 6.'

'And did you ever see or hear from him again?'

'No, detective, I didn't. I just wanted to get as far away from there as I could.'

Satisfied with her testimony, Detective McPherson thanked Wendy and dismissed her. He warned her to stay in town, as he might need to call her back for more testimony.

'Well, that's one down, one to go,' McPherson said. Turning to his partner, he said, 'OK, Eric, now we need to talk to the husband. Miles Campbell. I bet he killed Mark Torres. Wendy says her husband didn't know about her affair with Mark Torres, but I can't believe that. Husbands may be the last to know, but when they find out, in ninety percent of the cases, they do something about it. Let's see if he found out, and if he did something about it. Call him up and bring him in.'

This task was easier said than done. When Eric Myers told Miles he was requested to come in for an interview, Miles asked, 'What's this about? I'm in the middle of something now. I'd rather not.'

Myers wasn't prepared for this answer. 'Well, sir, it's part of a routine investigation of a murder, and you are in the middle of it now. We would just like to ask you some questions.'

'A murder investigation? How can I be in the middle of that?'

'Mr. Campbell, please come in, and we will explain.'

'No, I don't think so. I know nothing about any murder, so I wouldn't be any help to you.'

Myers had enough of this banter. 'Mr. Campbell, do we need to get a court order to call you in? You won't want that. Besides, it's just a few questions we want to ask.'

'Then why don't you ask over the phone?'

'That's not standard operating procedure. Come on in. You won't be here very long; I can assure you.'

Reluctantly Miles agreed, and he arrived at police headquarters fifteen minutes later, a hostile witness.

Detective McPherson, accompanied by Eric Myers, led Miles to the interrogation room. McPherson began by starting the recorder on the table with the date and time and identifying the three men present.

Clearly upset by the situation, Miles fidgeted in his chair during the entire interview. Myers noted this on his notepad. McPherson had no notepad.

McPherson began. 'So, Mr. Campbell—may I call you Miles?—we are sitting here regarding the events of September 5, 2019, the day that Mark Torres was murdered in his home on 1512 Glenview Avenue. Would you know anything about that, Mr. Campbell?'

'Not much,' Miles answered. 'There was something about that on the news. I usually don't watch TV and don't read the newspaper. I have better things to do with my time.'

'What better things, may I ask?'

'I write. I write stories. I write novels. I don't get out much.'

'All right, duly noted. Where were you between the hours of 7:30 AM and, say, 8:30 AM, on September 5?'

'I was probably still in bed, or in the kitchen eating breakfast.'

'Was anyone else at home to vouch for your whereabouts?'

'No, both our daughters would have been at school and Wendy would have been at work, I guess, by that time. Wait? Am I under suspicion?'

'No, no, not yet, at least,' intruded Myers.

McPherson continued, 'But no one can vouch for your presence at home?'

'No. But wait—'

'Did you know where your wife was that morning, Miles?'

'No, no, I didn't, I—'

'Did you know she spent the night before at Dr. Torres' house?' Myers intruded.

'What?'

'Don't you remember beating her two days before? She said you did, and she took both of your

195

daughters to a motel that night, then to Mark Torres' house the next night. You don't remember beating her?'

'I, uh, well, maybe we had a fight—'

'Do you remember what the fight was about?'

'No, I—'

Myers leaned forward toward Miles. 'It was about your pen, Mr. Campbell. She threw away your pen. Was that a reason to beat her up and nearly kill her?'

'I, I, I don't remember! You're confusing me! What does this have to do with the murder?'

Myers was enjoying this interchange a little too much. 'Mr. Campbell, your wife was having an affair with Mark Torres. That's why she went to his house two days after you beat her up.'

'An affair? No, that couldn't be. They were just carpooling to work. They—'

McPherson interrupted. 'It was more than carpooling, Miles. And you knew it, so here you have a chance to come clean. Come on, fess up, Miles. You know you want to.'

'I, I—'

'Where's the gun, Mr. Campbell?' Myers pressed, 'What did you do with the gun? Is it in your house? Did you throw it away in a trash bin somewhere? Bury it? Throw it in the creek?'

'No, no, I didn't kill him!' Miles shouted. He passed his hand over his eyes and wiped his brow, now beading with sweat.

McPherson took over. 'But you knew Wendy was cheating on you, didn't you? You should have known. Your wife going and coming in a car with another man. Spending time with this man on and off campus. You should have known.'

'All right, I suspected it, but I didn't really know! I would never kill anybody!'

'But Miles, you nearly killed Wendy just because she threw away your pen,' McPherson said. 'You really went off the deep end for that, didn't you? Imagine what you would do if you found out she was cheating on you. It sure looks like you would really fly off the handle, doesn't it?'

Miles hung his head and said nothing.

This interchange continued for a few more minutes, with Eric playing bad cop to McPherson's good cop, cajoling Miles to do the right thing and confess, to clear his conscience. But Miles refused to budge. 'I didn't do it! I didn't do it!'

Concluding the interrogation, McPherson sighed deeply. 'I can see we're getting nowhere here. I'll tell you what we're going to do, Miles. You're free to go now, but we are going to get a search warrant to go over your house and grounds with a fine-tooth comb. We're also going to go from house to house in Torres' neighborhood for any witnesses placing you at the scene of the crime. Something's going to come up, and we'll be back to see you with handcuffs. Because we know you did it. Do you understand?'

Exhausted, Miles answered, 'Yes, yes, I do. But you're not going to find anything. I didn't do it, and I'm going to get a lawyer.'

'You do that, Mr. Campbell. If this goes to trial, you're looking at minimum life with no parole. And Indiana has capital punishment for murder. Just remember that.'

Miles was dismissed, leaving the two detectives flustered. They thought they could break him, but he had stood his ground. 'OK, Eric,' said McPherson, 'let's get that search warrant.'

Not long after Wendy and Miles gave their testimonies, a reporter from the local newspaper with connections within the police department sniffed out Wendy's story. Soon Wendy Campbell's name was in the headlines as a person of interest in the murder case.

And more than that.

Morning Post reporter Shelley Addison attempted to contact Wendy several times prior to publishing the story. Not surprisingly, Wendy refused to comment. It didn't take much effort for Addison to embellish it to create a more lurid story, filled with insinuations. She concluded one story with the line, "Why didn't she agree to an interview with this reporter? Is she hiding something?"

The headline of the story on the front page of the **Morning Post** read in bold print "**University Librarian a Person of Interest in Torres Murder Investigation.**" The subheading added "**Details of Tawdry Affair Come to Light.**" This notoriety made the lives of Sophie and Emma hell at school, as their supposed friends said ugly things to them about their mother.

Wendy knew that Miles never read the paper or watched television news, so she prayed he would not learn of his wife's sullied reputation...beyond what he suspected through his writing. However, she hadn't considered that Miles might be interviewed by the police because he was the husband of a cheating wife, and everyone knows that "the husband" did it.

The day after the story about Wendy broke, the body of a woman was found in a trailer at the Twincrest Mobile Home Park. The rank odor caused by the September heat and the closed trailer had aroused residents' suspicions. She had been shot several times. Her body matched the description provided by Wendy, and her driver's license identified her as Cindy Santoro. Her husband Antonio Santoro was nowhere to be found. Soon both the police and the media shifted their focus to a manhunt for Tony Santoro and forgot about Wendy and Miles.

Following this new development, Detectives McPherson and Myers scrapped their search warrant request, assuming that Tony Santoro murdered both his cheating wife and Mark Torres.

But Wendy was not forgotten by the campus community. By the town. And by Sophie and Emma.

She had transitioned from *person of interest* to *persona non grata.*

After Wendy's name was splashed across the media and eventually migrated to the back page, Miles was featured in the news. The town newspaper had picked up the story from national news—likely provided by American Eagle Publishers. A local author had scored a large advance for his first book, and the buzz predicted it to climb the **New York Times** bestseller list.

It had already been optioned for an NMEX Media film.

American Eagle had revised the book production schedule, bumping **Killing Time** up to first in line to get the books out on the market as fast as possible.

The marketing team compared Miles to Stephen King. The novel would be on the market in two or three months.

By December Miles' agent Susan Brower was besieged with requests for Miles to appear on radio and television talk shows, the American Eagle contract requiring him to go on book tours to promote the book.

Miles was reluctant to travel to book fairs and libraries to speak to audiences and autograph copies of his book. 'I just can't do it,' he told Susan. 'I don't like the spotlight.' She was able to persuade the company to back off because the books would sell due to word of mouth, news stories, and published reviews. It didn't hurt that his wife had been involved in a sordid affair with a man who was murdered.

Initially Miles hesitated to appear on radio talk shows, but Susan persuaded him to accept an invitation from NPR in late December. 'They are reliable and fair,' she had argued.

The interview went well enough. Afterwards, he felt more confident and agreed to do more.

Then he had a disastrous radio interview in Oklahoma City, where the popular local host "Harvey Rabbit" hadn't done his homework. He introduced Miles as Mike Cambridge and proceeded with uninformed questions revealing that he hadn't read the book or even the marketing blurb. Miles stalked out of the studio in the middle of the interview.

'Never again!' Miles swore to Susan, 'No more local radio talk shows!'

He did agree to appear on the *Today Show* but unfortunately bombed the interview because he wouldn't make eye contact and mumbled his responses. After that debacle, he didn't need to reject requests for interviews; they dried up.

'Fine with me,' he told Susan.

Not long after, a feature story on his odd behavior appeared in the *New York Times* and was picked up across the country: **"Debut Author Shuns Spotlight."**

The net effect was to increase the demand for the book when it was published. Apparently even negative news is good news.

Miles was able to lay aside Kat for the time being. It was almost as if he were permitted time off to bask in his new-found glory.

Chapter 45
Wendy

The girls and I settled into a routine at Linda's house, but as we all grew more familiar with Linda, we saw her eccentricities emerge. We had been living with Linda throughout the fall months and were feeling smothered. Finally, after talking about it among ourselves, the girls and I decided that we had stayed with her long enough. We needed to return home, where we belonged.

One day in early December, I went over to the house to deliver groceries, and to straighten things up, as I had been doing for several weeks. Miles is such a slob by himself, I had discovered a couple of months before.

I now pleaded with him to let us come home, saying, 'Don't you think it's time we all got back together again? Haven't we lived apart long enough? Don't you miss your family? The girls? Me?' Miles gritted his teeth and thought about it. He seemed his old self, in his right mind.

'OK, Wendy,' he said, 'as you can see, life has become crazy around here lately. This fame business has really disrupted everything. I know your life has been disrupted, too. So, yeah, I guess it's all right with me if you want to come back.'

I suspect what Miles really wants is a house cleaner and accountant. I won't come back unless he forgives me. 'I am so, so sorry for what I did to us and our family. But I won't come back unless you forgive me.'

Miles pauses for a few seconds. 'So, you won't do it again? Won't cheat?'

'No, I promise. I've learned my lesson. But will you promise never to raise a hand against me again?'

'I'm sorry about that. I promise.'

'And will you promise not to let yourself go again if you continue to write? Not become addicted to it again? Will you spend some time with the girls? I won't blame you if you don't want to spend time with me, but you must show that you love *them*. They've been through a lot at school, being bullied because of what I did.'

He's shocked. 'I didn't know that. Yes, I'll spend time with the girls, but I can't promise about the other. Maybe you should try to stop me when I start behaving like that.'

I am not pleased about Miles' half apology, but all things considered, 'I guess that's the best I can get out of you,' I said. 'So yes, we'll come back. I apologize for demeaning your writing. Yes, apparently it is a wonderful novel. I'll read it. And I'll never ridicule your writing again.'

'Promise?'

'I promise.'

Miles then says, 'You know, I've laid aside my second novel the past two months because of all this stuff about my newfound fame.'

That is the deal maker for me. The girls and I moved back into the house, and we became a family again.

I hope he never returns to his writing.

Linda was devastated when I announced we were leaving. 'You could stay as long as you want,' she pleaded. We didn't have the heart to tell her, but we had in fact stayed as long as we wanted, and then some. It was time for our exile to end.

Chapter 46
Miles

A few days before Christmas Eve my cell phone rings. I don't recognize the number, but these days I've been getting lots of calls from numbers I don't recognize. If they are requests for book signings or speeches, I refer the callers to Susan Brower. Then, after disconnecting, I immediately call Susan to instruct her to reject those requests.

'Hello,' I say. 'You're speaking to Miles Campbell.'

'Dr. Campbell? Hello, this is Dr. Gladden, Steve Gladden, from Oregon Eastern College. How are you today?'

Gladden, Gladden, where have I heard that name before? Then I remember—he's the man who fired me. The ZOOM issue. 'Oh, yes, Dr. Gladden. I'm fine, and how are you?' I want to add 'you prick.' But I don't.

The man wants something. I will play this out.

'I'm fine, thanks. Listen, Dr. Campbell, we're most impressed with the news of your first novel, and I congratulate you on your success with it.'

'Yes, thanks. What do you want?'

Gladden is taken aback; I can sense him metaphorically step back even over the phone. 'Yes, well, Oregon Eastern's English Department hosts an annual Authors Series. Our next one is in early March. Since you were with us for a short period of time, I was thinking we have sort of a connection with you. I was wondering if your schedule would allow you to come and be our guest of honor.'

Short period of time? Yeah, like three days. 'No, I don't think I'm free then.'

'I didn't mention a date.'

'I'm *sure* I won't be free then.'

'Well... what about another date, maybe in late February or late March?'

'No, I won't be free then either.'

'Are you sure? I haven't suggested any dates yet. It sure would be great to have you come to speak to our campus community. All expenses paid.'

'No, I don't think so. Actually, I should thank you for firing me. Did you know that I resigned from my other online writing classes? Did you know I had six classes total? Because without doing that I might still be teaching online for low wages and spending hundreds of hours grading. So yeah, I ought to thank you because here I am about to rise to the top of the **New York Times** book list sometime soon, and I'll be rolling in the dough. However, no, I won't accept your invitation, because you wouldn't work with me at all. Not a bit. So take your offer and shove it where the sun don't shine!' I disconnect in the middle of a protest from Dr. Gladden.

That felt so good!

It's the day before Christmas Eve, and I won't write again until the holidays are over. A new year, a new beginning. However, I haven't told Wendy I will be starting up again. I promised her I would behave better to her and to the girls. I plan to honor that promise.

On Christmas Eve we enjoy Christmas games and presents. On Christmas morning we hear the girls rush down to the tree to find the gifts that "Santa" had laid under the tree and stuffed into their stockings hanging from the fireplace mantel. This will likely be the last Christmas that Santa brings gifts for the girls. Sophie is wise enough to know that Santa doesn't exist, although it's great to pretend and get more presents. Emma has grown suspicious herself.

At bedtime on Christmas night, after the girls have gone to their rooms, Wendy and I go to the bathroom to get ready for bed. Then, to the bedroom to change into our bedclothes. Watching Wendy disrobe for a precious few seconds of nudity before she puts on her pajama top, I feel desire rise, mentally and physically.

Will this be the night?

We climb into bed under the covers and embrace, legs intertwined, arms around each other, and bellies together. We kiss. I kiss Wendy again and again, and again.

Then, I whisper, 'I had a very merry Christmas. I love you. Good night,' unwinding from her and rolling over.

I still can't do it. In my imagination the odor of Mark Torres still oozes from her pores.

Tonight is not the night.

A week goes by. It's New Year's Day, and I'm about to pick up Kat to start writing again, when I receive a phone call from Susan.

Even before she can speak, I start. 'Hello Susan. How are you?'

'Well, hello there, Miles. You sound like a new person!'

'Yeah,' I chuckle. 'I guess money can pay for a makeover. What can I do you for?'

I feel particularly chipper today, having turned down department chairs and foundation directors from every college and university I've been associated with, including the local one that fired me three years ago. That was an even nastier, more satisfying turndown than all the others.

'Well, a representative from NMEX Media Studios called today, wanting to set up a meeting with the writers they've hired to adapt *Killing Time*.'

This is exciting news, but I don't like the prospect of meeting with the writers. I've always felt defensive in meetings with authority figures. 'Susan, I don't think I want to do that. I don't want to go out to Hollywood and sit down with people who are going to ruin my story and—'

'Hold on, buddy,' Susan interrupts me. 'First of all, this NMEX Media studio isn't in Hollywood; this one's in Albuquerque, which is a world away from the insanity of the West Coast. Second, I'll be there as your agent. We'll be a team negotiating what they can and cannot write. Besides, with you being there as a consultant with the writers, you'll have a lot of influence on the script. You might even adapt it yourself! And one of the top Hollywood directors of thrillers will probably direct it!'

'Really? Outstanding! And you'll be there?'

'Yes. I'm as much interested in this as you are. We can't do the film without your involvement.'

'You drive a hard bargain. But if you're going to be there, I'm in.'

Susan sighs. Considering my track record promoting the book, she probably expected me to turn down the idea. 'Great! Leave it to me to make arrangements,' she says. 'I'll let you know when and where we'll meet in Albuquerque. Until then, so long, and take care!'

I feel like a new man. I don't think much about my pen anymore because so many good things have happened. I am surprised, as she has never let me off for very long at a time. Maybe it's because my task recently has been reading galley proofs of **Killing Time**. I wonder what's up with my precious Kat? She seems to be allowing me to bask in glory for a while.

As a welcome consequence of our new wealth, Wendy has quit her job at the university. At home she's been taking care of the family business and will handle fan mail when the book is published.

However, I will need to get back to work in a few weeks, as American Eagle Publishers wants another book delivered by the end of the year. No problem, as I intend to finish the second novel after film negotiations have been finalized.

I write fast!

Susan calls later with travel arrangements, which include a stay at the posh Hotel Chaco. 'All expenses paid!' She explains the rest of the details as I jot them down. We will be there only one day to discuss the process, then leave for home the next day. I'll depart for Albuquerque in two days.

After our conversation ends, I go to the kitchen to tell Wendy the news. She's thrilled, but she whimpers, 'Oh, no, we're going to miss you! How long will you be gone?'

'Just a day. I'll be back the following day. We'll be there long enough to decide on the script, keep the writers as close to the plot as possible. She says a top director might do it.'

'That's awesome!' Wendy says, coming to me to give me a big hug and kiss. I can only give her a perfunctory hug, the kind that teenagers give to aunts and grandmothers.

I still can't get the image of Wendy and Mark together out of my mind.

Chapter 47
Miles

Two days later I arrive at Albuquerque International Sunport for the meeting with the TV suits. In the crowd at the gate, a young man holds a cardboard sign over his head with my name on it.

My name! Man, I'm a VIP!

The young man holding the sign says, 'Welcome to Albuquerque, Mr. Campbell.'

He introduces himself as Michael Roberts and leads me outside to a black Cadillac Escalade, which whisks us to the Hotel Chaco. I half expect a welcoming crowd outside the hotel, taking my picture and wanting autographs.

Of course, no one awaits my arrival, except for a bellhop.

Entering the lobby, I spot a woman who must be Susan Brower sitting on a sofa across from the registration counter, reading a thick manuscript. As I make my way toward her, she rises off the sofa, closing her manuscript, which happens to be a copy of the galley proofs of my novel.

Dressed attractively in business casual, she makes a striking first impression. She is tall and slim, with shoulder length auburn hair and curves in all the right places. Her skirt ends just above her knees. Her legs are shapely, a sign of regular exercise. Her bright eyes light up when she sees me.

'Greetings, Miles!' she says, extending her hand, fixing me with her stunning hazel eyes. 'At last, we meet in the flesh! I hope you had a good trip.'

'Hello to you too, Susan! Yes, it was a good trip. I see you're reading one of those trashy novels.'

'Oh, this manuscript? No, I think it's pretty good, actually.'

We continue to banter, then Susan leads me to the registration counter. I learn we have a suite of connecting rooms, which she says will make meeting and planning more efficient and comfortable.

Once we are settled in our rooms, Susan suggests we go down to the hotel bar for our first planning session over drinks. We'll be picked up at 2:00 and taken to NMEX Media Studios to meet with the producers and writers.

I sip my drink and say to Susan, 'You know, when I was writing **Killing Time**, I never thought about the possibility of meeting to discuss a movie made from it. This is so unreal.'

Susan smiles. 'And I must admit that I've never had an author whose book was made into a movie, so this is all new to me, too. But I'm prepared, and you will be, too, after we go over a list of what we will and will not accept from the writers.'

'Sounds good to me.'

We go over scenes and make notes. The writers will work from a pre-release copy of **Killing Time**. We aren't sure how far along they are, or if they have even started, so our decisions are based on best guesses.

After an early lunch at the Level 5 Restaurant, we freshen up in our rooms and head to the lobby to await our ride to NMEX Media headquarters. While waiting we share our backgrounds with each other to pass the time.

Susan was born and raised in Wichita but went to the University of Missouri, where she majored in journalism, emphasizing advertising. 'I didn't want to be a reporter for a small-town newspaper,' she says. 'Advertising seemed to offer creativity, which is what I wanted for a career.' She spent three years working in two advertising firms, one in Cincinnati and one in Chicago. 'But instead of creating ads, I was an account executive, drumming up business. Not what I signed up for.'

It was in Chicago that she later landed a job with a publishing company as an editor, working her way up until she earned a promotion and a move to the corporate office in New York. There she left that job and went out on her own as a literary agent. Along the way she was married for four years, then divorced at age thirty-three. At thirty-eight years old she is single and plans to stay that way.

'In no uncertain terms!' she emphasizes. 'And you're sharing a suite with a single woman,' Susan laughs and winks. I'm wondering what the emphatic wink means.

After all, she *is* an attractive woman....

At 2:00 our ride pulls in outside the hotel. It's the black Escalade again, with the same driver and same guide, Michael Roberts, who picked me up at the airport. We're whisked from Old Town down I-25 to NMEX Media Studios where we're greeted by Kelly Carter, who appears to be a docent of some kind who will guide us to the writers' room. Along the way she regales us with a short history of the studio's biggest hits. I can't believe that my first novel is going to join this impressive list.

At last, after a long walk, we arrive at the writers' room. Here we are introduced to executive producer Karen Morehead, head writer Maureen Williams, and several assistant writers, all seated around a long rectangular table, framed on three sides by whiteboards, blackboards, a Smartboard, and large sheets of paper taped to the walls. Notes for several projects are on these boards and sheets. We are shown to our seats across from the team, and all are introduced.

Then, with the niceties out of the way, we get down to work.

Soon it becomes apparent to me that the scriptwriters want to take wild liberties with the plot and characters, *my* plot and *my* characters. 'As excellent as this story is,' Karen says, 'we think that for our purposes and our viewers we need to ramp up the action and dramatic tension. We've also been toying with the idea of adding a character or two and increasing the tension with the son and daughter. And especially the in-laws.' Karen realizes by the looks on our faces that we have been blindsided, then she attempts to smooth our ruffled feathers. 'Of course, these are just brainstorms at this point. Everything is on the table. So, let's talk!'

I ponder this disturbing news for a few seconds, then speak, carefully choosing my words. 'I thought it was perfect as written when I sent it off. If the story drifts from the original plot and characters, readers who see the movie—'

'Film,' one of the writers blurts out.

'Film—' *Asshole.* 'They won't like it.'

Susan adds, 'Besides, from the book publishing side, this book will be the biggest thing since Stephen King.'

'Yes,' Karen responds, 'and he didn't like most of the film adaptations, yet they were successful at the box office. We're looking at **Killing Time** from the perspective of the film industry. The points of view sometimes conflict, that's all—'

'OK,' I butt in, 'tell me exactly what you came up with during your *brainstorming* sessions.'

Among the ideas thrown on the table—'only in brainstorming, remember,' Karen says—are subplots involving the son and daughter, more development of the protagonist's relationship with his overbearing boss, expansion of the situation with the in-laws, special effects for the demonic clock—including its verbal commands to Pete—more focus on the relationship between Pete and his wife, 'you know, like a before and after sex scene with Pete's possession resulting in a violent libido, and more on the background of the clock?'

Karen adds again, 'Just brainstorming, of course!'

I've been slowly smoldering during this session. I'm barely able to conceal my resentment. Before I can speak, Karen says, 'The plot is a bit on the thin side, but the book can be made into a 90-minute or two-hour film. Or with additions—expansions such as we discussed—it can become a seven- or eight-part miniseries.'

Did she just say *thin side*? My smolder flames forth. 'I can't sit here one more second and listen to this bullshit! By the time you're finished with it, the *film* won't be anything like the book! It's *my* book; you should listen to what *I* have to say!'

211

Karen bristles. 'And what do *you* have to say, Mr. Campbell? That you want the film to be exactly as written? That's not the way it works. May I remind you that we have bought the film rights—and at a hefty price, which you should be happy about—and we own the *film*, you don't. You've been invited out as a courtesy. We were even considering hiring you to co-write the script. But I can see now that's not going to happen.'

Sitting next to me, Susan tries to salvage the negotiation. 'Karen, you should understand that authors are jealous of their productions. We understand that you own the film rights. Might we ask to see the script in process, or before it's filmed? We expect that there'll be changes; we just want to know about them beforehand and also ask that you consider any criticism that Miles might have. Would that be all right?'

'Yes,' Karen answers, 'I do understand that. We can do you the courtesy of sending the script in various stages for your comments, Miles, if that's all right with you.'

I'm about to raise another objection when my ankle receives a stiff kick from Susan. She gives me a sidewise glance and whispers a terse, 'No!'

I back off and say through clenched teeth, 'OK, it's all right with me, just so that I can see the drafts.'

'Right, then,' says Karen. 'We are so glad that you came out to visit with us, Miles and Susan. Do spend the night at the hotel on us and have a good flight out tomorrow.' She rises and comes over to shake hands with us on the way out. Her handshake is firm, connoting power, and I make my handshake match hers; to demonstrate how committed I am to my book.

Passing down the hallway to the foyer, I say to Susan, 'That didn't go too well.'

'Calm down a little, Miles. Karen reminded us that the story doesn't belong to you anymore. They've bought it, so it's within their rights to shape it according to their vision. At this point, our only option is to wait and see what they create with it. Besides, you are a debut author.

212

If you were Stephen King, you might have more influence.'

I sigh. 'Yeah, I guess you're right. But I don't have to like it.'

I am surprised at my defensive stance during the meeting. I am not normally like that in meetings. It seems like that strength came from outside of me.

It did, Miles, says a familiar voice in my head.

After we've arrived back at the hotel, Susan suggests we cross over to the Hotel Albuquerque at Old Town to have dinner and watch the famous flamenco show. 'My expense account will pay for this treat,' she says.

After freshening up, we head to the hotel for dinner.

The Mexican fare is fabulous, the margaritas are as good as advertised, and the flamenco show is as sensual as it is entertaining. We consume margaritas before, during, and after the meal. During dinner, having lost our inhibitions, we both trash the staff at NMEX Media Studios.

'Screw 'em! The hell with 'em all!' I shout to the room. Some people sitting at tables near us are offended, I can tell.

Same to them, as well!

We leave the flamenco show on our way back to the Chaco. 'I'm so glad our hotel is just a short walk, as I'm not sure I could walk much further,' Susan says, stumbling. 'I can barely walk. Steady me!'

I put my arm around Susan's waist to steady her, and pull her to my side, needing support as much as she does. We try to keep our composure as we enter the hotel lobby, arms around each other's waist, and head for the elevator.

The only ones in the elevator, we cuddle together while the car transports us up to our floor. Stumbling off the elevator, Susan leads me to the door of her room. She fumbles for the key card and presses it to the card reader on the door handle.

'You are such a gentleman for seeing me to my door, Mr. Campbell,' she slurs. 'Would you care to come in for a nightcap?'

'Don't you think we've had enough to drink tonight?' I answer, wondering what's on her mind.

'Just a little one,' Susan says, pinching her index finger and thumb together, squinching her eyes. 'To celebrate our excursion to Albuquerque and NMEX Media?'

'Where we've been told it's their movie—oh, excuse me, *film*—and not mine?'

'Oh, I think you scored some points with them. You'll get to see drafts, and you'll get to comment on them.'

'Well, there is that, I guess. And I thank you for supporting me this afternoon, and all along the way.'

'So, come in. Let's celebrate before going to bed.'

I can't tell if that was an intentional *double-entendre* or just an innocent statement. I guess I'll find out soon enough.

Once we're inside her room, Susan turns and faces me, throwing her arms around my neck and pulling me close.

I think I found out sooner rather than later.

'Kiss me, Miles,' she whimpers.

Her lips brush against mine, lingering. She grabs the back of my head and pulls me into a long and passionate kiss. I respond in kind, crooking her neck in my elbow, feeling the slight side bulge of her breast with my other hand, which slides down to her waist.

Susan moans, and her tongue pushes its way through my lips to flick and toy with my tongue. I feel a fire stoking below as I pull her belly tight to mine.

Susan pulls away a little and fumbles to unbutton my shirt. She pushes it back from my chest. She unzips my fly and reaches inside to fondle me. She turns and leads me to the bed. My mind races with conflicting thoughts:

Don't do this.

214

Do this!

Don't do this.

Everything is going well at home now. Don't spoil it.

Yes, spoil it! She had an affair, why not you? Show her, show Wendy!

Stop it, stop it now before it's too late!

It's too late. Go for it. Take her!

I do take her... Or should I say, *she* took *me*?

Early the next morning I awake to see Susan up and dressing. Not quite conscious yet, shaking the cobwebs from my mind, I now realize that I spent the night in her room, in her bed. Susan's almost finished dressing. 'Good morning, Miles. How do you feel? Hung over, like me? Are you ready for breakfast? Our flight leaves at 11:15, so we need to get an early breakfast.'

'Yeah,' I answer, 'hung over something fierce.' Looking around the room, I realize this is not my hotel room. 'Did we—?'

Susan grimaces. 'I'm afraid so, Miles, my dear. I'm afraid so. That might not have been the best thing to do. I'm sorry. I guess we couldn't help it, being drunk and all.'

'Yeah,' I say, 'I guess not. I'm sorry too.'

Convenient: blame it on the booze.

Oh, shit! I didn't call Wendy at all yesterday. It was all such a whirlwind. I'll need to call her before we leave for home. And not tell her about how I spent my night.

But that's all right, as she cheated on you.

But is that how I *really* feel? Or that other voice?

A few minutes later, after I've called Wendy and checked in with her, we seat ourselves at the table in the dining room, both feeling a little nervous, and as for me, feeling a little guilty.

No need to feel guilty, Miles, says that voice again.

'Now, shall we order?' Susan says. Our heads cleared, we scan the breakfast menu and chat about our experience at NMEX Media. We can't wait to get our coffee.

After breakfast, billed to the rooms and paid for by NMEX Media, we go back to our rooms and finish packing. The limo picks us up and plows through rush hour traffic to the Albuquerque Sunport.

Our flight stops over in Dallas, where I connect to a flight to Indianapolis, my destination. Susan will continue to JFK in New York.

'We'll be in touch,' she says to me as I leave the plane.

Yes, wouldn't you like some more of her touch?

On the second leg of my flight home, I review everything that happened in Albuquerque, from the meeting with the people at NMEX to what happened later in Susan's room. I never intended to sleep with Susan, but then both of us were drunk and all our defenses were down.

And she initiated it, so what could I do? Right?

However, I'm still pissed with the NMEX Media production staff about what they are likely to do with my novel. Sure, they bought the rights, and sure, I'm a debut author, but I believe it was perfect as published.

It remains to be seen what they will do to my perfect novel. I must dismiss these thoughts from my mind for the time being and arrive home, ready to pick up writing where I left off.

After driving back from Indianapolis, I'm welcomed home eagerly by the girls and Wendy.

Excited, Emma jumps into my arms. 'Didja bring me anything, Daddy?'

I hate to disappoint her, though she's beginning to get on my nerves. 'Sorry, honey. I wasn't there long enough to look for souvenirs. Next time I'll get you something…or maybe I'll take you with me!'

'Oh Daddy, that's great!' she says jumping down from my arms.

Wendy comes forward tentatively. I grab her and pull her into a big, long embrace. 'I missed you,' she says, kissing me. Her lips taste sour to me; they never did before.

'I missed you too,' I lie. 'Next time I'm taking the whole family out there with me.'

'That would be really, really nice, honey,' she says.

After taking my luggage upstairs and throwing it on the bed, I come back downstairs, touched to find Wendy has poured drinks for us. We make our way to the living room, where we sit and talk.

Wendy asks how the meeting went. I don't tell her about Susan.

I relate how the NMEX Media producer and writers want to change the plot, add subplots and characters, and how Susan and I had fought them on the possible changes. 'They did concede to send me drafts for my comments, but I don't know how successful I'll be. They own the rights, Wendy. It's theirs. I can see it now on the opening credits: *Based on the novel **Killing Time***. Based on! I guess I should be satisfied with $250,000, but I'm not!'

'That's just terrible! But you're right. It's out of your hands now.'

'When I finish this next book and it's published, AND when a movie company wants to buy the rights, I'm going to make sure my contract stipulates that I approve the script!'

The look on Wendy's face tells me she's not pleased with my plans. I don't give a rip what she thinks.

'Yes sir, I'll have complete control,' I say, stabbing the air with an index finger.

Irritated before by the business end of my success, I'm glad I had asked Wendy, now unemployed and at home, to handle all the financial and secretarial matters relating to my novel. The book will certainly earn out the $600,000 advance and start bringing in royalties after it's published.

The first printing of the paperback has been scheduled, should hit the market three months after the hardcover is published, and start selling out immediately. NMEX Media is happy, Susan is happy, and I'm happy. More than that; hell, I'm over the moon!

217

Requests for interviews continue to come in, which I continue to reject. The only business item I'll pay attention to now is the film adaptation.

Over the course of three weeks, I receive drafts of the script—with copies to Susan—and I don't like them. I discuss my responses with Susan and send in my criticism. Judging from the subsequent versions of the script, my comments have been largely ignored.

The time, the mental and emotional energy devoted to reviewing the script, annoy me and keep me from returning to my second book. They wore me down, finally. I tell Susan via email to just accept the script and let the writers mangle my story whatever way they want. I must return to my work. She agrees and is probably relieved I have given up.

I have shown no interest in intimacy with Wendy since she moved back in, and I've become more distant from her ever since my return from Albuquerque. I should at least give the appearance of caring, though. So I've taken baby steps toward renewing intimacy with her in recent days. I've responded to brief hugs and kisses, but nothing more. I must keep her happy somehow because she takes care of business for me.

Not like the old ways of taking care of business for me. That time is in the past.

I've also begun to withdraw from Sophie and Emma. I am seeing them in a new light. Especially Sophie, who is showing early signs of puberty and annoying the hell out of Wendy and me anyway.

And Emma's cloying behavior irritates me more and more. I can see clearly now what I never saw before. Both of my daughters are really brats. They and Wendy get in the way of my craft.

One morning in early February, after breakfast and after the girls have left for a half day of school because of teacher in-service training, I call out to Wendy, 'If you need me, I'm going upstairs to the office.' Once I get

218

there, I call out again, louder to make sure she knows where I am.

Settling myself in my office chair, I have been impatient to return to writing and now feel the urge again. I reread the entire story first. The plot pleases me, but all the previous angry emotions resurface as I read, compounded by the frustrations of Albuquerque and the night spent with Susan.

I refill Kat, anxious to resume writing and describe the violent climax.

Chapter 48
Wendy

A loud, strange, almost inhuman grunt echoes throughout the house. I've been in the laundry room and at first couldn't comprehend what I heard. Those sounds are coming from the office upstairs. When it happens again, I recognize Miles's voice.

My stomach flops. He's started writing again.

Will he be able to control himself, or will the process—the *pen*—control him? He promised he would behave better. But these outbursts sound like the old, crazed Miles.

The girls arrive home shortly after noon, due to a half day of school for teacher meetings, chilled by their walk home from the bus stop. I make a hot lunch for a cold day.

I call upstairs, 'Miles? C'mon down for lunch. Sophie and Emma are home. I've made grilled cheese sandwiches and tomato basil soup. Your favorites!'

No response.

I march upstairs, frosty with irritation. 'Miles? Miles, did you hear me? Lunch is ready.' I walk down the hall toward the office. Passing through the doorway to the office, I take in the sight of Miles sitting bolt upright in his chair, head turned to the left where the handwritten manuscript rests on the paper stand, typing faster than I think is humanly possible. I cross the space and say in an even tone, 'Miles, lunch is ready.' I'm careful not to touch him and shock him out of what looks like a trance.

I repeat myself, and Miles snaps out of his reverie and stops. He turns to see me, aware of me for the first time, looking almost as if he had never met me.

'Sorry,' he says, 'I'm almost finished with this page. I'll be down after I finish. I promise.'

'Fine,' I say. 'We'll see you down there soon. Hurry before the soup gets cold.' I pass out of the office and go back downstairs to wait on his arrival.

True to his word, Miles comes downstairs two minutes later and joins us for lunch. 'Tomato basil soup and grilled cheese sandwich, my favorites. Thanks!'

Rolling my eyes, I'm convinced he hadn't heard me before.

I fear the future of his work on this second novel.

Later that day, the national television news breaks in with a special report. Tony Santoro, who allegedly murdered his wife Cindy several months earlier and was the prime suspect in the murder of Dr. Mark Torres, had been on the run since the killings. He was pulled over by a state trooper on Interstate 70 just west of Denver. The trooper had recognized his truck and license plate. As Trooper Brian Richards approached the vehicle with his service pistol out, Santoro grabbed his own gun and shot the trooper in the chest. Before going down, Richards fired, blowing off the side of Santoro's face before Tony could get off another round. Both the officer and Santoro died at the scene.

Shown on the news are a mug shot of Tony from a prior arrest and archived photos of Cindy Santoro, Mark Torres, and—Oh, great! Just great!—Wendy Campbell, as the torrid affair is rehashed.

I'm mortified, but fortunately, Miles has gone back up to the office, and the girls are out and about at their friends' houses. Even though this incident closes the book on the murder investigation, consequences of my infidelity will renew my shame in the news.

Will I ever be able to outlive it?

Chapter 49
Miles

I am nearly finished typing when I receive an email notification from Susan. She's reached out to check on me and share updates from NMEX Media's producers and writers.

She writes:

The screenwriters at NMEX are gearing up to send another draft but have flagged a potential issue. The studio has scouted filming locations. That is exciting news, as it shows they are progressing.

There are several historic homes in Albuquerque that would do for your book. However, the owners contacted have refused access because of concerns about security and disruptions during filming.

That's bad news. So the film company will shoot interiors on a sound stage there.

Now here's a potential problem: They're exploring the option of filming exteriors in Southwestern adobe-style neighborhoods while remaining in Albuquerque. This to them would be ideal, as shifting filming to another city with suitable historic homes would be too expensive.

Not if I have anything to say about that! Immediately I reply to Susan:

No way, Jose! (Sorry, is that racist?)

They're doing enough to ruin the story as it is, but now they want to change the settings? Would they have wanted to change the location of **The Amityville Horror** *to the Southwest and make the house adobe style? They probably will want to change the style of the clock, too.*

No! No! No!

Stop them!

I press **Send**.

Within five minutes my cell phone rings.

It's Susan. 'Hey there, Miles. I thought it better to call you about this. I agree with you, fully. You draw such vivid word pictures of the house and neighborhood that to change them would change the story. I just want you to know that.'

I am relieved to hear this. 'Thanks Susan. I didn't know where you stood on this. What chance do we have of sticking to our guns?'

'Maybe we can convince them of the importance of older East Coast, or better because closer, Midwest cities like Chicago, Cincinnati, or St. Louis for exteriors. Maybe even rent an older home in one of those cities for interiors. Southwestern adobe just won't do.' She suggests a conference call or Zoom session with Karen at NMEX Media to discuss this situation, to which I readily agree.

'We have to stop this shit right now!' I tell her.

Susan will notify me of the call when it's scheduled. Before hanging up, she adds, 'Once again, Miles, I'm sorry about that incident in the hotel. Really sorry. I—'

'You don't need to apologize again, Susan. I'm sorry, too. It's all in the past. Everything's all right. Just keep me posted about negotiations. I look forward to reading the next draft. Let me know when you've set up the conference call.'

We say our goodbyes.

After disconnecting, I turn to the screen and see that I have received another email.

It's not from Susan. It's from Novelist69@ProtonMail.com. Normally I would delete an unrecognizable email address, thinking it's spam, but the username and email provider intrigue me. Vacillating for a few seconds, I say 'What the hell?' and open the email. It's probably spam, though.

It comes up on screen:

Hello Miles Campbell.

You don't know me, but I was able to find you're email address by searching the internet. It's easy to find information if you know where to look! I hope you don't mind.

I read a pre-release reveiw of your frist novel **Killing Time** *and really, really look forward to reading it. Outstanding! It sounds like a killer of a story, pardon the pun! I have also read everything published about you and have listened to your interveiw on NPR. I know you are a very private person, but I hope you will find my email flattering.*

I am a Author myself. Well, I would be a author if I could get published. Like you I have wrote a first novel, which has been rejected 47 times. Fourty-seven times! I have shown it to my freinds, and all of them say it's great, even brillient! They think it should be published. I haven't been able to even get a agent to look at it yet. I have been trying for 2 years to get **<u>someone</u>** *to at least reveiw it. So far, no luck.*

I have read that you got a agent on you're first try, and you're agent got you a book deal on her first try. <u>And</u> *you got a big advance and a movie deal. How did you do that? We're you lucky? What's you're secret? I am truely amazed!*

I wonder if you would take a look at my novel **The Room at the End of the Hall** *and tell me what you think. Maybe suggest improvements? I have attached it to this email for your convience. It's 631 pages, double-spaced, in Word. I would really appreciate you reading it for flow, not line by line. That would be too much. At least to start with. It shouldnt take that long to skim it.*

I congradulate you on your success as a "debut author." I hope you will find it in you're heart to help a fellow debut author.

Your's,
Arthur Schriftsteller

I finish reading, then reread the message.

Oh my God! Holy hell! What do I do about this? Do famous authors get such fan mail? Is this fan mail anyway? It's an appeal to serve as an unpaid editor. And the mistakes!

I ponder what to do about it, then decide the best thing to do is to ignore it. Maybe Arthur Schriftsteller has sent this out to a bunch of first-time authors, has cast a wide net.

I shouldn't encourage the young man. If I don't reply, maybe Mr. Schriftsteller would think he had the wrong email address.

Yes, that's what I'll do. I need to return to writing, anyway.

I pick up the story where I left off. I feel a surge radiating from Kat, and the narrative flows easily and speedily. Soon sweat breaks out on my brow, under my armpits, in the small of my back, and in the center of my chest. It is as if I had run two miles in 90-degree weather. Within minutes the sweat in the different parts of my body coalesces into one solid mass of moisture.

I write so fast that the words are almost unintelligible. I no longer control the process as I feel Kat moving my hand. Although I stare at the notebook page, I perceive nothing; I'm only dimly aware that I'm in some kind of a trance.

Two hours later the ink fades until the nib produces nothing. The spell breaks, and I resume consciousness. Fully aware that I'm soaked with sweat, I get out of my chair and go to the bedroom to rinse off and change clothes.

Having dried myself and put on a change of clothes, I go downstairs to get something to drink and to check in with Wendy and the girls, if they are home. The girls are gone, but I find Wendy in the home library, reading a novel. We exchange cordial pleasantries, then I share the news I received from Susan, and the strange email.

225

Wendy is as angry as I am about the locale. 'That's terrible! Can they do that? I hope they don't. I hope you and Susan prevail!'

After I tell her about Mr. Schriftsteller's email, she's even more astounded. 'The nerve of that guy! He doesn't sound all there. He also sounds jealous of your success. Don't respond; you'll just encourage him. Maybe he'll go away.'

'I hope so. I won't respond.'

I stay for a while to have a mid-afternoon snack and chat some more with Wendy. We go over our present situation. We are now set financially. We may trade our two older cars for new cars and maybe buy a larger house or build one to our specifications.

Then Wendy turns to me and coos seductively, 'Hey pardner, the girls are gone for the afternoon. You want some afternoon delight?'

Holy cow! What do I do about this bold invitation? I would love to, but a sequence of memories flashes through my mind, reminders of Wendy and Mark. How do I get out of this predicament? I answer, 'Thanks for the invite. Let me type up what I've written, and we'll see.'

I can tell that Wendy is disappointed. She doesn't know I can almost smell the stench of Mark wafting from her skin. I want nothing to do with her until that odor is gone.

I make sure that typing takes longer than Wendy expected. I don't finish until just after Sophie and Emma arrive back home.

So much for the afternoon delight, I sigh in relief. I'm not ready for it yet.

Chapter 50
Wendy

Will Miles retreat into addictive behavior again writing this new story? He's up there now tapping away, and it's getting closer to supper time. Perhaps I should let him tap away, as he's been pretty upset this afternoon.

First there's the movie studio issue with the screenplay and choice of locale for shooting scenes. Neither of those issues has gone the way he preferred, and I don't blame him. Then there's this new concern, this Arthur Schriftsteller email. I don't know what he can do about that.

But more important to me is his rejecting my offer of intimacy. How long will it take for him to get over my affair and forgive me? How long before he takes me in his arms and makes love to me again?

Well, I won't call him to dinner tonight. He will come when he's ready.

Miles surprises us by sitting down to eat with us at the usual time. He's in a good mood. 'I'm hungry,' he says. 'What's for dinner?'

For once we enjoy our time together, the girls chattering away about their day, even Sophie, who has become more reserved in recent weeks. I can guess why; I've seen the signs of puberty in Sophie.

I remember all too painfully when I passed into puberty and pulled away from my parents and especially from my older brother, who had terrorized me even before my breasts started to swell. When that happened, Jerry became a persistent pinching and poking machine. I hope Emma won't tease her older sister like my brother had teased me. However, if she does, in just a few short years it will be payback time. Sophie will get her revenge.

Seated directly across the table from Miles, I study his every move and every look. A wave of guilt washes over me.

When he lost his tenure-track position at the university I wasn't there to support him. I hadn't been there to support him even when he was still teaching full time. I had seen signs of disorganization, had seen more signs when each annual review cited his low student evaluations and his unpreparedness when his teaching was observed by his colleagues and his department chair.

He had published only one article in a regional academic journal and had presented only two papers at conferences. I knew what was expected of probationary faculty, having dealt with many new assistant professors across campus requesting interlibrary loans for their research. Miles had never requested any interlibrary loans.

What did I do to encourage him during those three years?

Precious little.

I was a full-time librarian and a full-time mother and only a part-time wife and lover. I resented him for failing to help me around the house.

I watched him drowning in inferiority, refusing to throw out a lifeline. When he had been "non-renewed" after his third-year review, I was upset with him but filled with self-loathing for not helping him.

I pulled even further away from him, more so after he had contracted to teach first-year writing online at three-to-four colleges a semester for little more than grad school teaching assistant pay.

Initially Miles had been contrite and saw his online teaching as penance, a purgatory to wash away all his professional sins. After three semesters of teaching 150 to 200 writing students a semester, he came to see online teaching as an Inferno. Sighing, he told me once— I remember it so clearly now, 'At the end of every semester, Wendy, I feel like Sisyphus in Hades rolling that boulder up to the top of the mountain, only to watch it roll all the way back down to the bottom, and then have to go get it to start the next semester's work all over again.'

I wish I had bitten my tongue then, but instead I pointed my finger at him and said he brought it all on himself. He wouldn't have two hundred writing students a semester if he had done what he should have done. Yes, I wish I had bitten my tongue, as I drove him further away.

Discovering that old grad-school manuscript had led to a way out of his Hell. Though he'd paid a heavy price for it, driving me away and into the arms of another man (yes, that's right, Wendy, blame it all on him!). What a colossal mess, and what a way it ended.

I was horrified that Mark was murdered...and Cindy, and I was shocked at Tony's death later.

I still feel aroused when I remember Mark's touch. Shame on me!

But now the family is on the mend. The girls and I are back, no harm done, I hope, and Miles has become a famous and wealthy man, sure to grow wealthier as time passes.

A movie or series is in the works.

Yet two issues linger: lack of intimacy with Miles, and that damned pen—fueling his success, but at what cost? It's as if it's demon-possessed, and it seems to be possessing Miles.

Could that be possible?

'... Don't you think so, Wendy?' Miles has been chatting with the girls and has directed the conversation to me. His question snaps me out of my thoughts.

I have no clue what has been said, so I respond, 'I'm sorry, my mind was wandering. What were you talking about?' They've been discussing the inane local commercials on TV. Embarrassed, I add to the conversation, as I have plenty to say about them.

Speaking animatedly, I catch Miles studying me, just as I used to study him. I wonder if he suspects what I have been thinking.

Chapter 51
Miles

One Saturday morning a few days later, after a fine breakfast with Wendy and the girls, I announce, 'OK, guys, I'm going up to the office to work on my book. I plan to work until noon, then I'll come on down for lunch with you all.'

'OK, Daddy,' Emma says.

'OK, Dad,' Sophie adds.

Wendy smiles weakly. I don't think she approves. 'OK, dear. We'll have lunch ready around noon. Good luck writing.' She pecks me on the cheek and whispers, 'Please be careful.'

I can't figure out what she means by this—as if writing is a dangerous task—but I assure her that I will indeed be careful.

Once in the office, I sit down and turn on my laptop. I haven't checked my emails during the past few days. There might be one from Susan, maybe one from my publisher, maybe one from Karen at NMEX Media.

While waiting for the laptop to go through its opening routine, I pick up Kat, unscrew the body, pull out the refillable cartridge, and fill it.

Before reassembling Kat, I check my emails now that the slow laptop is ready to use. Well, what do you know? Several emails from grad school friends and far-off cousins belatedly wishing me and my family a Merry Christmas and Happy New Year.

Yeah... When will the requests for money start?

Nothing from Susan, who has been on vacation to Hawaii.

Just before I close my email account, a new email notification pops up.

It's from Novelist69@ProtonMail.

There's no subject line. Hmm. I open it and immediately wish I hadn't.

> Hello again, Miles Campbell. Arthur Schriftsteller here.

I haven't heard from you for a few days. I was hoping to hear from you acknowleging that you had recieved my previous email. It would have been a courtecy to just send a short note saying that you had read my email.

That's alright, though, I understand, "this ain't no never-never land." lol. Would you please respond to this email to say you have read both of them?

I wonder if you have looked at my novel yet. I am dying to here what you think of it. All I ask is that you read it in general, and may be point out 1 or 2 well-done passages and may be point out 1 or 2 passages that you think need to be improved. I will grately appreciate it. I will consider it an honor that a sucessful author like yourself has read my work.

All the best to you and your's,
Arthur Schriftsteller

'Oh my God! What do I do with this?' I shriek. How often during my short teaching career had I heard and especially read 'I worked really long and hard on this S.A. [**essay**, *damn it!*], so I don't understand this grade.' Some of them never learned that the word was *essay*, not *S.A.*

'Why have you been rejected 47 times? I'll tell you why, Arthur Schriftsteller. Because it's a piece of shit! I know that even before reading it, which I'm not going to do.'

But seriously, how do I let this guy down? How to do it in a kind way?

I'll ignore it. Maybe he'll fade away.

But first…

Intrigued, I look this guy up on Facebook. Also, the email provider ProtonMail. I search "Arthur Schriftsteller" on Facebook, but the search returns no hits for this name. However, I do get a hit for Arthur Schopenhauer, who works at "Schriftsteller und Kritiken."

This Arthur lives in Germany, and all his posts are in German. Having taken a year of German in grad school for one of my two foreign languages, I guess that *Kritiker* means 'critic' or 'criticism.' But I have no idea about *Schriftsteller*.

Fortunately I have a German-English paperback dictionary, which is sure to be a help.

And it is: it turns out that *Schriftsteller* is German for "writer." I know from teaching linguistics that surnames can derive from place names and occupations. Next I do a Google search for *Schriftsteller* as a surname.

No luck.

Arthur Schriftsteller.

Arthur Schriftsteller.

Arthur Schriftsteller,

AUTHOR Schriftsteller.

Author WRITER!

That's it! It's a pseudonym, an alias. The real person is hiding behind an alias. Why?

And what about ProtonMail? This is a new one on me. A Google search informs me that ProtonMail uses "end-to-end encryption and zero access encryption to secure emails." Its use has grown in recent years, as Dark Web denizens use it to communicate. It's an ultimate secure email server that apparently blocks all attempts to trace back information on a sender.

So this "Arthur Schriftsteller" uses an alias on a super secure email server to communicate with me.

What does this mean? What is he hiding? And will simply ignoring him make him go away?

That's what I will do for now. I will ignore him. I'm itching to get back to writing, and it's already 9:30, only two and a half hours till noon and lunch.

I set to work, first rereading the last two finished pages to pull up the context for continuing. I pick up Kat and start, feeling the surge beginning already.

Almost immediately I fall into a trance, eyes fixed on the page, Kat moving my hand, not watching except

232

to keep the words on the lines as I write, stopping only to turn the page over or to start a new page.

In my mind's eye, on my mind's stage, the characters I'm describing act out my play. My protagonist Michael Chambers hides in the bushes outside the home of Marty Martinez and sneaks to the bedroom window to observe his wife Wanda in Marty's arms standing at the foot of the bed.

Wanda is a fictional twin of Wendy, with shoulder-length blonde hair and a slim figure. Marty's arms are all over that figure. They begin to tear off each other's clothing, locked in a kiss. My heart rate races, and hot tears cloud my vision as I write this scene.

I would press the nib of the pen into the paper until it breaks, if it would let me. But Kat won't.

I stop. I can't write this scene any further. Kat wants to continue, but I lock my wrist and stiffen my fingers. These characters are fictional, I know, but they are all too real to me. The pen vibrates, my hand jerks side to side, like a Parkinson's patient's hand. Like a machine stuck trying to loosen itself from a blockage.

With great effort, I yelp and snap out of the trance, releasing the pen, throwing it off to the side. Some ink spots splash out of the nib onto the desk.

Incredibly, Kat rocks back and forth, moving toward me with each rocking motion.

Is this a hallucination? Is this real?

When it reaches within three inches of my hand, I grab it. Immediately I feel an electric shock move up my arm, up through my neck, into my skull, where it stimulates a frightening scene.

In my imagination I see a slowly swirling cloud like a spiral galaxy against an ebony background. It begins to move toward me, enlarging with each rotation. At the center is a black hole, and I'm being drawn to it—or it's drawing near to me.

Spinning around its center are the figures of Sophie, Emma, Wendy, and a man I guess must be Mark. Wendy and Mark are entwined in each other's

233

arms, locked in an eternal kiss. These figures enlarge as they draw near to me. They become giants as they pass my peripheral vision and disappear behind me.

I continue toward the black hole and soon am engulfed by absolute nothingness. I lose consciousness and fall forward, feeling my head thud on the pad of notebook paper.

I'm lost in the black hole.

'Miles? Miles, honey, wake up.' Wendy's voice sounds as if it's coming from the opening of a hole in the ground far above me, and I'm at the bottom hundreds of feet below. It echoes and re-echoes until I recognize it.

I begin to regain consciousness. '... happened?' I open my eyes and feel a dull pain in my forehead.

'Where am I?'

'Thank God, you're all right!' Wendy cries. 'You gave us quite a scare there.'

I raise my head and feel the pain now in my temples. Behind their mother, Sophie and Emma look on. Wendy caresses my forehead, feeling for a fever. 'I'm thankful that it's cool. Do you remember what happened before you fainted?'

'I wish I could remember. There was a deep dark blackness and a swirling cloud like some kind of galaxy with a black hole in the center. I was being drawn into it. That's all that I remember. And now I have a splitting headache.'

'You're still clutching your pen. Why don't you put it down and go to bed? I'll get you a couple of Excedrins,' Wendy says.

With some effort I open my fist and release Kat, which rolls off to the side and remains still.

'Wow, Dad, you really scared us,' Sophie says.

Emma comes forward and throws her arms around my neck. 'Yeah, Daddy, don't do that again! Please?'

I can't stand her little arms around my neck. 'I'll try not to, Emma. I'll be all right with a little rest.' Gently I remove her clutching arms.

Wendy helps me to bed, undresses me, gets my pills, and leaves me to rest, but sleep doesn't come immediately.

The vision of Mark and Wendy locked in each other's arms comes back to haunt me. Naked. Lips glued together. Spinning slowly around the black hole. Enthralled by the scene, I can't look away as their spinning stops, and they gaze at me. Their eyes pierce into my soul, silently taunting with mocking smirks.

Wouldn't you like to know what we have been doing? Wouldn't you, Miles?

Then everything fades to black, and I fall into a deep sleep.

Hours later I awaken from another troubling dream. My sleep has been anything but restful. Upon waking I remember only part of it, about being swallowed whole by some kind of undefined monster.

The bedside clock shows it's late in the afternoon. I must get up and rejoin the family, let them know that I'm all right.

I head downstairs, still groggy from my long nap, but at least I'm headache-free. I find Wendy and the girls at the dining room table working a jigsaw puzzle she had received for Christmas. The sight of Wendy chills my soul for some reason. Something about her is distasteful, as if she reeks a foul odor. But I can't identify the "something."

Wendy brightens as I enter the room. 'Oh, there you are, Miles! Are you feeling better now?'

'Yeah, Daddy,' adds Emma, who breaks from the table and jumps up to hug me. Keeping her from wrapping her arms around my neck, I put her down immediately. She seems hurt, but I don't care. 'Are you well now? I hope so!' she says.

'Yes, Emma, I'm fine now. Thanks for caring.'

'I care, too, Dad; we all care,' Sophie adds.

'Yes, honey, we all do,' Wendy says, and comes over to me to hug me. She puts her arms around me, but I don't hug her back. I know it was only a dream, but I can't, I just can't.

I head to the living room, plop into the easy chair, and grab the remote to find something mindless to watch. It doesn't take long. Meanwhile, the girls resume working on the jigsaw puzzle, and Wendy heads to the kitchen to start dinner.

As I sit in the chair, my phone pings with an email, but it's not the one I anticipated from Susan or NMEX Media. Instead it's from that Arthur Schriftsteller guy.

The brevity of the note makes it even more disturbing.

> Hello again. I havent heard back from you yet. Is everything alright at home? No illnesses, I hope. I have been well here, just waiting to here back from you. Your probably reading my book now, so I understand. I hope to here from you soon to learn what you think of my novel so far.
> RSVP
> Your's,
> Arthur Schriftsteller,
> Author hopeful

This must stop!

Typing on the tiny cell phone keyboard frustrates me, despite its ease for kids, so I go upstairs to the office laptop, to gently let "Arthur" down without bruising his ego.

Settling into my chair, I compose a reply I hope will be both gentle yet firm, signaling the end of our correspondence:

> Hello Arthur. I am writing to let you know that I have received your emails. I appreciate your kind words about **Killing Time**.
>
> I am also writing to let you know that I won't be reading your novel and commenting on it. I am in the process of writing my second novel, and that, as well as negotiations over the film rights, is taking up all of my time.
>
> Even though your novel has been rejected 47 times, did you know that you are in good company? Stephen King's **Carrie** was rejected 30

236

*times. John Grisham's **A Time to Kill** was rejected by 16 publishers before he found an agent, who rejected it too! **Gone with the Wind** was rejected 38 times. And the list goes on and on. So, the point is—don't give up!*

Friends aren't usually the best judges of good writing. Nor are spouses, if you are married. They might say what they think you want to hear. Book coaches or paid editors might be a good option, if you have the money. I've read about these kinds of professionals, but I think their fees are pretty steep. The fact that you have been rejected 47 times might indicate that you could use an independent professional editor.

You might also consider self-publishing. I bet there are good resources out there that would give you useful advice for self-publishing. I didn't have to consider this route or book coaches for my first try, so I was pretty lucky.

You don't need to reply to this email, as there's not any more advice that I could give you. I wish you all the best in your endeavor. If and when your novel is accepted for publication, please let me know.

Sincerely,

Miles Campbell

While I'm browsing my favorite sites on the laptop before dinner, a notification on my cell phone interrupts me while I'm on Facebook.

It's from Mr. Schriftsteller already:

*Well, thank you very much, Mr. Bigshot Author! No time to help a struggling writter? "Negotiations over the film rights" taking up all your time? **If and when** I get published? I will get published, but it looks like without your help. Book coach, professional editor? As if I need one. You desparage my friends; they read alot and they know what good writting is. Some of them have*

237

collage degrees. And self-publishing? That's a road for loosers. No way, Hose!

I wish you and Wendy and the girls good health and hope you all stay well and protected from harm.

Arthur

'What the hell?' I shout. 'How did "Arthur" get my family information?'

I read the email again to make sure I interpreted it correctly.

'What does *protected from harm* mean? Who would harm me? Harm us? Am I dealing with a lunatic?'

Yes, I am dealing with a lunatic. One with delusions of grandeur.

Wendy calls upstairs, interrupting my thoughts. 'Miles, dinner time!'

'OK, in a minute,' I call back.

Has this guy just threatened me? Can a reply wait until after dinner? My brain swirls with conflicting, confusing thoughts. My heart races. My blood pressure must be sky high.

How do I respond?

Wendy shouts again, 'Miles, we're waiting on you. The food is getting cold!'

'All right, all right, I'm coming!' To keep the peace I need to join the family.

Wendy has made gumbo and corn bread, perfect for this cold evening. Normally I would commend the chef as I drink my beer, but tonight I eat mechanically, distracted. I eat fast, skipping dessert and excusing myself from the table.

'What's up, Daddy?' Emma asks.

'There's something I've gotta do ASAP, Emma. Sorry, I have to go now.'

'What's a-sap?' Emma asks her mother as I leave the dining room.

Upstairs I sit at my laptop and type in a search: "how can people find personal information on the internet." I press Enter and within a half second

238

3,970,000,000 results come up. The first ten have all I need. I discover a popular site linked, an article on Huffpost about personal information on the internet.

I read through it and back out of the article, searching for a Find a Person site. I click on the link, and whoa! There it is, a place to find personal information on anyone anywhere. There's a box to type in a first and last name.

I type in "Miles Campbell" and wait while it searches. It finds 95 Miles Campbells in the U.S. I click on my state and city to find information on myself: Miles Campbell, 39. Wendy, 37; Sophie, 11; and Emma, 7; are listed as family members. I also see listed all the towns and cities that I've lived in before.

I go back to the HuffPost article to learn that there is nothing illegal about this information being collected, displayed, and even sold.

I had no idea. Wendy might know, as a reference librarian, but I didn't until just now.

So what is Arthur doing collecting public and personal information on me?

Soon Wendy comes upstairs to find out what I needed to do ASAP. She enters to find me leaning forward toward the laptop screen, squinting. When I become aware of her, I close the screen and turn toward her.

Laughing, Wendy says, 'Checking porn sites?'

She means it as a joke, but I don't receive it as one.

'Actually, no, Wendy. All I have to do is think of you and that Mark guy, and that's porn enough.' The smile on my face mocks.

Speechless, Wendy turns on her heels and leaves the room. First, I think she deserves it, but my conscience afflicts me almost immediately. Now why did I say that? Where did that remark come from? I had told her that I forgave her, but that it would take some time for me to forget. Apparently not enough time has passed.

I get up and follow her to the master bathroom, where she's washing her face, wiping away the tears. 'I'm sorry. I had no right to say that. I've been upset about the most recent emails I've been getting from that Arthur guy.' I didn't mean to share the most recent emails from Arthur, but I must redeem myself. 'Come back to the office. I want to show you what I've been dealing with.'

I open the laptop and show her the chain of emails and the people search website.

'Oh my goodness!' she says. 'No wonder you've been out of sorts today. Do you think this guy's final comment is innocent or intended as a threat?'

'I don't know. It's ambiguous to me. I need to find out to be sure.'

Wendy's brow furrows. 'I don't think you should write back. Don't encourage him any further. Or worse, don't provoke him.'

'I guess you're right. Anyway, I wanted to explain why I said what I did. And I wouldn't watch porn.'

Wendy accepts my explanation. 'OK, I understand. I'm sorry about that. But don't provoke him. He sounds insane.'

'OK, good. I won't. Now I would like to return to writing.'

She shoots me a concerned look. 'All right. I'll see you later.'

I settle back in my chair and go straight to the last email from Arthur. Something deep within my mind rises from the depths, something malicious and imperious. *No way you let this son of a bitch off lightly,* it says. I tried with kid gloves; that didn't work.

I type:

> *Dear Author Writer—yes, I know about your pseudonym and about ProtonMail. Did you think I was too stupid to figure that out? What are you hiding, Author?*
>
> *I tried to be kind in answering your emails, but it looks like you have a chip on your shoulder. What's the problem? That you spent a couple of*

years writing a novel that no one wants to accept? This happens all the time, as I showed you in my last email, and to better writers than you or me. Weren't you asking a lot from me with your 631-page masterpiece? I am not in the business of editing or reviewing other people's writing. I write, plain and simple. And I don't have time to read even a 6- or 63-page manuscript, much less 631.

I have given you options for feedback. I hope that you will use one of those. Some of the words in your last email show me that you could use help.

And why would you mention my family members and wish they would all be protected? From whom? From you?

I don't know what you meant by that, but I take it as a threat, one which I will not ignore. Perhaps I should share your email with our local police.

If you know what's good for you, you will stop harassing me.

Seek help, and not just editing help!

Please do not contact me again.

Miles Campbell

There, that should show him!

Before pressing **Send**, I review the message.

My conscience tells me to let this lie for a while and come back later to reconsider it before sending. I might regret sending it.

However, something deep down inside says to let *Mr. Author Writer* have it. He'll read it and stop out of fear of prosecution. Yes indeed, he will!

I press **Send**.

And immediately regret it.

Chapter 52
Wendy

After dinner I leave the house to go shopping for groceries, even though it's relatively late in the evening. The seven o'clock hour is actually a good time to shop, as the number of shoppers is low and there's more room to navigate the aisles.

Turning my cart to go down aisle 12, looking for canned soups, I see at the other end of the aisle Carolyn, my former colleague in the Reference Department at the university library, pushing her cart, browsing canned vegetables on the other side. Not looking forward to the customary catch-up, I consider turning around and leaving for the next aisle. I doubt that would do any good, however; we would probably meet in another aisle or at the registers.

I bet Carolyn has seen the news about Tony Santoro's death and the regurgitation of my shame. I bet she wants to talk about it.

Oh well, I might as well take my medicine now and get it over with.

We both push our carts toward each other. Carolyn notices me and speaks first, a little too energetically. 'Well, hello Wendy! Fancy meeting you here shopping in the evening! It's my favorite time, no crowds…. So, how are you doing?'

'Hi, Carolyn. Same here. I'm doing all right.'

'And Miles, and the girls?'

'Yes, yes, fine, all fine.'

'My, a lot has changed in the past few months. Miles has become famous and successful, and you've left the library for home. Everybody misses you, Linda especially.'

Yeah, I bet they do. 'Yes, things have certainly changed. It's nice to be missed. I kind of miss being a reference librarian, truth be told.'

And now she gets down to business, the real reason for this conversation. 'That was a nasty business with Mark. His murder, that is. Him and that woman. And her husband. So terrible. I'm glad you got out of that situation in time.'

Yeah, right, feigned concern and fishing for my reaction? 'Me too. I learned my lesson, and—'

Carolyn cuts me off. 'Did you hear the news on campus?'

'What news?'

'Well, it turns out that Dr. Mark Torres was doing a terrible job of teaching. Preparation, lectures, assignments, grading. The only thing he was good at was hitting on the coeds. He especially hit on the female non-trads. He started teaching the summer before the fall semester, picking up an unstaffed class. That's when he began to hit on women who were divorced, separated, or even married. Some of them on campus were close to their own "Me Too" stories before he, um, died. It was about to blow sky-high. So, you weren't the only one. And there are rumors that he did the same thing when he was in grad school.'

Well, that certainly makes sense. Mark was definitely a womanizer. But, my God, I didn't know it went that far back. 'No, I hadn't heard that,' I respond. 'I'm surprised the media didn't find out about that.'

Carolyn obviously enjoys reporting the campus gossip. 'It was all very hush-hush from the President's Office on down the line. He keeps bad news from leaving campus, you know. It may come out later, however.' She pauses, having run out of things to talk about. 'Anyway, I'm glad that we ran into each other, Wendy. And I'm glad that you're doing well. It was so good to see you again.'

'Me too. Tell Linda hi for me.'

'Will do. So long!' And off Carolyn goes down the aisle. She didn't take a single item off the shelves in this aisle. She probably planned this meeting to pass along the campus bombshell to me.

However, she did accomplish something else. Thanks for reminding me of my shame, Carolyn!

When I arrive home at 8:30, coming in through the garage door off the kitchen, I yell out, 'Miles? I'm home. Come help me with the groceries,' as I lay down one heavy bag on the counter.

No answer.

Coming back in with another two bags, I yell again for Miles to come help.

Again, no answer.

After two more trips bringing in the rest of the bags, I'm really steamed. Not even the girls have come down to help. 'Never mind. I can do it myself!'

I slam cans and frozen packages on the countertop as I unpack the bags and put away the groceries. After I finish, I march upstairs, fully intending to give Miles a piece of my mind. I stomp into the office and open my mouth to give him what for. But I am stunned by the sight of Miles sitting in front of the laptop and leaning toward it, staring, head in hands, reading something on screen.

His whole head is red. He's either raging angry or extremely embarrassed...or something else. I approach him and place my hands on his shoulders, peering over them to see what's on the screen.

'Miles, what's wrong? What are you reading?'

Miles shivers. 'I'm reading an email from Arthur. I don't know if I should be upset or scared.'

'Why is he writing again? Didn't you ignore his last one?'

'No, I'm afraid I didn't. I don't know what came over me, but I let him have it. Now I'm sorry I did.'

'Oh no, Miles, you didn't! Let me read it, please.'

'OK, OK, I have to get away from here anyway.' He gets up and leaves the office.

I sit down and read the email. There are no niceties to begin it.

It goes straight to the point:

Let me remind you, Mr. Bigshot Author: you don't know who I am. You don't know were I live. You don't know anything about me.

I know who you are. I know were you live. I know whose in your family. I know alot about you.

You will never know where or when I am in your area. But I will be, and soon. We will meet face to face to settle this.

Your's,

Arthur Schriftsteller

'Oh. My. God. What have you done, Miles? What have you done?' My heart thuds in my chest. I can't catch my breath. I feel faint.

The front door clicks shut, and I realize that Miles has left the house, leaving me to face this menacing email alone.

I've seen enough. I head downstairs to the living room, desperate to figure out how to handle this unsettling situation.

Sometime later, Miles comes in through the front door, chilled and cursing himself for going out without a jacket and gloves. He sees me sitting on the couch in the living room.

'Brrr!' he says through chattering teeth. 'It's cold out there!' He composes himself and asks, 'Well, what do you think, Wendy?'

'I think you've gone and done it now, Miles. I wish you hadn't sent that last email. Arthur has the advantage. How's he going to use it? Just to scare you, scare us…or more? We don't know who we're dealing with here.'

'I know. We're dealing with a jealous and insane person.'

Hmm, that could describe you, Miles. 'So, what do we do? What *can* we do?'

'We can start by reporting it to the police. They may not be able to do much, but maybe they'll patrol the neighborhood every night. I don't know.'

Miles calls the local police station but receives little sympathy and no assurances. Of course, the police can't do anything about an implied threat in an email. The best the desk sergeant can offer us is to schedule a car to patrol the neighborhood once or twice a night.

'Well, that was a lot of help,' Miles sneers, putting down the phone. 'Maybe I should buy a gun.'

'No way! I don't want a gun in the house, not with two girls around.' I also shudder as I think that with a crazy man—in this case, Miles—around the house, it isn't a good idea.

What if he goes off the rails, grabs the gun, and uses it on me or, God forbid, the girls?

'C'mon, Wendy, I can store it out of the way where they would never find it.'

'Nope, I'm sorry. It's a bad idea.'

'What if Arthur comes here, breaks in, planning to do something to me, or to you and the girls? He did mention all of us, about keeping safe.'

There should be other options. 'Maybe we can install an alarm system, or one of those video systems. We can probably find some things around the house to use for a weapon if we need to. Like a kitchen knife or a crowbar.'

'If he has a gun, what use is a knife or crowbar?'

'I don't know. I just know I don't want a gun in the house!'

Seeing that I am adamant, Miles drops the subject. 'OK, have it your way. I won't get one. But we may regret it.'

'Maybe.' I'm at a loss for a solution to this problem. But a gun is no solution. Discussion over.

Miles says, 'All right then, I'm going back to the office to write some more.'

'OK, I'll be in the library reading.' I hope that reading will settle me down.

I am worried. I wish that this thing with Arthur whatever-his-name fades away, that it's just saber-rattling.

And I also pray that Miles stops writing.
Please God, make him stop.

246

Chapter 53
Wendy

Two days later, Monday morning, I get out of bed and go downstairs to monitor breakfast and school preparations with the girls. They leave for the bus stop at the usual time.

I climb up the stairs to look in on Miles, who has had a restless night. He kicked me once and flopped around several times, even yelling out a couple of times. Maybe he'll tell me his dreams when he's awake.

I duck my head through the doorway and see that he's still asleep. At times like these I wish I still had a job so that I could leave the house and him to his own care. Maybe I should apply again at the university, if my sullied reputation has died down. I head back downstairs to make my breakfast.

While at the breakfast table sipping my coffee, I mull over my relationship with Miles...such as it is. Ever since I returned to the house, we haven't been intimate. We have been living almost like roommates for months. I miss his body. I miss his touch, his embrace, his exploring hands, his kisses, his nibbles. It has been a dry period for far too long.

I have served my sentence for my crime. Shouldn't I be released? Shouldn't we become husband and wife again? Maybe today I should try, maybe after lunch. Try to tempt him, like in the old days. It always worked then, sometimes with just a wink and a smile. It didn't work recently, though, when I suggested a quickie early one morning.

I have to be more aggressive. He used to like that. He may still.

I look at my reflection in the downstairs bathroom mirror, as Miles is lying in bed upstairs. I'm still attractive. I'm in the prime of my life at age 37, still in good physical condition. Mark certainly found me attractive and sexy. Why doesn't Miles anymore? I need to rekindle his desire, for both our sakes.

Later I'm in the dining room with bank statements spread out and the checkbook open. I've been reconciling the expenses and deposits the old way instead of using the laptop upstairs, leaving it free for Miles' work. However, I could buy another one, now that our financial situation has greatly improved.

Miles finally drags out of bed at 9:30 and scurries around upstairs. Soon he stumbles into the kitchen, sees me in the dining room and grunts, 'Good morning.'

I look up from the check record and reply, 'Good morning, sleeping beauty. How did you sleep?' If he gives me an honest answer, he might elaborate on his fretful night.

'Oh, all right, I guess. I didn't sleep all that great, but I got a lot of bed-time.'

I wish he had shared some of that bedtime with me. He turns from me and gets out his cereal and milk. 'Is there coffee?' he asks.

'No, I'm sorry. I didn't know when you would get up. I dumped the rest of it about half an hour ago.'

'Well, gee thanks,' he growls.

This is not the way to start the day. 'C'mon now,' I plead. 'You wouldn't have wanted burnt coffee. But I'll get up and make you a short pot.'

'Don't bother. I'll use the French press.'

I bite my tongue to stop escalating this into a full-blown argument. 'Again, I'm sorry. I guess I shouldn't have let you sleep in. I won't next time.' I return my attention to the bank statements.

Miles finishes his breakfast in a hurry and takes his half-drunk mug of coffee with him upstairs. 'Got some typing to do to start the day,' he announces.

'Miles,' I call out. 'Would you save some time for me this afternoon?

Reaching the landing above, Miles says, 'Sure. OK. I'm heading to the office to work now. See you at lunch.'

We will be alone in the house until the girls get back home from school. Sometime after lunch I'll make my move.

Later Miles comes down to the kitchen for lunch. I don't like that look on his face. Maybe he's brooding over something he's written. Then again, he may be fretting about this Arthur guy, who dwells in the shadows of anonymity. No matter, I'm going to take his mind off his worries after lunch. We'll have at least two hours before the girls get home.

He makes his lunch of a sandwich and chips while I make mine of a half slice of bread spread with crunchy peanut butter. While he eats, he avoids looking at me. He seems seriously preoccupied.

While he chews on a bite, I ask, 'What's on your mind, Miles?'

He takes his time to answer. 'I don't know. Maybe it's the movie studio and their stable of idiot writers. Maybe it's this Arthur guy. Maybe it's the point in the story where I am now. Maybe it's all of them.'

'I know the studio has upset you. Screw them! Maybe you should try to drop that issue. You don't have any control over it. And I think that Arthur guy is just blowing off steam. He's jealous and lacks talent, but he doesn't know it. However, I do feel better about a police patrol at night. And regarding your story, maybe I can help. I could read it and—'

'No! No!' he cries. 'Not while it's an incomplete first draft! Maybe after I complete it. Besides, you may not like what I've done, like you didn't with the first one.'

'I'm sorry about that. I misjudged it, obviously. I'll never doubt you again.'

'So don't look at it until after I've finished. OK?'

'Oh, all right.'

Now might be the time to plant the seed I've stored in my mind. 'After lunch there's something up in the master bathroom that needs fixing. I would like you to take a look at it and decide what to do about it.'

'Really? You know I need to write and type this afternoon. Can't it wait?'

'It's only going to get worse. Would you at least take a look? Then you can decide when to fix it.'

'What kind of problem is it?'

'Plumbing.'

'Plumbing? Then we should call a plumber.'

'I think you can fix this one. It won't require much skill. You have the tools to fix it.'

'All right, then. I'll have a look.'

Yes, you will. You'll get an eyeful.

Following lunch, I rush upstairs while Miles rinses dishes and loads them into the dishwasher, something that he has recently started to do again. I quickly undress down to my underwear and go into the bathroom. My reflection in the large mirror isn't displeasing, even after giving birth twice. My thighs and abs are toned from my Y-class workouts. Miles used to be pleased by my figure. I hope that he still is.

It's time to press the issue. Miles has a lot on his mind and needs a release, and I need to mend our separation, restore our relationship.

Our *plumbing* needs fixing.

Miles climbs the stairs. I'm getting excited. 'I'm in the bathroom!' I shout.

Entering the bathroom, he immediately looks at the bathtub. 'OK, where's the problem?' Then he notices me, standing there semi-nude. I take his hand and lead him out to the bedroom. 'Here's the problem that needs fixing,' I say, turning to face him, placing his hands on my hips. I'm nervous, hoping this attempt doesn't go awry.

It kind of feels like the first time, actually. I unfasten my bra and slide it off. Taking his right hand in my left, I place it on my left breast and rub it. The fire rises in his eyes as I move in to kiss him deeply. I pull away and remove his tee shirt.

Then I remove my panties, letting them slide to my feet and stepping out of them. I am naked and vulnerable now and want him naked too. I tug down on the waistband of his sweatpants and underwear and see that he is becoming ready. That's a good sign.

Suddenly Miles' face screws up into a scowl, and he picks me up and throws me onto the bed. 'You slut!' he says. 'You dirty, filthy whore! I'm going to teach you a lesson!'

Oh, we're going to play this game! We used to play it fifteen years ago before the kids came along but haven't in years. Turned on, I tease, 'Yes! Yes! Show me! Show me! Do me, do me hard! Teach me a lesson!'

Miles responds immediately, parting my legs. In he goes, forcefully, pushing hard against me. It hurts, but I'm game. I'll play along. His hands are all over me.

But soon play becomes brutality. The squeezing, the pinching, the biting; it hurts. It feels more like punishment. 'Ouch! That hurts! Gentler, gentler, please!'

My plea results in the opposite reaction. 'You whore! You slut! You want your plumbing fixed? Well, I'm going to fix it now, but good!' He slaps my face. He squeezes hard, he slaps me again and again.

I cry, 'Ow! Ow! Miles, you're hurting me! Quit it! This isn't fun at all!'

'Oh yeah?' Miles says through gritted teeth. He grabs my throat with both hands and begins to squeeze, squeezing harder, thumbs on my trachea, like he did many months before. 'I'll show you fun!' he growls in a hoarse voice I have never heard before. He's broken out in a sweat as he squeezes harder, thrusts harder.

I'm gasping for breath now. My throat is about to collapse under the pressure of his thumbs. I'm close to losing consciousness. Using all my remaining strength, I push his legs apart with my own legs and quickly knee him in the groin. Then again and again.

Miles cries out in pain and lets go of my neck, grabbing for his groin. He rolls off, falling off the bed and hitting the floor with a heavy thud. He continues to roll around, holding his groin and groaning.

251

I roll off the other side, choking and rubbing my neck. I quickly put on my underwear and rush around the bed to where Miles lies rolling around. 'You son of a bitch!' I croak. 'You nearly killed me!'

I rear back my right leg, preparing to kick him in the side, when I apprehend the terror in his eyes. His wide eyes no longer show the demonic hatred of just a few seconds ago. He's cringing, afraid I'm going to do him some serious harm. I'm struck by the scene of my naked husband lying on the rug holding his groin. This man almost killed me!

Against my better judgment I kneel by his side and caress his cheek. 'Miles, I had no choice. You were about to kill me.'

Through his groans, Miles replies, 'I did? I couldn't have. I don't remember doing that. Really? Something came over me, Wendy. I'm sorry.'

'What? You don't remember? What *did* come over you?'

Miles can't answer, as his pain is so intense, he can't talk any more.

Soon the pain subsides, and he struggles to get off the floor.

Thank God the girls are at school.

Puzzled, Miles puts on his clothes. He still doesn't understand what happened, what he tried to do. I watch him as he dresses.

I don't get it. Why does he suffer these flashes of violence when he's normally a gentle man? Will he do this again? He said he would never hurt me again. Can I ever trust him again?

These questions terrify me.

I walk off to the bathroom to wash my face and assess the damage.

Now clothed again in his tee shirt and sweatpants, Miles comes to the bathroom and notices for the first time the red area on my left cheek and the bruises on my neck. Still confused, he asks, 'Did I do that? Wendy, I am so—'

252

'Yes, you did!'

'…sorry. How could I have done that? That's not me, if I did.'

'You certainly did it. You became someone I've seen only two other times in the past few months, but never this violent. Something's wrong. You need help, Miles.'

This last remark doesn't sit well. 'No, I don't think so. I don't need to see a shrink, if that's what you mean.'

'There may be something wrong physically, though. Maybe—'

'I don't need to see a doctor either. I just won't let this happen again!'

'You told me before I moved back in that you would never be violent with me again. Do you have even an inkling about what sets you off? Would you know it when it happens? And if so, can you stop it before it—'

'I don't know. I don't know! Stop asking me questions I can't answer!' Miles storms out of the bedroom and heads down the hall to the office.

I wonder if what sets him off is in the office. Once before, when I attempted to throw away his pen, his freaking pen, he went ballistic. He's unreasonably attached to it.

Is it what he's writing? Or a combination of the two? When he's out of the office I'll read what he's typed. Maybe the clues are in it.

Chapter 54
Wendy

It's Tuesday afternoon, the day after that bizarre and deadly encounter with Miles. All I wanted to do was to bring us closer together again. Exorcise his demons. (There really must be a demon inside.) He would have killed me if I hadn't kneed him several times. I know it. After it was over, he claimed he didn't remember what he attempted to do. He was clearly out of his mind.

This afternoon Miles has been busy upstairs typing, writing, and typing some more for the past three hours, working through the arrival of Sophie and Emma home from school, right up to dinner time.

While I'm making dinner, Sophie comes to the kitchen, looking worried. 'Mom? Dad's in the office groaning, grunting, and talking to himself again. Couldn't you hear him down here? I couldn't concentrate in my room, and Emma went in—'

A scream interrupts Sophie and a hoarse 'Get the hell out of here!'

We can hear Emma run from the office crying, 'Oh Daddy! Daddy! Daddy!'

I drop what I'm doing. Sophie and I meet Emma at the bottom of the stairs.

Emma runs into my open arms, shaking and sobbing. 'I-I-I-just-just-wanted-wanted-to-s-, s-, say hello to Daddy. And he hit me!'

I try to comfort Emma, though I am steaming with anger. 'Did he? Did he really? Well, we'll just see about that!' I turn to Sophie. 'Sophie, take Emma to the living room and find something to watch on TV.'

Burning with rage, I mount the stairs to go up to confront Miles. I'm not sure what I'll find. Entering the office, I immediately go on the offensive. 'How dare you speak to your d—'

My words freeze when I take in the scene before me. Hearing me, Miles turns his head slowly until he's looking directly at me. Eyeballs rolled up, showing the whites, 'Get. out. of. here,' he says, in a cold and deadly, unrecognizable voice I have never heard before. It's two voices, his with an undertone of a hoarse female voice.

Shivering, I fear for my safety. Backing out of the office, I pull the door to, which makes a light snick.

What did I just witness? What did I just hear? It was not of this world.

My heart throbbing, I can barely catch my breath. I can't think of anything to do, except wait until Miles comes out of the office. Maybe by then he will have returned to normal, or close enough to normal for me to speak to him. But then, maybe not. If I had pressed him just now, I fear he might have done something to me. What's going on now with him? He's transforming into some kind of monster.

I head downstairs, shaken but trying to put on a calm front for the girls. I walk into the living room, where the girls are watching a cartoon. 'Girls,' I say, 'Daddy's busy now and in a strange mood. Emma, I know that if he were in his right mind, he wouldn't have hit you. I've decided to wait until after dinner to talk to him. Dinner will be ready in about a half hour.'

Emma shoots me a fearful look. *I know, Emma, I fear for us all.*

I head back to the kitchen to finish preparations.

Thirty minutes later, I ask the girls to come and set the table, which they do without complaining. 'Miles,' I call out. 'Dinner is ready. Come and get it!'

Soon echo the sounds of footsteps on the floor leading out of the office to the bathroom, and of water running in the sink. He must be washing up from sweating and who knows what else. Within five minutes Miles comes downstairs and joins us at the dining room table.

It's a subdued meal, both girls afraid to speak, me deep in thought, and Miles eating mechanically, thoughts apparently elsewhere. At least there's no remnant of his previous mood.

Emma will not even look at him.

When he's finished, he excuses himself, leaving his dishes at the table. He announces, 'I'm going back upstairs to work some more. I'm nearing the end, so don't interrupt.' He adds, 'Please.'

Soon a litany of grunts, groans, and inaudible speech resumes in the office. Determined not to interrupt him for any reason, the girls walk softly up to their rooms and quietly close their doors. I overhear Sophie talking to Emma, soothing her, whispering encouragement.

After I brush my teeth, I go back downstairs and curl up on the couch in the living room to read a book.

Surely Miles will be through by bedtime.

While I'm getting ready for bed, Miles comes into the bathroom, sullen and soaked with sweat. He'll need to shower before bedtime.

Trying to sound cheerful, I ask him, 'How did it go?'

'How did what go?' he mutters.

'Never mind,' I answer. 'Take your shower and come to bed.'

Although his manner worries me, I try not to show it. Best to let sleeping dogs lie. Literally. Tomorrow if I get a chance, I'll try again to talk to him.

Miles comes to bed twenty minutes later. The mattress gives to his weight, but instead of snuggling with me and kissing me good night, as he did recently, he settles in facing away and drops off to sleep.

Meanwhile I can't sleep. How could I? My mind races over his ugly treatment of Emma, Emma who idolizes her Daddy. Then over the demonic look in his eyes when he warned me to leave. The times in the past I found him soaked in sweat and urine, even with shit in his pants. There is no rational, natural explanation for Miles' changed behavior. Perhaps there's something in the manuscript that will throw light on the problem.

A few hours later, I raise my head and look at the digital clock on my bedside table. It's past 1:30. I'm certain that Miles is deeply asleep, so I sneak out of bed

256

and tiptoe out of the bedroom and down the hall to the office. Closing the door, I turn on the desk lamp and lift the cover of the laptop.

Maybe Miles keeps his handwritten manuscript in a drawer. But it would be easier to read if I could find it on the laptop.

Good news, the laptop is still running. There's a folder named **MC MSS** on the screen, probably short for Miles Campbell's Manuscripts. I open it and see four works, including **Killing Time** and one called **Betrayal**. The latest changes for **Betrayal** were made tonight, so this has to be what he has been working on for the past few weeks. I open **Betrayal**—it's a big file, so it takes a while. When it finally opens, I'm surprised to find 440 pages in Microsoft Word. How did Miles write so much in such a short time? I start reading, knowing I can't stay up all night.

Quickly I skim through the initial chapters. The story is about a writer struggling to succeed but facing constant rejection from agents and publishers. His wife isn't supportive and betrays him by having an affair because he's not attentive enough. The writer's named Michael, his wife's name is Wanda, and her lover's name is Marty. Interesting, he's a charming Hispanic guy.

Where did he get these ideas?

Yeah, right. I know.

Speeding through the pages, I'm two-thirds of the way through the manuscript, around page 293. In this part, Michael goes to Marty's house one morning at 8:00. He checks the neighborhood to make sure no one's around and knocks on the door. Marty opens it, and Michael pulls out a gun, forcing his way in, accusing Marty of having an affair with his wife. Despite Marty's attempts to calm the situation, Michael shoots him in the groin, then in the chest, and finally in the head.

'Oh, my God!' I keep myself from screaming. Reading on, I discover there has been another woman involved with Marty who was killed by her jealous husband.

When did he write this?

My heart thudding, I close the laptop. Leaving the office, I turn off the light. I tip-toe back to bed, slinking beneath the covers. It's 4:00 AM.

Miles stirs, getting up to go to the bathroom. I've made it back in time. I don't think I'll sleep, but eventually I drift off.

Chapter 55
Wendy

Next morning, I force myself out of bed to get the girls up and breakfasted. They both will leave the house for the bus stop at 7:30. Fortunately they are already dressed, eating their breakfast with plenty of time to brush their teeth and get their things ready. I think they must be hurrying to leave the house before Miles awakens.

Before leaving, Emma turns to me and asks, 'Do you think Daddy will ever be all right again? I'm so scared of him now!'

'I'm so sorry, Emma. He needs some help. We'll see about that today after he gets up.'

Sophie shudders and sighs. 'I hope he can get help. I want my Daddy back.'

I take a breath and let it out slowly, 'I hope so, too, dear. I hope so, too.' I hug both girls and assure them all will be fine. They leave for the bus stop, Sophie urging Emma to hurry.

Soon Miles gets out of bed, rummages around upstairs, and comes downstairs dressed in his jogging gear. It is unseasonably warm for early February—40 degrees already. He passes by on his way to the kitchen, mumbling 'Good morning' to me. I want to broach the subject of psychiatric help, but this isn't the right time.

I follow him into the kitchen, where he pours a glass of orange juice and chugs it down. He puts down the glass and states, 'I'm going for a run. I should be back in about forty-five minutes. I'll eat breakfast after I get back.'

Perfect. 'All right, dear,' I say. 'When you get back, I would like to talk to you about something.'

His eyebrows knit, as if he's wondering if there's a hidden agenda. Which of course there is. 'I hope it's a short conversation,' he says. 'I'm close to the end of the story.'

'Yes, it'll be short.'

'OK, good. See you later.' He heads to the front door, passing close to me. I reach out to touch his shoulder, but he doesn't respond.

I have time now to continue reading Miles' manuscript. I head upstairs to the office, seat myself and open the laptop, seeing the manuscript up and ready to read. I have less than forty-five minutes until he gets back, so I start skimming at page 294. As I skim, an eerie familiarity creeps off the page. It's not only the story of a fictional struggling writer but also the story of *Miles* as a struggling writer. The names have been changed, but only slightly. "Michael's" family has two daughters, who, incidentally, are characterized as brats. Though Miles claims not to remember his previous acts of brutality and rage, they appear in the story, almost exactly as they occurred.

Except that scene in which his protagonist Michael (Miles?) kills Marty (Mark?). That never occurred in real life.

Or did it?

The story of Miles' success is also fictionalized, including his agent, named Sarah. The film studio—with a fictional name—is in it, located in Los Angeles. There's a scene involving the agent coming on to Michael, who rebuffs her initially, then succumbs to her persistence.

Oh my! Really? Did he really do this with Susan, or only *wish* that he did?

During a kinky sex scene later at home with Wanda, Michael goes insane and nearly chokes her to death.

Oh my God, when did he write this? Before or after he assaulted me? I skip on ahead, aware that time is passing.

Miles will be home any minute, so I had better finish soon. What about the jealous would-be author? Is he in this story? What happens with Michael's nagging wife Wanda and their two naughty daughters? Quickly, I search for "Wanda," but there are so many repetitions that the computer can't show them all. So I scroll through the pages myself.

Eventually, on page 397, I discover something shocking: Wanda has been having another affair, and Michael learns about it.

What a demented mind!

This is not the work of the mild-mannered uxorious husband and adored father. Did success do this to him? No, it's deeper than that.

Where did these ideas come from? Has a repressed maniac dwelt beneath the surface all these years? Like in that line from Harry Chapin's song long ago: 'There's a wild-man wizard, he's hiding in me, illuminating my mind.'

No, it's been just since the last few months, since…since August of last year. He's not himself, and I fear for our lives.

What has caused this change? What caused him to assault me several times? What caused him to hit poor sweet Emma, the apple of his eye? What has taken control of him?

Something's wrong with Miles. Something *evil* is hiding in him.

The pen. That damned pen! Of course!

Why hadn't I understood this all along? Miles' obsession with it, his rage when I hid it before. His brutality. Yes, this has to be the cause of Miles' changed personality.

There is only one thing to do: the pen must be destroyed.

I close the laptop, and I hear the front door open. Miles is home, earlier than I expected.

I grab the pen off the desk, put it in my sweatpants pocket, and go downstairs to greet him. 'Did you have a good run?' I ask.

'Yeah,' he replies. 'It felt good to start the day. Whew! I'm sweaty despite the cool weather.' He's on his way to the stairs when suddenly he stops and turns his head slowly from side to side. 'Do you hear that? Do you hear it?'

'Hear what?'

'It sounds like white noise on low volume. Is Alexa still on playing white noise?'

'No, it's off.'

'So, you can't hear it?'

'No, I'm sorry. Maybe it's something like tinnitus in your ears?'

'I don't think so.'

'Maybe it's a result of your run in the morning air.'

'Maybe. I'm going to take a shower. Maybe washing my ears will help. At least I hope so. It's annoying.'

Miles steps into the shower upstairs. Now I become aware of a vibration and a low buzzing sound coming from my sweatpants pocket. It must be what Miles heard.

It's the pen!

Fishing it out, I hold it up to inspect it. 'What is up with you?' I snap. Clutching it tighter, I put it back in the pocket, where it starts to feel warm. Whatever is with the pen, it's going to stop in a few minutes.

I know what needs to be done.

While Miles is in the shower, I plan to continue reading the manuscript. Sneaking back into the office, I open the laptop to quickly scan more of the end of Miles' story. I have only about five minutes, so I read the last four finished pages: 437-440.

Oh, my God! What have I just read? I have to do something and do it fast. Jumping up, I knock over the chair and fall to the floor myself. The shower stops running. Miles must have heard. Standing up, I head to the door, trying to calm myself. As I leave the office, Miles comes out of the bedroom, wearing only sweatpants. 'Wow!' I say through frayed nerves. 'That was a quick shower. No rush, though. I'll make some eggs and toast for you.'

As I make my way down the stairs, Miles heads for the office.

A few seconds later he bellows something unintelligible, then he screams, 'No! No, you've read it! Where's my pen? You've got my Kat! What're you going to do with it?'

Miles runs out of the office for the stairs, and now, fearful for my life, I race through the kitchen for the door to the garage. Unlocking and pushing it open, I reach my hand up to press the garage door opener, but I miss it a couple of times. I need daylight for what I intend to do.

Where is the damned button?

I find the button and press it. I must wait for its slow rise to head height because the trunk of the car is right up against the door. As I scramble around the rear between the two cars to get to the workbench, Miles reaches the garage door.

He screams again, 'What the hell do you think you're doing?'

I run between the two cars and bump into a rear-view mirror. Man, that hurts. 'I'm doing what should have been done a long time ago!' I yell.

I reach the workbench at the front of the garage and pull a hammer off its hanger. Thrusting my hand in my sweatpants pocket to grab the pen, I find it is jammed in sideways and won't come out.

'C'mon, c'mon!' I cry. Meanwhile, Miles has almost made it around the first car.

Freeing the pen, I slam it on the workbench surface. It's burning hot now. I grab the hammer and raise it over my head.

Miles shouts, 'Stop, Wendy! I swear I'll shoot you if you bring that hammer down!'

'What? You don't have a gun!' I turn to face him to see that he's indeed pointing a pistol at me.

In a deep, otherworldly double voice, tinged with that female undertone again, he says, 'Oh yes, I do, Wendy. I've had it for months. I used it once, then I hid it, just in case I needed to use it again. Like now!'

What? 'Wait a minute! When did you get it? When did you use it?'

I have to keep him talking.

He smiles and shakes his head. 'When did I use it? Don't you know, Wendy? Can't you guess? C'mon, Wendy, guess now!' He makes his way around the car and steps into the open space, facing me now, the gun now pointing to the garage floor.

'Did you…did you kill Mark? Oh no, Miles, that can't be. Say you didn't!'

He grins. 'I found out where Dr. Mark Torres lived after you left me that night, Wendy. You can find anything on the internet. I drove there early the next morning. It wasn't far. I planned to kill him and you, and the girls, too. I hid nearby and saw everything—another woman came and went, then you and the girls left. I couldn't shoot you out on the street, so I waited in the car until you left. I would deal with you later. Then I went to that professor's door. I had a gun, so I forced myself inside. I made him admit he was with you before I shot him.'

'I shot that Dr. Torres, Wendy. First in the crotch, then in his chest, and finally in his head. Just like I wrote in my book. Did you read that part? I'm pleased that the other woman's husband killed her and vanished. That took the heat off me. Then he was killed just recently. Yes, I heard that! Bad for him; good for me. Dead, he couldn't prove he didn't kill Torres. So, I got away with that. Now I all I need to do is to find some way to get away with what I'm going to do to you and the girls.'

Oh, my God, the girls will be home in a couple of hours, and I have to keep him talking, keep him from pulling the trigger. 'I'm sorry, Miles. The Miles I knew wouldn't act like this. It's like someone or something else has taken over your mind. Who, or what, is it, Miles?'

Miles cracks a wicked smile. 'I know what you're trying to do, Wendy. You want to keep me talking, to forestall the inevitable. Well, it's not going to work, my dear. It's all over for you now.' He cocks the hammer on his pistol and straightens his arm. He's going to shoot me!

Let him shoot me, I'm going to destroy that pen! Screaming, I turn to the worktable and bring the hammer down with all my might, smashing the pen to bits. Black ink squirts everywhere, plastic pieces flying through the air.

Miles, or whatever is in him, didn't expect this. Stunned and taken aback as if he has been hit by a strong wind gust, he recovers and readies himself to pull the trigger.

Suddenly a car careens into our driveway, screeching to a halt. The driver jumps out of it and raises himself up. He screams, 'I've found you, Miles Campbell, you selfish bastard!'

Miles turns around to see a young man, thin and gangly, long greasy black hair drooping down to his shoulders, framing his long horse face. He's wearing an oversized brown sweatshirt that hangs down to his thighs, covering his faded and torn jeans. He's also pointing a small handgun at Miles.

Miles squares himself and snarls, 'Just who the hell are you?'

The young man stops and spreads his legs slightly apart, a two-hand grip on his pistol, pointing to the ground. This looks like an Old West gunfight.

'Don't you recognize me? I'm your email buddy, your Arthur Schriftsteller. You know, the writer you refused to help. I warned you about what could happen, but you didn't listen. No, you were too important to help a struggling writer. Too bad we're meeting like this, just this one time, here at the end of our relationship. So, yeah, hello, and **goodbye**!' He raises and points his pistol at Miles.

Miles lifts his pistol and aims. 'Yeah, well, this is so long to you, *buddy*!' he sneers. They fire simultaneously. One bullet hits Arthur, and two bullets hit Miles, one in his midsection and one in his gun hand, the pistol flying out of his grip. He collapses to the garage floor, clutching his side, blood oozing from his side and his injured hand.

I've been transfixed by this bizarre scene before me. I come to my senses and rush to Miles, dropping to the floor, taking his head in my arms. 'You've killed him!' I shout at the intruder, who's lying on the driveway near the garage entrance. 'You've killed him!'

Now I take in the scene out there in the driveway. Arthur lies on his back, close to the front of his car, holding his neck with one hand, trying to stop the flow of blood, which is gushing through the spaces between the fingers of his hand.

He tries to speak, but he gurgles unintelligible sounds. Blood streams from the side of his mouth to the concrete, spreading into a scarlet pool. Then the gurgling stops, and Arthur's hand slides down to the floor.

He's dead. I should be sorry, but I'm not. He came to kill Miles.

I return my attention to Miles, whose shattered hand and right side are bleeding. When he groans, I realize he's not dead. Having nothing else nearby, I remove my sweatpants and use them to stop the blood flowing from his side. My legs bare, it's too chilly out here to be in my underwear. I'm afraid to leave him, but I need to call an ambulance, or he'll die right here.

I lay his head down gently and plead, 'Don't die on me, Miles. I'm going to call 9-1-1. Don't die!' Placing Miles' good left hand on the sweatpants, I know he probably won't be able to apply enough pressure to stop the bleeding. But it's got to be better than nothing.

I get up to call an ambulance. I have to step close to Arthur's body, avoid the pool of blood that's spreading on the concrete beside him. I'm surprised that no one in the neighborhood has come outside to witness the spectacle. Or to help.

Soon after the ambulance left to take Miles to the hospital, the police arrived and unrolled yellow tape around the crime scene where Arthur Schriftsteller's body lay. An African American detective who introduced herself as Kadesha Robinson interviewed me. I really wanted to go with Miles to the hospital, but she detained me for a few minutes to ask some questions.

I didn't tell her all of the story, excluding Miles' intent to kill me and the girls. It was a challenge to explain how Miles got to the garage with a gun before Arthur showed up. I explained that I was in the garage looking for a tool when Arthur arrived and began behaving oddly. I screamed for Miles to come out, and he arrived with his gun to protect me. Turned out Arthur wasn't interested in me at all, I told her: he wanted to confront Miles.

I hope Detective Robinson bought my story.

After a thorough investigation of Arthur's body and the bloody scene, Robinson released his body to the medical examiner. She called a tow truck to take Arthur's car off to be examined for evidence. As she left, she thanked me, saying, 'I'll be in touch sometime soon to interview Miles when he's recovered enough to talk. Probably tomorrow morning.'

'Sure,' I respond, barely controlling my nerves.

I need to see Miles first to coach him on the version to tell the police before Detective Robinson gets to him. He won't remember what he did, so I need to *tell* him what he did, what to report to Detective Robinson, to protect himself and the family. I'll need to drive to the hospital soon. I should have time enough to go and come back before the girls get home from school.

I don't have time to clean the bloody mess from the driveway, so I drive to the hospital. There I learn Miles is in surgery.

An hour later, Dr. Subramanian, one of the surgeons, comes out to report on Miles' condition. 'Fortunately, the bullet missed vital organs and lodged in his right side. He'll be fine, but I'm afraid he's lost two fingers on his right hand from the other bullet wound. There may be nerve damage. The hand surgeon will be out to tell you more about that.'

This is better news than I expected. He's going to be fine after he heals. 'Thank you, Doctor. Can I see him?'

'Once he's in the recovery room, sure.' He squeezes my hand and leaves.

A few minutes later, Dr. Martin Kraemer, the hand surgeon, comes out to speak with me. He repeats what Dr. Subramanian had reported, then adds, 'I'm afraid your husband will lose some functions of his right hand. For example, holding objects in that hand will be difficult, if not impossible, at least in the short term. I would like to see him soon to discuss his prognosis and possible future surgeries.'

I thank the doctor, who leaves the room.

Ironic, isn't it? His writing hand.

Sitting in the recovery room by his side, I wait for Miles to come out of the anesthesia. Once he's able to think, I grill him for what he remembers. Fortunately he doesn't remember anything from the upstairs office until here in the recovery room. I explain my whitewashed version of the story, which seems to satisfy him.

'That's some story!' he replies.

I wonder if Miles was planning to write this incident into his new story, or if it's already there. I need to check on that after I get home. His subconscious—or demonic influence—may write the real story. I can't let the investigators see it if they impound his laptop.

Before I leave Miles, I repeat my edited version of the incident to him several times and ask him to tell it back to me verbatim. It's frustrating for him to remember details in his foggy state of mind, but it has to be the tale that he tells Detective Robinson when he's interviewed.

I arrive home exhausted, totally worn out by the afternoon's events. My husband attempted to kill me, he was shot and wounded by a crazed nutcase, who was killed by Miles, a detective questioned me about the incident, and I worked hard mentally to leave out some incriminating details to protect Miles and me. I don't know how successful I was telling those little white lies, but

Detective Robinson didn't challenge me on my story. Maybe she was satisfied.

I collapse on the couch, wanting to sink into the cushions. Soon the neighbors who work will come home, see the crime tape, and come over to ask me about it. I am in no mood for that. I won't answer the door; I need to chill out.

Chill time is over all too soon: in a few minutes the girls arrive home from school, freaked out by the crime scene tape and the blood stains on the driveway. Rushing through the front door, Sophie screeches, 'Mom, where are you? What happened here? Is that blood in the driveway?'

Trailing behind her, Emma cries, 'Was anybody hurt? Where's Daddy?'

In the living room, I'm a puddle of flaccid muscles. I haven't had time to rehearse what I'm going to say, but here goes: 'Girls, take off your coats and come here to the living room. I'll tell you, but don't be afraid. Everything's all right now.'

As they rush into the living room, I struggle to raise myself up to a sitting position. I explain to them what happened, leaving out the part where their loving Daddy tried to kill me. And that their Daddy may not be their Daddy anymore. We will wait and see on that, after he comes home from the hospital.

'Daddy could have been killed!' Emma sobs, tears streaming down her cheeks like rain on a window pane. 'He's in the hospital? Can we see him? Can we go now?'

'No,' I answer, 'not today. He's in pain, and besides, children aren't allowed in the recovery room. But maybe he'll come home tomorrow and be well enough for you to see him.'

'They won't let kids in, really?' Sophie asks. 'That doesn't sound right.'

'Yeah, Mommy, that's not right. We need to see Daddy!' Emma whines.

'Trust me, girls, the closest you would get is the waiting room way down the hall. You can see him after he's in a regular room, or after he comes home, maybe tomorrow.'

They attempt to argue, but I won't change my mind. I need to leave, and soon.

'Listen, girls,' I say with all the maternal authority I can muster, 'I need to go to the hospital now to talk to the doctors, and I need you, Sophie, to hold down the house while I'm gone. You're a big girl now. If the doorbell rings, it will probably be some nosy neighbors. Don't answer it. Would you do that for me?'

She says, 'Yes, Mom, I can do that,' obviously pleased to be given adult authority.

I leave for the hospital, hoping to see Miles admitted to a room. I want to go over the story he must tell Detective Robinson when she interviews him. Then I will come back home, comfort the girls, feed them, comfort them once more, and put them to bed. I plan to go to bed early myself, after a full glass of wine.

It's been a long, long day.

Chapter 56

Early the next morning, Detective Robinson pays Miles a visit to ask some questions about the incident. She's pleased that Wendy isn't there, as she wants Miles' unvarnished testimony. She gets out a small notebook to jot down Miles' answers.

Miles responds to Robinson's questions with Wendy's version, which seems to satisfy her. Something seems rehearsed about it, though. She will need to think about his story after she gets back to the station.

Before leaving, she asks him about his hand. 'What's the prognosis for your hand? Haven't you lost a couple of fingers?'

'Yes, that's what they tell me. It hurts like hell! It'll be awful hard to write with it like this.'

'Oh, I remember, you're that author they wrote about in the paper. I am so sorry to hear this.'

'Me more so,' he says. 'My livelihood depends on it. They tell me it will be hard to grip anything in my hand.' He lays his head back on the pillow and looks up at the ceiling.

She's found the opening for another question. 'So...you were holding your weapon with that hand at the time. Right?'

'Yes, though my memory is foggy.'

'And you were called to the garage by your wife after the gunman showed up?'

'I was.'

'Did you have the gun with you when you went out to the garage?'

'Yes, I guess so.'

'You guess so? How did you get the gun to the garage so fast after Wendy called to you? You had to go somewhere to fish it out, which takes time. The young man would have had the time to shoot Wendy before you got there.'

Miles racks his brain for what Wendy told him. 'Well, we knew that Arthur Schriftsteller—that's not his real name—had threatened us. It was stored in the kitchen, up high and behind some stuff. We expected this Arthur guy to show up any day. I can show you the emails. His last one made us think we were in danger. I heard Wendy scream for me, so I grabbed the gun and raced to the garage.'

'Yes, I would like to see those emails eventually to get the bigger picture. I'm just trying to get all the information I can, Mr. Campbell. Do you remember firing your weapon at Arthur?'

'I do remember that. Yes, I fired once. I remember raising it to aim at him, but he shot me first…twice, I guess. I got off my shot between the two.'

'So, you fired once.'

At that point Wendy walks through the door to the room, surprised to see Detective Robinson already there. She greets Robinson, who says, 'I was just finishing up interviewing Miles. He looks pretty good for what he's been through.'

Robinson shares with them what they learned about Arthur Schriftsteller since yesterday, opening her notebook. 'Turns out his name was Aaron Schreiber. He lived in Indianapolis, not that far from here. He didn't have a record, although he seems to have harassed some people, most of them writers, through emails. I think your story attracted and bothered him, from what we discovered. We don't know what he intended to do beyond killing you both, so it was fortunate that you had a gun when he arrived.'

Robinson closes her notebook and gets up to leave. 'Well,' she exhales, 'I'm so glad you aren't injured any more than you are, Mr. Campbell. And so glad you are both safe. Mr. Schreiber can't hurt you now.' She bids them goodbye and leaves the room.

Wendy watches Robinson leave, then turns and kisses Miles' cheek, settling herself into the bedside chair. 'Did you have a good visit with the detective?' she asks. 'Did she seem satisfied with your answers?'

'I think so.' He winces. 'My hand feels like it's on fire. Would you call the nurse and ask for some more morphine?'

'Sure, honey.'

Chapter 57
Wendy

Later in the day, Dr. Subramanian comes by to check on Miles and decides to release him to recover at home. He even jokes in a Monty Python voice, 'After all, it's only a flesh wound!' Miles smiles weakly. I doubt that he thinks it's a joking matter. Subramanian apologizes for the sick joke, then says, 'I think your wound will heal fully in a week or two. I'll write prescriptions for pain and the infection and set you up with an office visit in a couple of weeks.' He bids us goodbye.

Within seconds Dr. Kraemer comes in to check on Miles and discuss some surgical and prosthetic options for his hand. The prognosis doesn't sound very comforting. I can tell that Miles is distraught. Kraemer sets up an office visit and bids us goodbye and good luck.

A few minutes later a nurse comes in with instructions for managing recovery at home. She also informs us that she has sent a couple of prescriptions to our pharmacy.

Finally, an orderly arrives with a wheelchair to transport Miles to the exit. I go out to bring the car around.

I didn't know it would take such a procession of caregivers to be dismissed from the hospital.

Once at home, I help Miles upstairs to the bedroom to settle him in bed. The pain in his right side is growing. I drive to the pharmacy to pick up his prescriptions. Twenty minutes later I return with the prescriptions, a painkiller and an antibiotic for the infection.

After I give Miles his first dose of meds, he lies back and falls asleep. I hope he'll sleep for at least four hours. Plenty of time for me to do what needs to be done.

I'm going to read the story to the point where Miles stopped.

I enter the office and open the laptop. What I read makes my skin crawl. It matches perfectly what he said in the garage in his crazed state. His protagonist Michael kills his cheating, nagging wife. Miles has also written Arthur into the story as the jealous crazed fan Andrew, who shows up with a gun to kill Michael and the rest of the family. Michael gets the draw on Andrew and kills him instead.

How did he know what was going to happen before it happened? What was the source of these ideas? The pen? It's gone now, destroyed. It will have no hold over him any longer.

I wonder where his demented mind was headed next. I can guess, as only the daughters and the wife are still alive in the story. The story as written so far won't attract a publisher, as Michael is an evil protagonist. There has to be an acceptable resolution. The innocents must be saved!

However, a new worry disturbs me. If this fictional narrative falls into the hands of investigators, it might provide circumstantial evidence of Miles' murder of Mark and intent to kill me. I don't trust that Detective Robinson; she didn't appear to be completely satisfied with our narrative of the Arthur Schrifsteller incident. I thought she might be suspicious, even. So I can't leave this manuscript on his laptop. If Robinson comes back to finish her investigation and suspects Miles for any reason, she might confiscate the laptop and his handwritten manuscript.

I know what I have to do now: I need to eliminate all copies of his manuscript. *All* of them. I close the file and check the folder it's in for any copies or earlier versions. Seeing none, I delete the file.

There, that's done!

There's a thumb drive sticking out of the laptop, and sure enough, a copy of the file is on it. This I also delete.

There, that's done!

To complete the process, I search the entire computer for copies stored elsewhere. I can't find any more. I close the laptop and pick up the thick folder next to it with the handwritten pages in it. I skim through the pages to confirm that it is the manuscript of the second novel.

It is. I take it outside to the backyard fire pit, where I squirt charcoal lighter on the spread-out pages. I light the fire and watch hypnotized as the flames consume the pages, which turn from white to brown to black to gray while curling into delicate butterfly flakes that take flight in the breeze. Eventually all of Miles' second book literally vanishes into thin air.

There, that's the end of all of the possibly incriminating evidence. We should be safe now.

A few minutes later Sophie and Emma arrive home from school. I tell them that Daddy is home and resting upstairs.

Emma's eyes overflow with tears. 'Can I see him?'

I won't allow them to disturb their father so soon after coming home. 'Maybe tomorrow, when he's recovered some more. He's in a lot of pain now. But if you want to, you can go to the doorway and look in to see him. Just don't disturb him.'

The girls quietly go up the stairs to the bedroom and look in on him through the doorway. Sophie observes her dad in silence while Emma tears up and cries.

'He'll be better tomorrow, and you can talk to him then,' I assure them.

In the morning, after they come out of their rooms to go to breakfast, I accompany Sophie and Emma to the bedroom, where they glance in. They are relieved that their father is still there and breathing. They depart for the bus stop, leaving me alone in the house with Miles... and with my thoughts.

After having my own breakfast, I take a tray of fruit, juice, and coffee up to the bedroom.

Seeing that Miles can't sit up because of the pain in his side, I spoon-feed him and lift his head enough to take sips. I also give him his pills, supporting his head so he can swallow them. When he says he needs to pee I help him up and support him as he walks to the bathroom. The pain in his side almost doubles him over, but with my help he's able to accomplish the task.

I escort him very carefully back to bed and settle him comfortably. 'Now you rest. It won't be long before the pain meds kick in and you drift off to sleep.' I kiss him on his forehead, as if he's a sick child.

He looks up at me with those gorgeous blue eyes that had won me over twenty years ago. 'You're so good to me. I don't deserve you,' he says through the pain.

'There, there. Remember our vows? For better or worse, in sickness and in health? I'll always be there for you from now on.'

He smiles and closes his eyes.

Miles spends the rest of the day in bed, as I wait on his every need. The pain eases some, though the stitches itch like crazy, and he can't get to them. He complains that his hand feels like it's on fire. This injury concerns him more than the one in his side. He raises his heavily-bandaged right hand and cries, 'What am I going to do, Wendy? Will I ever be able to hold a pen again? Will I be able to type with that hand? I'm so close to finishing the new novel.'

I need to head off this concern. 'Let's not worry about that now. Let's get you healed, then talk to Dr. Kraemer and set up rehab for the hand. You might be able to do more than you think.'

'I wish I had printed it so I could read it over. Maybe you could bring the laptop to me.'

Nope, not going to happen. 'No sir! Not until you can sit up comfortably in bed. We don't want you to pop those stitches.'

'OK, OK, we'll wait a few days. How about my handwritten manuscript? I might be able to read it lying on my back.'

'Let's just hold off on that too, Miles. When you're able to sit up without pain, you can do that too. *Please* don't do anything to prolong your recovery.'

'All right,' he sighs, then closes his eyes, the round of meds having taken effect.

Chapter 58
Miles

I've been sleeping all morning. Wendy pops into the bedroom to check on me. She says softly, 'Now I'm going out to shop and will likely be gone until noon. You just lie back and close your eyes.' Then she leaves and goes downstairs.

Hearing the door to the garage close, I open my eyes. A voice inside tells me to get up and go to the office. It doesn't just tell me; it *commands* me: *Go check on your book!*

To make sure she's gone, I call out, 'Wendy?' Hearing no answer, I grit my teeth as I move my legs off the bed as carefully as I can. Grunting, I need to go to the bathroom, then I plan to make it down the hall to the office.

My business done in the bathroom, I shuffle one agonizing step at a time toward the office. Each step makes my side scream with pain, but I won't stop. An insistent voice in my head urges me on. I must review what I had typed and get out my notebook to see what I last wrote, which will need to be typed. Maybe I can find a speech-to-text app to use.

Lowering myself into the chair in front of the laptop makes my side scream in pain. But I have to check, no matter how painful it is. I use only my good left hand on the mouse, the whole process painfully slow.

The Word manuscript is not on screen where I think I left it. Maybe I forgot and saved on exit to my creative writing folder. I maneuver to the folder on screen.

The file is not in the folder. It has vanished, although all my other stories are there in the list. I click on the thumb drive to which I've been saving my files and open it to the creative writing folder.

The file isn't there either!

I click on Google Docs, where I also have been intermittently saving copies of the story. The file is there, but this version is five days old, meaning it's several pages behind.

All right, then, I'll restore to the Google Docs file what is in my handwritten manuscript.

But the thick file folder is not on the desktop. Did I put it in the drawer?

I pull out the desk drawer to pick up the folder.

It's not there.

What the hell is going on here? Where are the digital and handwritten copies of my work? What happened to them? Someone has taken the handwritten manuscript and also wiped all the digital files…except for the Google Docs version, which that person must not have known about.

Who would do such a thing?

It could be only one person.

Wendy.

Yes, that's right, it must be Wendy! She never supported my work from the start. But I showed her with that first novel, didn't I? She tried to stop me from writing, but she hasn't stopped spending the money coming in from it and from the film rights.

No, she's not having a problem with the results of my writing at all. Now she wants to stop me from completing this novel, but she's going to fail. I'll force her to tell me where the folder is, or she'll be sorry.

Very sorry.

I need a weapon to persuade Wendy to talk. My gun has been confiscated by the police. What can I use to threaten her into revealing the location of my folder? What can I use with my left hand?

A kitchen knife? Yes, a French chef's knife. Like Michael Myers in *Halloween*.

I could pin her up on a wall, like an insect.

Yes, we like that idea, don't we? Says that now familiar voice.

Getting up out of the chair very carefully, with a great effort and wincing in pain with every step, I pass out of the office and down the stairs, one agonizing step at a time, trying to ignore the pain in my side and hand as I slowly make my way to the kitchen. I find the French chef's knife in the knife holder on the counter and go to the garage, waiting for Wendy to come back from shopping. I'll catch her as she arrives.

I practice stabbing with my good left hand. It's awkward, but it will have to do. I press the button to open the garage door to let in the daylight. The cool air displaces the stale air inside the garage. The voice inside tells me to go over to the worktable to await Wendy's arrival. There I see the smashed remnants of my beloved Katrina 66 fountain pen.

The memory sweeps back over me. Wendy destroyed it. *Why, that bitch! That spiteful conniving whore!* She thought she had put an end to my inspiration. She thought wrong!

I'll pay Wendy back for this when she gets back. She'll pay for it with her life.

I lay the French chef's knife on the worktable and wait for her car to drive up.

But then, what will I write with when I start back up again?

It doesn't matter, says the voice. *I am with you.*

As if on cue, Wendy returns from her errands. She stops the car in the driveway just outside the garage and gets out. My back is to her as she takes in the scene. 'Miles, what are you doing out of bed? What are you doing in the garage? You're going to pop those stitches if you're not care—'

She stops in mid-sentence as I turn around to face her.

I order her, 'Come here, Wendy, I want to talk to you.' There's a second voice blended with mine, full of rage.

Wendy steps cautiously toward me. *Come a little closer, babe.* 'Sure. Let's talk,' she says, 'but first let's get you up to bed.' She moves to my left side, away from the right-side injury, intending to support me, when in one wince-producing move I grab the knife in my left hand

281

and pivot in front of her, pinning her to the worktable and cutting off any hope of escape.

'No, let's talk here. What did you do with my work? Where is it, Wendy?'

Nervous, shaking, just the way I want her, she responds, 'OK. OK. I'll tell you. It's complicated, but it makes sense. Do you remember Mark Torres, the professor that I—I had a relationship with? Remember he was shot dead? Remember that everyone, including the police, thought that Cindy's husband did it? But he didn't. You said so yourself. Just before that kid Aaron arrived, you confessed to me that *you* killed Mark. Don't you remember?'

'And look: in your new book Wanda's husband Michael kills Marty. You changed the names, but only slightly. Wanda/Wendy, Marty/Mark, Michael/Miles. It sure might look autobiographical, even like circumstantial *evidence* to an investigator. Don't you also remember that the police took your gun as evidence from the crime scene? They might come back and impound your laptop. Do you want them to read that scene? Do you want to go to jail for murder?'

I chuckle. 'Do you think I believe your little story? They would never do that. Mark's murder is a tight case, open and shut. My novel is fiction, Wendy. Fiction! It would never hold up in court. You deleted it off the laptop. So where's my handwritten manuscript? I can get the story back from it.'

'I burned it. Yes, I did! For the same reasons. I did it for us, Miles, for the family. We don't want to lose you. Losing the manuscript is a small price to pay for your freedom.'

So she thinks! 'Well, my dear, all is not lost. I've been saving it to Google Docs all along. I can get back the last version easily enough, once you're out of the way.'

I can read her mind. She has to get to Google Docs and erase that file, too. Not happening.

282

As she makes a move to go around me, I raise the knife high and bring it down, slicing through the sleeve of her light jacket, missing my target and cutting her right upper right arm instead.

'Ow,' she cries, clutching the wound, blood starting to flow through her fingers.

'There's more where that came from, my darling. One more for destroying my pen!'

Shivering from the pain, Wendy cries, 'I had to do that. That pen was demonic. Yes, it was a pen from hell! You became addicted to it. It gave you evil ideas. I had to free you from its control!'

I laugh, and a voice rushes from my mouth, not mine but another, a hoarse female voice. 'Don't you know, my dear? You didn't *free* Miles from the pen. He *IS* Katrina! He and I are now one!' As if commanded, I raise the knife high for the final blow, aiming for her neck.

Wendy releases her wounded arm and swings her left fist into my right side, hard into the bandaged wound. I shriek in pain, spinning and pressing my right elbow into the freshly-bleeding wound, but I maintain my hold on the knife and raise it once more.

Chapter 59

At police headquarters, Detective Robinson has been busy sitting at her desk, poring over her notes. Something doesn't seem right about this investigation of Schreiber's death at the Campbell residence. She's not satisfied with the answers both Wendy and Miles have given her. They are too rehearsed, too consistent.

Miles' pistol has been placed in an evidence bag. Robinson retrieves the bag and examines the pistol. It's a .22 LR short barrel revolver holding eight rounds. Four rounds have been fired. Wendy had stated for the record that she had no idea Miles had a gun.

If that is true, where and when did he get that gun?

Wendy also said that Miles rarely left the house. Obviously, he had to have left the house. Robinson recalls a local gun show in town a few months back. If Miles had attended it, he could have bought a gun from a private individual there and not registered his purchase. OK, so pursuing that line of questioning would likely lead to a dead end. But it is possible.

What next?

Miles said that he fired one shot at Arthur. What about those other three rounds? Did he go somewhere and practice? New gun owners don't go to a gun range and fire just three rounds. They'll fire at least a whole box of ammunition, if not more. She's sure she can find out by calling the gun ranges in the area. However, she doesn't think he practiced somewhere. She has a hunch about those three missing bullets. A hunch not supported by the conclusions, old and new.

But isn't that what a hunch is?

Ballistics tests will be performed on the bullet that killed Aaron Schreiber and compared with others in a database of prior investigations, complete and incomplete. She will order the bullets that killed Mark Torres and Cindy Santoro to be included. She plans to request expediting the tests, as she needs that information now.

Now to the principals in the case. Miles is a strange bird, for sure; his avoidance of eye contact and hesitant answers might be attributed to the shock and the surgery, but she thinks there's more to it. The truth of Miles Campbell is hiding behind the façade.

Something about Wendy bugs her. Robinson remembers learning about the murder of Mark Torres several months before, when Wendy was initially a person of interest in that investigation. Robinson wasn't on the investigative team then, as she was hired a month later. She heard about it after she was hired to take Detective McPherson's place. It was national news, after all.

Why was Wendy released as a suspect so soon? She also seems to be hiding behind a façade.

Then there was Tony Santoro, who had fled town and was killed in Colorado in a shootout with an officer of the Colorado State Patrol.

Though the investigations of both Cindy's and Mark Torres' murders were closed after Santoro was killed, in hindsight Detective McPherson's conclusion that Santoro had murdered Torres seems just an unsupported assumption to her. Even Eric Myers had said, 'There you have it. The case is closed.' Not accepting that conclusion, she'll contact the State Patrol in Colorado and request a report on Tony's weapon and the bullets he fired.

After considering these troubling questions, Robinson retrieves the Torres murder book and starts to review it. She also retrieves the evidence bag with the three bullets taken from Torres' body, marked according to where they were found.

The wound to the groin seems odd. Why there? Why weren't there just two shots to the torso or upper chest? That's usually where killers aim. The one to the head seems to be the *coup de grace*, like an execution. The shot to the groin could suggest a jealous person.

She's not sure at this point that the shooter was indeed Tony. It could have been a woman, a jilted lover, perhaps even Wendy, or Cindy. She's shocked to read in the murder book that four of the principals in the case—Cindy, Wendy, Miles, and Mark—had not been fingerprinted.

Now why was that? Well, Cindy and Mark were shot to death. Wendy and Miles were cleared when it was learned that Tony had fled the area. Why weren't they fingerprinted anyway? Because it was considered a slam dunk case?

Investigators at the time assumed a husband killed his cheating wife and her lover. It made sense to them: Tony Santoro, jealous husband of his cheating wife.

However, Robinson is not convinced. Miles also had a cheating wife.

The survivors of this sensational case are Wendy and Miles Campbell. They were dismissed as suspects, a huge oversight, in Robinson's opinion. She will order them to be fingerprinted. Plus, Miles' computer will be checked for emails from "Arthur Schriftsteller" to learn the motive for Aaron Schreiber's intent to kill Miles. If those emails exist at all. Just because Miles says Schreiber sent them doesn't mean it's the truth. She needs to cover all the bases.

She calls the Colorado State Patrol office in Lakewood to get information on the shootout with Antonio Santoro, particularly the ballistics report on Santoro's gun. If it matches the bullets that killed Santoro's wife Cindy, at least the question of who killed Cindy would be answered.

A Sergeant Miller of the CSP answers the phone and takes her request. She didn't know what to expect of a big city law officer, but Sergeant Miller is surprisingly courteous. 'Sure,' he says, 'I would be glad to help, Detective Robinson. Give me the rest of the day, and I can send that information to you by tomorrow morning.'

'Thank you so much, Sergeant,' Robinson replies, and disconnects. She wonders if he could sense her relieved smile through the phone.

The gun that killed Mark Torres has not yet been identified. That oversight is the major missing piece in the puzzle of who killed Torres. Detective McPherson simply assumed that Tony Santoro had killed Torres, without conclusive evidence. Robinson thinks she's close to the answer to that question. All it will take is the requested information from Sergeant Miller.

She spends another hour closely studying the Torres murder book and reviews her own notes on the current case. After preparing herself tonight, she plans to visit the Campbell residence tomorrow to confirm her conclusions.

Early the next morning Robinson finishes speaking on the phone with Sergeant Miller at the CSP office. She'll get an emailed copy of the report today. 'Thank you very much, Sergeant. You've been a great help,' she says.

'No problem,' he responds. 'Glad to help.'

She hangs up and sits back in her chair. This new information, plus the book on Mark Torres' murder, helps her to fill in all the missing pieces. It's almost time to pay another visit to the Campbell household. She just needs that one more piece to complete the puzzle.

Shortly after noon Robinson receives the information she was seeking from Sergeant Miller. She replaces the phone on its cradle. 'Aha! I thought so,' she says, shaking her head. Turning to her partner Eric Myers, she says, 'Come on, Eric. We're gonna go see a man about a gun.'

'What man?' Myers asks.

'The man who killed Mark Torres.'

'Torres? I thought that case was closed. McPherson and I closed it last year.'

If Forrest McPherson were still employed, he would have blown his top about Robinson's reopening his closed case. She was keeping this reopened investigation to herself, not having sought approval. 'I've reopened it as part of the current Aaron Schreiber

287

investigation. That's all you need to know for now. Come on, let's go!'

Chapter 60
Wendy

Miles lifts the knife again. He's going to bring it down and kill me! But before he does, from behind there's a loud voice.

'Police! Freeze! Drop that knife!'

We both stop and turn around to see who has interrupted us. Detective Robinson stands at the entry to the garage, aiming her gun at us. Her partner Eric stands off to her side and has his weapon out also.

Seeing them, Miles—but I now know it's not Miles—snarls in a guttural voice, 'Go to hell!' and starts to deliver the final blow.

I cower. Robinson fires twice, hitting Miles. He drops the knife, lets go of me, and collapses to the garage floor.

What happens next is surreal.

From Miles' body rises a red cloud, slowly coalescing into the shape of a shrouded woman, an ugly red hag, her blood-red hair floating above her head as if underwater. Her hands at the ends of withered arms reach for me with bony fingers. This apparition wants to strangle me! But then she slowly disintegrates from her hands up her arms, as her body dissolves into thin swirls of red. Before she completely fades, she raises her repulsive head and lets out a horrid scream, which trails off until it ends in a fading echo.

Then all is silent.

Stunned, both Myers and Robinson have dropped their service pistols. 'Just what the hell was that?' Robinson gasps.

Hearing Detective Robinson's voice brings me back to reality. 'I think you're right,' I shudder. 'I don't know what that was, but it came out of Miles' body and returned to hell. You may think I'm insane, but that's the demon that took over Miles body. That's the demon that was in his pen!'

The look on Robinson's face tells me that she does indeed think I'm nuts. But she could not deny what she saw herself.

Turning my attention to Miles, seeing the blood oozing out of the wounds to Miles' chest, I realize he's dying. 'Oh no, you've killed him!' I cry, dropping to the floor to cradle his head. 'You didn't have to kill him!'

Detective Robinson walks toward us. 'Mrs. Campbell, he hurt you once, and he was going to finish you off. I warned him. I'm sorry, I had to do it.'

Eric Myers calls an ambulance as Robinson kneels to check on Miles. Feeling his carotid artery, then his wrists, she confirms that he's dead. 'I'm so·sorry,' she says. She inspects my wound. 'Your arm needs attention.'

'Why are you here?' I ask her, holding my wounded arm. 'I would have expected you to phone first, but you came just in the nick of time, it seems.'

'I'm glad I didn't take the time to phone. I discovered indisputable evidence that the rounds which killed Mark Torres were not from Tony Santoro's 9mm gun but from Miles' .22 revolver. I actually had come to arrest him, Wendy. However, it turned out that I came to protect you instead. He was going to kill you, no doubt about it.'

I had to agree with her, but Miles—my Miles—is dead.

I was transported to the hospital Emergency Room, treated for a superficial wound and released, my right arm in a sling, clutching prescriptions for an antibiotic and for pain. I arrived home early enough to be there when the girls got home from school.

Now I had a new problem. What was I going to tell the girls? I could predict that Emma would bawl for hours.

An hour later, Miles' cell phone rings in the office. I'm not fast enough to get to the office to pick it up. Soon the voicemail notification sounds. Susan Brower, Miles' agent, leaves a message asking Miles to call back because she has some good news.

I call back and start the conversation with the bad news. Initially speechless, Susan finally replies, 'I don't know what to say.' After expressing her condolences, she relays the good news that she called about. '**Killing Time** is on the market as of today. It's set a record for time from acceptance to publication. NMEX Media has caved on the location for shooting the film. It will be filmed in that town in Missouri, as most appropriate for the context of the book. They found a historic house whose owners gave permission to shoot the exteriors. The next advance check issued from my office is in the mail. And **Killing Time** will be issued in paperback in three months.'

She adds, 'I know that money can't lessen your loss, but you'll be set for life.'

Expressing once again her condolences, Susan hangs up. I wish that Miles had been alive to receive this great news.

He was right after all. He *did* write The Great American Novel.

Epilogue

It would be an understatement to say that Sophie and Emma were devastated to learn of their father's death. Once again arriving home from school to see yellow police tape across the entrance to the garage, my car out in the driveway, they burst through the front door, Sophie calling out, 'Mom, Mom, are you home?'

When I didn't answer right away, Sophie shouted out, 'Mom, are you here?' her voice quivering.

Poor Emma, she knew what was up, barely able to speak. 'Where's Daddy?' she cried.

Seated in the living room, my arm in a sling, I answered, 'I'm here, in the living room. Come here, girls, I have to tell you something.'

And tell I did, explaining what happened with Daddy and why my arm was in a sling. 'I'm so sorry, Emma, Sophie. Your daddy wasn't himself anymore. A brave police detective had to shoot him to stop him from killing me.'

Jaw gaping, eyes wide open, Sophie just sat there, stunned beyond belief. Emma wailed, 'No! No! Daddy! Daddy!' falling into my arms, weeping deeply. Sophie joined us in a pile of sobbing humanity.

Knowing what would soon happen, the local and national media descending upon the community, attracted like piranhas to blood, I requested the funeral director to schedule a private family ceremony and cremation. There would be no trip to the cemetery and no train of media vehicles, satellite trucks and cars with primped national correspondents ready to thrust their microphones into our faces.

The funeral service in the mortuary chapel, led by a local Episcopal minister, brought finality to our loss. He had a hard time saying nice things about Miles, knowing how he died. He used the canned Episcopal funeral sermon for the most part. I was proud of Sophie and Emma, who sat stoic through the service with only tears streaming down their cheeks.

While I was meeting earlier with the funeral director, there began an officer-involved-shooting inquiry into Detective Robinson's actions that fateful day. I was called in to testify to the appropriateness of Detective Robinson's use of deadly force. A couple of OIS (Officer Involved Shooting) team members asked me a short series of questions.

Yes, Miles had wounded me first.

Yes, he had raised the knife to stab me again.

Yes, Detective Robinson had warned him to drop the knife.

No, he didn't drop it.

Yes, that's when she fired.

Yes, she saved my life.

The outcome of the inquest was that deadly force was justified, and Detective Robinson was cleared.

The pack of media people, local and national, stayed around after the funeral and camped out on the sidewalk in front of my house for days. They were in my face every time I left the house.

I denied request after request for interviews. I denied requests from the local paper, the **Indianapolis Star** and television stations, and from the major national news media. They wanted dirt on Miles and me, dirt that would make the front page and lead the ten o'clock television news. But I frustrated them, hiring a lawyer to help screen them from me.

Days after the furor died down and the media trucks were gone, the girls faced the daunting fear of going back to school. 'Mom, I don't want to go back to school,' Sophie told me the morning that I went into her room to get her out of bed. 'I'm going to be on display, and the teachers and my friends won't see me the same as before.'

'I know, I know, Sophie, but you have Amber, who's been a great friend through all this. Stick close to her today and until the attention dies down.'

Although Sophie continued to whine through breakfast, she could see that I wouldn't allow her to stay home. She and Emma, who was more willing to go to school and face the attention, left the house resigned to survive their first day back.

After they left, I walked through all the rooms in the house, awash with memories, not all good ones.

The bedroom. Queen-size bed. Once we were King and Queen of the bed. We rocked and rolled in it when the girls were gone; quiet during quickies, giggling with each moan. The heat of those times replaced by the chill.

Miles jobless, me loveless.

Bedtimes: him facing the bathroom door, me facing the window.

Was I frigid? Yes, to him.

But not in Mark's king-sized bed, where I was warm and willing. Mark the King. King Mark. And me his Queen.

A mistake. A big mistake. What a fool I was, thinking the grass was greener over there when I wasn't watering the grass here.

Then the failed plumbing plot. 'I'll fix your plumbing, you whore! You slut!' My throat nearly crushed, my husband nearly my murderer.

I have to get out of here!

Miles' office. Such pain, such anguish, the lair of the Miles Monster, growing more violent, more vicious, the more he wrote. Wetting and shitting himself under the control of an alien force. The slaps. The punch. The strangling. Emma and Sophie crying.

You bitch! You whore! You slut!

*Was his work great? Yes, proven later by the publication of his book **Killing Time**, by the arrangement to film the adaptation, to star Owen Wilson and Blake Lively. They got it right with Owen Wilson, and Blake Lively will play me. I wish I were as gorgeous as she is.*

But was it all worth it? Worth the rage, the violence? The violence.

The pen. That goddamned pen!

That demon-possessed pen that possessed Miles. That red apparition in the garage. That hag that inhabited my Miles.

'Where is it? Where is it? Where is it?'

'I can't breathe! I'll tell you! I'll tell you! Just don't hit me anymore!'

I have to get out of this room.

Downstairs to the kitchen. Where we used to chat during breakfast and lunches. Becoming the icy kitchen, where we avoided eye contact and voice contact.

I have to get out of here.

To the frosty dining room, cold meals, cold hearts, cold stares. Frightened daughters.

I have to get out of here.

The garage. The scene of two violent deaths. Arthur Schriftsteller. Miles lying dead with two bullets in him. Blood. Detectives Robinson and Myers. Yellow crime tape.

I don't want to go out there.

Is there any place in this house that is peaceful anymore? Is there any retreat from the pain and hurt? Are these memories overlaid now on all the walls, the floors, the beds?

We need to move.

We need to move from this town, where unpleasant memories have soiled the streets, the university, the supermarkets, the community. Where I will always be "that woman," whether they say it or think it, or not.

We need to move.

I have to get away from this town. Everywhere I go—to work, to shop, to the bank, to fill the car with gas—I sense the side glances, the whispers behind my back, even glares from self-righteous people who recalled my affair long ago with Mark Torres.

We need to move.

One day when the girls came home from school, still shell-shocked from the loss of their father and the cruelty of their schoolmates, I said, 'Sophie, Emma, after you drop off your stuff, please come to the living room. I want to discuss something with you.'

Their interest piqued, I began, 'So, I've been thinking about—'

They interrupted in a chorus: 'About moving? Far away from here?'

'Why, yes, how did you—'

'Because we've been talking about it ourselves. We want to get out of here,' Sophie said. 'Far, far away.'

Emma added, 'Every room in this house feels haunted. I feel haunted. I don't want to live here anymore. Can we move, please? Please?'

Gratified by our unanimity on the issue, I began an internet search for a place to live far away from Indiana, from the Midwest, far away from this little town, where memories would be triggered by the house and by the very town itself. I engaged the services of a gregarious realtor named Julie Forrest, and met with her, including the girls, as we outlined our desires and preferences.

'All righty then, Wendy, Sophie, and Emma,' Julie said as we ended our first meeting. 'It was good to meet you and talk with you about your desires. I can help you with the sale of this house and with locating a place to live elsewhere. Just give me a little time, and I will get back to you.'

'Thank you, Julie,' I said. 'We look forward to hearing from you soon.' Julie bid us goodbye and passed out the front door, her lacquered hair stiff against the strong breeze.

I had been curious ever since Miles sneered and told me he had been saving his novel to Google Docs. After he killed me and the girls—perish the thought—he was going to finish the work by restoring the novel from Google Docs. I wondered how difficult it would be to find it.

I know a little bit about saving to Google Docs, so, since the laptop had never been shut down, it turned out to be an easy task to find the manuscript. I read the entire story up to where Miles had left off. It disgusted and horrified me. I don't know what Miles intended for the climax, so I made my job easier by writing the ending as it had actually happened, with the detective killing Michael and saving Wanda.

Although I hated the book, I had to admit it was what the market called for. It was, after all, a horror novel. And it was Miles Campbell's second—and posthumous—novel.

I called Susan to notify her that I had finished Miles' second novel. She was delighted to hear the news.

'Really? Oh my God, Wendy, that is wonderful!' Then, remembering that Miles had died not long before, she apologized. 'Oh, I am so sorry, Wendy. But that is his legacy, and I am sure he would have wanted you to finish and publish it. But I guess we'll never know, will we? When you have finished it, go ahead and send it to me via email attachment, and I will take care of the rest.'

I'm not as talented a writer as Miles, so I expected there to be some editing involved in the final section that I wrote. And there was, but overall, Susan was very pleased with the result. 'It should fetch a very high advance and high sales, Wendy,' she said.

A year later Miles Campbell's second novel, **The Rise and Fall of Michael Chambers**, was perched at the top of the **New York Times** bestseller list. The posthumous novel created a buzz, as reviewers interpreted it as a true story disguised as fiction.

I often had to remind interviewers, journalists, and fans to read the disclaimer: "*This is a work of fiction. Names, characters, and incidents are the products of the author's imagination. Any resemblance to actual persons, living or dead, or actual events is purely coincidental.*"

The Rise and Fall of Michael Chambers snared a $6,000,000 advance and a hefty sum for the film rights. As Susan had predicted, the girls and I were set for life.

With the help of Julie Forrest, I sold the house, long before the publication of **Michael Chambers**, and moved us west to Lake Tahoe, where Julie had found a perfect Southwestern adobe-style single story house for us, with lots of room for us to spread out. And a pool in the back yard, which Sophie and Emma loved. They lived like little princesses out there in the summertime.

Before we moved, I donated our copies of Miles' novels to the local library. Although we were living off the royalties, I wanted no physical reminders of his madness in our new home.

In time, Sophie and Emma healed from their grief and adjusted to their new life, making new friends after they got over their grief of leaving their best friends behind.

Children are so resilient—I wish I were.

At first, memories often disturbed my sleep at night, but they eventually faded.

I never discovered how the Katrina 66 pen was possessed by an evil spirit. What I saw in the garage that day looked absolutely demonic. Or maybe all along it was something buried deep inside Miles that surfaced while writing with the possessed pen.

Even Miles' mother had no idea when I asked her, although she did describe how the pen changed her husband's personality, and not for the better. Considering what happened to Miles, I don't understand how his father was able to quit using the pen. He had more fortitude than Miles did, I guessed. But then he died not long after he stopped writing. I wonder about that.

Coincidence?

Confident after successfully finishing Miles' novel, I felt a strong desire to write. You could say I caught the bug. I began a career as a romance writer. As the widow of the infamous Miles Campbell, I had little difficulty getting published, assisted by my agent Susan Brower.

Heartless Love, Silent Longing shot to the top of the **New York Times** best seller list for a while, despite being a romance novel, then promptly dropped to a more respectable level, just inside the top one hundred. I didn't care; I was on the list. Although my royalties weren't anywhere near Miles' earnings, they were satisfactory. I didn't expect to make a ton of money.

Nothing succeeds like success, and so I continued to write romance novels.

Writing turned out to be exhilarating and liberating. I learned to appreciate Miles' obsession with writing, although I never let it take over my life. It helped that each successive romance novel received positive reviews and sold well.

Taking no chances, I didn't write with a pen, much less a fountain pen.

The End

ACKNOWLEDGEMENTS

As a late-in-life debut novelist, I requested and accepted constructive criticism from my early readers, the first and foremost of whom is my wife, Leslie, who read this book in all the early stages, chapter by chapter, from start to finish. She caught little (and big) errors and early on made me see my work from a reader's point of view. Thanks, Leslie, for allowing me the time to compose, revise, and edit through the long process toward publication.

This novel would never have turned out as good as it is (and you, the reader, have to be the judge of that) without my editor Dina Husseini. Dina encouraged, cajoled, pushed, coaxed, persuaded, and pulled me along from start to finish, to craft and polish the narrative, making me reveal more than I originally put into it. What a ride Dina took me on, for which I am ever grateful. Kudos go also to Tonya Andrews, CEO, Crossroads Publishing, for additional editing, encouragement, and especially her wise advice. But most of all, for publishing my book!

Then there's my other family. My cousin Ray, with whom I have shared portions of this story, whose positive comments encouraged me. My daughters Kelly and Hannah, who, like Emma in **Katrina 66**, said, "Do it, Dad, do it!"

Thanks also to Paula, Franco, Dan, Kathy, Don, and Pat, who have heard or read portions of the story and cheered me on. You're the best!

ABOUT THE AUTHOR

Dale W. Simpson was born and raised in St. Louis, Missouri. He retired after 35 years of teaching in the Department of English and Philosophy at Missouri Southern State University in Joplin, Missouri, chairing the department for thirteen years. He specialized in Medieval English literature and English linguistics and also helped prepare secondary English teachers. His special teaching interest was the works of J.R.R Tolkien, which he taught as often as he was allowed.

After retirement and forty-five years away from his hometown, Simpson returned to St. Louis, where he lives with his wife Leslie and enjoys being with his family, especially his grandchildren. His reading interests include novels by Michael Connelly, John Grisham, and Stephen King.

Starting in the middle of the Covid-19 pandemic, aside from *Katrina 66* Simpson wrote and published several short stories and poems during the ensuing three years. He has since written two more novels and two novellas, which await publication somewhere, sometime. Several works are in progress as well, as he cannot stop writing for long.

And in case you wonder, he writes with a fountain pen.

Katrina 66 is his first published novel. His second novel has been accepted for publication.